HAMO  A

STOLEN
MOMENTS
of JOY

Unrolling Script

Washington, DC

Published by Unrolling Script in the United States of America.

Publisher's note: This is a work of fiction. Names, characters, organizations, places, and events are the products of the author's imagination or are used fictitiously. Any resemblance to actual persons, living or dead, is purely coincidental.

Cover design by Jessica Bell
Interior design by Mirajul Kayal

ISBNs:
978-1-7346337-9-5 (hardback)
978-1-7346337-7-1 (paperback)
978-1-7346337-8-8 (ebook)
Library of Congress Control Number: 2021922074

www.HamourBaika.com

To boys who have lost their innocence
to powerful men's lust

Hazard

/ˈhæzərd/ *noun*

That night, we succeeded and yet failed tragically. Rakesh had warned me to not come here. I knew it wasn't safe, but I wanted to help. I could hear the music from outside. The metal gate to the front yard was left ajar. A middle-aged man guarded the door. I knew he was armed. Slowly walking by the gate, I peeked inside. The translator was sitting on the ground, among the crowd of spectators. But I couldn't see Rakesh. The rescue mission involved appealing to the greed of the host.

I heard the bells of a boy's anklet, but I couldn't see him. The music got louder, and the audience's excitement grew. All I saw was a green lace covering that hid the boy's face. It might have been Jabbar.

"Go home," the guard yelled at me. "Unless you want to join him," he laughed. His teeth rotten.

I had to be reasonable, so I went away.

Even a decade later, I still shivered at the memory of that night.

Abrasion
/əˈbreɪʒn/ *noun*

My demon takes the shape of the desire to hide. I wished I could stay under the blanket and cry myself back to sleep. Lie in bed until the bruise got healed. But I had to get up and somehow find a way of concealing it. Or explaining it. At least, it wasn't bleeding anymore. I had to admit that this was my own fault.

I looked at the clock. If I wanted to get to work on time, I had to leave quickly. I got out of bed and washed my face with cold water, careful not to touch the carpet burn on my face. Breakfast was out of the question. I wore my uniform, but I needed more layers in the cold. My bag was ready on the armchair. All I had to do was to shove the SAT book in there. Its covers were wrapped in paper. I didn't want anyone to judge me for still dealing with the SAT at my age. In the closet by the front door, I found a brown knitted hat that didn't go with my black suit and tie. What did match with my outfit was Cliff's baseball cap with silver plaques that said "Boss." I'd look ridiculous wearing that. Then his *ushanka* hat attracted my attention. I wished he would get rid of that Russian thing.

I put the ridiculous hat back on the shelf, thinking of the Soviet occupation of my country that forced my family to escape. And here I was, decades later, stopping myself from tossing my boyfriend's Russian headgear into the trash can. I couldn't tell if it was fake. But as much as Cliff liked fancy clothes, he wouldn't buy fur products. He'd never do anything to harm animals. Did that mean I was less than an animal?

My eyes got watery. No, I couldn't do this again. If the tear drops reached the bruise, it would burn, or worse, bleed. I put on my green jacket and glanced at the picture on the wall. I had chosen to frame this particular photograph. It showed my profile, with my eyes closed, as I kissed Cliff on the cheek. He had a big grin on his face, staring at the camera, tongue sticking to the side. He was wearing a tank-top, his bicep bulging at the corner of the picture. He took this selfie during the DC Pride weekend, excited that we could make out in public near DuPont. He loves to show me off. An admirable sense of pride that rubbed off on me over the years. If only we could live in that frozen moment forever.

I locked the door on my way out. Thank God no one was in the hallway. I almost ran down the stairs to leave the building before any of the neighbors saw me. Not that they'd care but I didn't want anyone to see me like this. Cliff really overstepped the line this time, bruising my face. We'd have to talk about that later. The cold air outside served as a painkiller for my face. The snow had started to set.

I walked down Robinson Street and stopped a few meters from the bus stop, where several people were already waiting. A guy was wearing cordless headphones, bopping his head to the beat of hip-hop music.

I thought back to last night. I shouldn't have provoked Cliff, when I saw he was getting mad. "Well, it didn't look like nothing. I saw you leaning over him and showing him something in your phone," I criticized as we entered the apartment.

"So what? I'm here, aren't I? Maybe instead of coming with me to the gym and complaining the whole time, you should just come home and make some freaking dinner."

"You think I'm just gonna be a good housewife while you go and flirt with every hungry bottom in the city?"

"Whatever."

"Oh, go to hell, Cliff," I answered.

"What did you just say?"

I should have kept quiet. "I said, go to hell."

"Who do you think you are, talking to me like that?" He walked closer, his voice louder than I expected.

"I'm the one who—"

He slapped me so hard my ear whistled. "That was a rhetorical question," he warned with his index finger.

I punched him on the arm. He bumped me with his chest, causing me to fall backward. "You really got some nerve. I can throw you out like the sack of garbage that you are."

"This is *our* apartment," I stung back.

"Oh yeah?" He loomed over me and extended his hand to slap me again.

I imagined kicking him between the legs, making him fall over and even get teary-eyed. I tried to kick him, but he took my foot and dragged me on the carpet all the way to the front door, giving me this bruise on the face. Then he let go. I sat on the floor and pulled my knees to my chest. I touched my face and complained, "See what you did."

He hung his foot next to my head and gave me a slight tap, making me turn my neck so he could see the bruise. "That will shut you up for a couple of hours." He took off his shoes and dropped them right next to me.

The young man at the bus stop turned up the volume on his headphones and looked at me for a second. He saw the bruise and immediately looked away. I was ashamed. What was wrong with me? Cliff's little outburst did not even compare to what I'd endured before I came to Baltimore. But even a cursory thought of my previous life brought tears to my eyes.

A girl stood next to me, forming a line that I wanted to avoid. She looked fifteen or so. She sounded like she was digging for something in her bag. I checked to see if the bus was coming.

"Here," she said.

I didn't want to look at her, thinking she was talking to someone else.

"Excuse me?"

I looked. She was holding out a pack of Kleenex. I tried to take a tissue.

"Just take the whole thing."

"Thanks." I chuckled at how absurd I looked.

She smiled and looked away.

I wiped my face, searching my mind for something pleasant to think about. Learning vocabulary was essential to my plan. I opened my covered-up SAT book and looked for a word to distract me: Abrasion.

The bus stopped in front of me. Not too crowded today. I sat by the window near the back door.

Soon, the bus approached Albemarle Street and I pressed the "stop request" button. I got off and made a left onto President Street. A police officer was standing on the sidewalk, like trash that disgraced the face of the city. In my twenty-four years of life, I'd learned that the police only protected the powerful from the powerless. I walked away. Two blocks later, I entered the Patapsco Fleet Inn.

"Good morning, Ms. Grace."

"Morning, sugar. How are you?" She was focused on whatever she was typing.

"Good, and yourself?"

She looked up from her monitor. "What kind of nonsense?" She studied my face. "What's happened to you?"

I just shook my head. "You know how you can glide on the hardwood floor with your socks on, as you dance? Like in that movie? Turns out you can't do that on carpet." I never danced, but she didn't know that.

"Oh my." She sounded like she could see it.

"Yeah. My face did glide though."

"That must have hurt."

"I'll survive." I always did.

"What was the song?"

I love Bollywood movies, so there is never a shortage of good songs. "Jashn-e Ishqa. It's from a movie. I'll forget all about it once I start working."

"Are you messing with me? Boy, you can't stand at the reception desk looking like that. You wanna scare off our guests?"

"I'm just standing here."

"Not looking like that, you're not. Why didn't you call out?"

"I don't wanna be home. Plus, it's gonna take a few days to heal."

"Well, you for sure won't be standing here like that."

"What do you want me to do?" I had to find a way of covering up the carpet burn. "I could put on some makeup. Do you have some foundation I can borrow?"

She just looked at me sideways and then broke into laughter. "You hit your head, didn't you?"

I realized why she was laughing.

"Go to CVS and get some. Look in the mirror, put it right next to your face. It should have the same hue."

"Will you teach me how to apply it?"

She shook her head no, but I knew she would.

"It's no big deal. I'm fine. I'll be right back."

I followed her instructions and did my best to look presentable. Around 10:45, I was at the front desk when someone attracted my attention. He looked like a model, wearing tight pants and a military jacket. He was carrying a backpack and a red suitcase that he pulled on the floor. His dark skin glistened in the dim light of the lobby. His thick lips were adorned with a thin strip of mustache and his chin with a patch of beard. The rest of his stubble was neatly trimmed to accent his jawline. He raised his eyebrows to make three wrinkles on his forehead, as he looked at me.

"Good morning, sir."

"How you doing? I have a reservation for Tyrique Williams."

I typed his name into the system. "Hope your flight wasn't delayed or anything." His suitcase had an airline tag. "With the snow and all."

"It's all good. Although to be honest with you, I expected it to be chillier."

I couldn't find his name. I switched his first and last name, just in case someone had mistyped it. "It feels colder with the gust."

"So I've heard."

I brought up the full list of rooms and the names they were booked under. Maybe Rebecca had completely butchered his name. But spelling "Tyrique" didn't seem difficult. I had to say something to hide the fact that I couldn't find his booking. "What brings you to town? A quiet stay in Baltimore on the way to New York's fashion week?"

"Fashion week? Nah, why you say that?"

"I'm sorry, I didn't mean to…"

"It's cool," he interrupted. "I try to look fashionable so the TSA won't harass me. You know how they tend to randomly pick on you if you don't look a certain way." He looked at my name tag and raised one eyebrow, "I'm sure you know what I mean, Abdul."

"Yes, sir." I still couldn't find anything similar to Tyrique or Williams in the system.

"This is heavy." He took off the straps of his backpack and placed it on the ground. "Is there a problem with my reservation?"

"I'm so sorry, Mr. Williams. The computer is acting up today. Let me go ask my colleague." Staring at him, I reached for a pen to write down his name, but my finger ended up in a pack of tacks on the desk. I pulled my finger and sucked on it to prevent bleeding.

"What's wrong?"

"Nothing. I just put my hand into a box of tacks. I'm stupid."

"I'm sorry," he touched his heart as if he could feel my pain. "Happens to the best of us. Don't blame yourself."

He was in fact the best of us. Something in me was being pulled toward him. He emanated magnetic energy.

I went to the back and found Ms. Grace in the office. "Could you please help me? I can't find the guest's name in the system: Tyrique Williams."

She stood up and followed me to the lobby. "Good morning. How are you doing?"

"Hi."

She typed his name. Still nothing showed up. She closed the program and opened a spreadsheet that she kept as a backup to our reservation system. Still, the "find" function didn't return anything.

"Mr. Williams, did you make the reservation directly with us or through a third party?"

"I made it through an app. Hold on." He reached into his pocket and took out his cellphone. He had manicured fingernails. Six or seven bracelets were wrapped around his wrist. "Right here." He gave the phone to Ms. Grace.

"Mr. Williams, you made a reservation at the Patapsco Paradise. That's the hotel next door. You're on the thirteenth floor. You'll have a perfect view of the Inner Harbor. We only have four floors here."

"Oh," he shook his head. "My bad. My cab brought me here. I didn't even think to read the... Wait, the thirteenth floor?" He paused, leaned in, and lowered his voice, "You think that's bad luck?"

Ms. Grace smiled, "You're not superstitious, are you? You'll be just fine in your *chambre avec vue.*"

"OK, OK. I trust you." His smile lit up the room.

"Have a good day, Mr. Williams."

"You do the same."

"Let me help you, sir." I intervened, wanting nothing more than a few more minutes in his presence.

"Nah, I'll be fine."

"Please. I couldn't help you here. It's the least I can do. Plus, you just said it's heavy."

"You don't think I can manage?"

Damn, had I just implied he was weak? "I just wanted to help."

He winked and motioned for me to join him. "Just messing with you."

I went around the reception desk, lifted his backpack, and opened the door for him.

"Thank you," he nodded at me. "You don't wanna grab your jacket or something?"

Not for crossing the street to the Paradise. "I'm used to the cold. I've lived in much colder climates."

"Abdul, you have this accent that I can't place. I don't want to pry, but it's piqued my curiosity." He walked down the steps.

"Where do you think my accent's from?"

"I don't wanna make a poor presumption and risk sounding uninformed." He stopped walking as if to conjure his energy to think. "If you're used to the cold and have a Muslim name... so... maybe Afghanistan?"

I couldn't believe it. "Yeah. How did you...?"

"Yes," he punched the air.

"A lot of time, I get China. Even Korea a couple of times."

"A Korean Abdul?"

He made me laugh.

"That's funny. I mean Uyghur could be another educated guess. But I doubt most people would even know about that."

"Exactly."

"My dad is from South Carolina. My mom from the US Virgin Islands." He was more courteous than most people.

"Nice to meet you."

"Pleasure." He extended his hand. "I feel like it's insensitive to ask questions and not volunteer anything about oneself. I hate it when people think they're entitled to ask you whatever question comes to their mind."

"I know what you mean."

"Well, I noticed your hand is cold. You should go back. I'll manage it from here."

"I'm OK."

But we had already reached the hotel.

He took his backpack from me. "Hopefully, I'll run into you again before I leave town. I'm just across the street."

"That'd be amazing." My face got hot. "Have a good one." I rushed back into the inn before I could say anything else embarrassing.

"Well, aren't you sweet to help out the most good-looking customer we had in weeks," Ms. Grace noted.

"I was just helping out. Nothing like that." Of course, I would use any excuse to talk to someone like him.

"Mhmmm. I don't blame you. That was a fine young man. And so are you, sugar. Don't you forget it."

Flirting with Tyrique had happened organically, like pollination did without the bees' conscious effort.

Maybe that was how Cliff felt, when boys gathered around him. The incident last night at the gym could have been benign. And yet I'd made such a fuss about it.

A deep frown formed on Ms. Grace's face.

"What happened?"

"Just reading about the police shooting of another unarmed Black man."

"The one in Kansas?"

"Right here on Mosher Street. Last night."

Already, more than one police shooting since yesterday. The police were always there to harm black and brown bodies. Most people abroad don't know about these incidents. America is advertised as the land of the free.

When I got home, I prepared two bowls of *salad Shirazi*. I put some chicken breast in the frying pan and let it simmer in a yogurt sauce on the stove.

Cliff came home around eight, half an hour later than usual. I went to the door, not saying anything. He just put his gym bag on the floor and said, "I went to the gym early so there are fewer guys trying to chat me up."

"I'm sorry, Cliff." I took off his coat. "I'm stupid."

"You're my stupid." He cupped my chin in his hand and kissed me on the cheek.

I rubbed the back of his arm, enjoying his tender side.

Cliff took off his jacket and boots. He loosened his tie and opened the top three buttons of his shirt. He had blond hair and a trimmed beard. Chest hair showed from under his shirt. And I could see the lion head tattooed on his arm. His tight shirt showed off his muscular pecs and biceps. He looked at me with his deep blue eyes and said, "I'm sorry I hit you."

"You can hit me anytime you want," I brought his hand to my lips and kissed it.

"I'm serious." His voice low and small, his eyes locked on mine. "It makes me feel loved when you get jealous. Just..." He exhaled. "I love you."

I felt so free now that our fight was over. Now that the real Cliff was back.

Liaison
/liˈeɪzɑːn/ *noun*

The next day, covering up the wound took less effort. Cliff called me resourceful and apologized again. I was standing at the front desk at work when Tyrique walked in. A pink scarf was hanging from his neck on both sides of his jacket. I smiled as I felt my heart pounding heavier.

"Good morning, Mr. Tyrique."

"Mr. Abdul."

"How are you doing? Are you enjoying your stay in the Paradise?"

"It feels like paradise right here."

His response surprised me. I had to say something to flirt back. But I couldn't think of anything. Asking how I could help would bring the conversation to an abrupt end, but I didn't know what else to say.

"I heard about this Lebanese coffee shop that is supposed to be nearby. But I forgot the address. I was hoping you can help me out."

"Morning in Beirut? Yeah, absolutely. It's only a couple of blocks away. It has its own style of coffee. They have American coffee too, but you should try theirs. Kinda like

Turkish coffee, but better. They add cardamom and a bit of sugar if you like. No milk. It's the best thing in the world." I got carried away.

"Sounds wonderful."

"Yeah, just go past the circle, the Katyn Memorial, down on President Street and turn left on—"

"I was hoping you could perhaps show me." He interjected. "I'm not good with directions. As you recall. I'd treat you to a coffee."

I probably stared at him for too long without saying anything.

He went on, "You know, to say thank you for helping me with my luggage yesterday."

"You're too kind, sir. It was nothing. I didn't even carry it all the way."

"Come on, Abdul. Don't leave me hanging. It's pretty quiet in here. I guess you don't get a lot of tourists in November."

Ms. Grace walked in. "No problem, he'll show you how to get there." She put my green jacket on the countertop. "He was about to clock out for his break anyway."

Did she want to live vicariously through me?

"You were?" He sounded excited. "That's serendipity."

Not knowing what that meant, I turned around and whispered, "Ms. Grace, what are you doing?"

"Go. Take your time."

"Not like I'm single." I mouthed, almost without making any sound.

"I know that," she swatted my concern away.

"Thank you so much for covering for him." Tyrique interrupted our murmurs.

"It is all right. It's been a slow Saturday," Ms. Grace announced, flirting on my behalf.

"I'm eager to taste this best thing in the world, Abdul."

Did I imagine the double meaning? Of course, I did. He would not be so upfront.

My heart wouldn't ease on the way. Why was he interested in me? Did he want only the directions to the coffee shop, or did he want something more? I wondered if my face was red. I was so excited I could hardly pay attention to what he was saying.

I decided to pay attention to my surroundings to stop thinking about his intentions. The barista behind the counter was beautiful. His locs were wrapped in a black scarf. He handed Tyrique two cups of coffee. He asked if I wanted any pastries. I declined. We sat down.

"This smells amazing."

I nodded. "Cardamom. Be careful. It's hot."

"I like hot," he reassured me.

A smile formed on my lips, probably looking quite cheesy, like a schoolboy on a first date.

"Those dimples though. Ahhh!" He bit his lower lip.

I blushed and looked down at my hands.

"Tell me, Abdul," he leaned back and hooked his arm on the back of the chair, "what brings an Afghan prince to Baltimore? Aren't you supposed to be reigning in your palace?"

I giggled. I couldn't be any farther from royalty. In fact, I once had been picked to become the worst type of servant. But I distracted myself from that thought, "You're the first American guy who uses the word 'Afghan' right."

"I like to learn about other cultures. You're Hazara, right?"

Delving into my ethnicity was a bit too much. I thought he didn't feel entitled to other people's past. "How do you know all this?" I deflected.

"A few trips and many books." As he put down his cup, he extended his hand on the table. Our skin touched. I felt the same magnetic power emanating from his fingertips. I squeezed them between mine.

"You're not drinking?" he asked.

"Oh… I forgot."

A sip of coffee had never tasted this good. I took a deep breath to take in more of the cardamom aroma. It felt like heaven. The innocent touch. The bittersweet of the coffee. The beauty of his eyes staring at me.

"You approve?"

I wanted to say, it was not only the coffee I relished. But instead, I just gave him a smile. "How did you find out about this place?"

"This coffee shop?"

I nodded.

"I came here yesterday to write. I love writing in coffee shops."

"You didn't need directions, then!" I shouldn't have said that. It sounded like I was complaining that this gorgeous man took an interest in me.

"A little harmless lie."

If he kept talking like this, I wouldn't be able to control myself. What did he see in me that he liked so much?

"I'm sorry. Wasn't it worth it though?"

"Yeah."

"Good."

"What is it you write?"

"I'll tell you. But first, I need to show you something and I won't take no for an answer."

"You gonna kidnap me?"

"Don't put thoughts in my head. I very well might."

If Cliff found out, he would blow up. Good thing he was so busy working on his app these days, because I couldn't resist the invitation.

We left Morning in Beirut and walked down toward the river. We walked by the Electric Boat Rental. The streetlights along the river against the backdrop of cloudy sky gave the scenery a dream-like character. It was beautiful to take a break from reality and walk alongside this beautiful young man, who, for some reason, wanted to spend time with me.

When we reached the corner, we turned right toward East Falls Street. He told me to close my eyes before I could see much of the MECU Pavilion. He wrapped his scarf around my head so that I couldn't see where he was taking me. I pretended to complain but part of me hoped he *would* kidnap me. Maybe he could break my reality and manifest my dreams. My heart melted as he took my hand to guide me.

"Where are we going?"

We giggled as we walked. I tripped on something in the snow, but he pulled on my hand and helped me balance myself. To prevent me from slipping again, he wrapped his arm around my waist under the jacket. I loved his touch. Tender yet strong. I could smell his cool sea breeze cologne. I resisted the urge to pull him closer to catch more of the fragrance.

We climbed some steps and entered a building. The air felt warm, and the street noise was now muffled. I heard an elevator. I really didn't care where he was taking me. It felt like he was elevating me high into heaven.

I hoped he could hide me well so that I wouldn't fall off the clouds, back into reality.

He finally unwrapped the scarf and told me to look. I saw the Inner Harbor skyline, with the MECU Pavilion and the National Aquarium on the right, the Patapsco River, and the skyscrapers on the other side. It had started to snow again. And from here, it felt like we were on top of clouds. The snow looked like a lace dress that was slowly descending on the city.

"Isn't that breathtaking, baby?"

Tyrique just called me "baby." He turned to me, his hand still wrapped around my waist. I knew we were in his room at the Paradise. The thirteenth floor if I remembered correctly. I felt his breath on my cheek. He looked into my eyes and then I felt the tip of his nose touch mine. Then I welcomed a kiss. He lowered his hand and touched my butt. I kissed him again, and then a third time, before I opened my eyes.

"The soldier spellbound the prince with a kiss," he narrated.

I swallowed. A thought of Cliff was about to form in my head. I forced it out, wishing to stay dreaming.

"That was a terrible verse of a poem that will never see the light of day."

"You are a poet." I observed.

"Aspiring. Not usually as corny as that impromptu verse. I mostly write articles. For Modern Man. It's a magazine for elegant, sophisticated professionals. Not to be confused with the sleazy Playboy-type thing from the fifties."

"A poet and a journalist."

He smiled, showing his perfect teeth.

"That's why you know so much."

"I know I wanna do this," he leaned into me and kissed me on the lips, taking off my jacket.

I had no control. I was light and soaring. My body compelled me to let him do as he pleased. My heart yearned for him. My brain flashed me a warning about the consequences, but I ignored it.

His skin was soft, and I was determined to feel as much of it as I could. To savor as much of him as possible. Somehow our clothes ended up on the floor and we on the bed. It felt as if I had died and gone to heaven. And this angel welcomed me at the gates of paradise. I wasn't sure how long it lasted. We were suspended in time.

I ended up laying on my chest. He lay on top of me, our fingers still interlaced. I felt his heartbeat quiet down. I loved the weight of his body on mine. After I could no longer feel the beating of his heart, he lifted his body.

"Sorry, did I smash your chest?"

"I'm fine." I lifted my face.

"You *are* fine."

When he got up, we were no longer on clouds. We were in a guest room on the thirteenth floor of the Patapsco Paradise. I had to go back to work. "What should I tell Ms. Grace when she asks what we were doing this whole time."

"Everything," he announced, grinning. "Tell her we did everything. She won't ask any more questions after that."

"You're terrible."

He didn't have to exit the dream. His reality wasn't anchored in Baltimore. He remained an angel, me a mere mortal.

"Hey, Abdul?" His tone turned serious.

"Yes?"

"What is this?"

He touched the pillow that had a tan stain on it and a few brown spots. I panicked. As I laid my face on the pillow, the foundation had rubbed off and the bruise on my cheek had become visible.

He sat next to me and grabbed my chin. "How did you get this?"

I looked around for my pants.

"I'm listening."

"I fell down trying to dance. I was drunk."

"You fell down cheek first?"

Ms. Grace had believed it. Why wouldn't he?

"Don't insult my intelligence," he reprimanded.

We were both back to reality now, and the worst part of it at that.

"I really have to go." I rose from the bed.

"You don't seem like the type that would get into bar fights." He exhaled slowly. "You're not single, Abdul. Are you?"

I hurried to put on my clothes.

"I know you heard me."

Those words dispelled my haste. His look made me feel ashamed. I shook my head to answer his question.

"Do you have an open relationship?"

"Something like that," I managed to mumble as I buttoned up my shirt.

"Listen to me, Abdul." Tyrique walked over to me and grabbed my shoulder to emphasize what he was about to say. "A boyfriend that hits you is just a boy. He's not a friend."

I looked down and felt tears well up in my eyes.

"And he's definitely not a man."

I'd given the impression of being a regular cheater. A tear rolled down my face and dropped on his foot. "We fight sometimes. It's no big deal. I hit him too." I wiped my face with my sleeve and looked for my black tie.

"Love doesn't hurt, Abdul."

I grabbed the tie from the chair and forced my feet into my shoes.

"He shouldn't hurt you."

I wore my blazer and grabbed my green jacket. "I'm sorry, Tyrique."

"I hope to God I'm wrong but…" He rubbed his forehead as if to clear his mind of unwanted thoughts. "You deserve better, Abdul."

I glanced at his eyes for a second.

"This is not acceptable."

Pretending I engaged in more than just defensive strikes, I answered, "I will never raise my hand to him again. I

20   Hamour Baika

promise." I sounded angrier than I thought. Angry that he had discovered my secret.

He put up his hands, preempting my resistance.

I ran out of his room. What did he think of me now? A violent guy from a violent country? Wasn't that how American media portrayed us? In a few moments, I'd lost all respect in his eyes. I took short breaths, hoping my tears wouldn't turn into loud sobs. At least not until I'd left the hotel.

As I walked out of the elevator, I almost ran into a young woman with long black hair. She looked familiar for some reason. Her nametag said "Trilce." I apologized and rushed out of the building.

When I got back to the inn, Ms. Grace had already gone on her lunch break. Rebecca was behind the reception desk in her wheelchair, visibly upset with me.

"How many hours do you think your lunch break is?" she questioned.

Within minutes, she gave me a verbal warning, which in contrast to its name, was written on a personnel form. That was the price of daring to dream: I was now chastised at work, alone, and my bruise unmasked.

The guilt of cheating on Cliff was boiling my insides. I deserved the beating he had given me Thursday night. I deserved much worse. The humiliation of Tyrique seeing the wound and Rebecca writing me up didn't compensate for what I'd done. I wanted to feel the physical side of this emotional pain.

Tyrique was so judgmental all of a sudden. What was so wrong with fighting a little? Boys fight. And I had promised to never hit Cliff again. So be it. After what I'd just done, I deserved a good beating. If I pushed his buttons, he would get mad. Explode with anger and let me taste my own blood. I could feel it. It tasted like metal. As if I licked a coin. I already had enough makeup to cover up the next bruise.

Why did I ever think someone like Tyrique would show interest in me? By now, he must have moved on. Found someone good-looking, successful, educated. Soon, he wouldn't even remember me at all.

When I reached home after work, I stood paralyzed at the door. There was something wrong with me. I couldn't appreciate my man. The gorgeous man I was with. I always found a way of making a mess of my life. Now I was harming Cliff's as well. Would he be able to smell Tyrique's breath on me? How long before Cliff threw the first punch? Or would he slap me first? I wouldn't raise my hand again. I promised I wouldn't.

I turned my key and opened the door.

"There you are," Cliff greeted me. "Come. I'm starving."

"Hi. I'm sorry I'm—"

"I got Chinese. I know how much you like lo mein."

He'd forgotten I loved fried rice. But he was there, and that was what mattered.

"Remember, we had lo mein on our first date?" Cliff reminisced.

On our first date, we went to a Chinese restaurant. Cliff was hungry and interrupted as I was trying to order. Then he said the love of lo mein was something we had in common. If liking a different dish meant he would take me on a second date, I could live with that. Even if it meant I would never have fried rice again.

He snapped his fingers to bring me back to present. "Hey? You drowned in your thoughts again?"

I had.

The news was on, showing the picture of the guy that the police had killed yesterday. He was so young, still a teenager.

Cliff clicked on the remote control and turned off the TV. "Come."

I sat at the table and smiled at him.

"Just so you know, I do my best to look unapproachable and cranky at the gym." He put a forkful in his mouth. "I know you get upset when boys check me out."

"Of course, they check you out. You're beautiful."

"Just beautiful?"

"Magnificent."

"Just magnificent?"

I didn't know what was better than magnificent, so I busied myself with putting some food on my plate.

"Yeah I am," he answered his own question. "It's good you get jealous. Makes me feel loved. Except you get," he drank some water, "bombastic."

"You know how embarrassing it is walking around with a bruise on my face?"

"I'm sorry. I acted like a fool."

I also had acted like a fool earlier today.

He grinned and said, "I'll make it up to you."

Maybe I didn't have to start a fight after all. It felt good to just have dinner and talk to my loving boyfriend. If he wanted to make a nice gesture, why stop him?

He gave me a pack of soy sauce. "Let's go on a fun date." He sounded excited. "What about going to ski?"

"Well, you know how I feel about skiing."

"Wine tasting?"

"We wouldn't even be alone most of the time."

"A game night? We can invite Mason and his flavor of the week and make fun of them after they leave." He looked at me expectantly for a few seconds. "I take that as a no."

My facial expression betrayed my disdain. "We could watch a movie," I suggested.

"OK, I'll check the schedule."

"The type of movie I like is hard to find in a movie theater. Plus, a Bollywood movie would go great with a kebab delivery."

"Fine," he capitulated. "If that's what you want."

I didn't deserve to get what I wanted. But I enjoyed seeing the caring side of Cliff. There was no need for me to trigger his anger. My desire for Tyrique's touch started to dissipate. I already had a good man who'd got us dinner and wanted to make up for our quarrel.

Fiber

/ˈfaɪbər/ noun

Pedaling a bit faster on the elliptical machine, I kept an eye on Cliff. With only a few guys in the gym today, I quickly noticed Cliff's admirer of the day. The white boy was positioned almost upside down on the leg press machine. One could only assume that pushing against the metal sheet supporting so much weight would be terrible for the knees. It also had no benefit for the calves. I never understood the point. Biceps and calves were the two muscles most visible. Yet, few people bothered to work on their calves. The boy pushed and grunted. I thought he was hurting himself on that knee-breaker of a machine. But his eyes still followed Cliff's every move.

Working out wasn't my idea of fun. But after our fight last week, Cliff wanted to prove he could behave. Plus, he wanted me to build muscle. "No one is chiseled enough," he remarked.

As usual, Cliff looked better than anyone else in the gym. He was wearing a yellow tank top and green short shorts to induce as much lust as possible and signal to any interested women that they had no chance. He liked to flaunt his gayness, knowing full well no one dared attack him for it. He would win such a fight.

Sweat sparkled on his skin. He climbed a power tower, a label that described him more than the equipment. He placed his arms on his favorite structure, his back against the support. He lifted his legs ninety degrees into the air, knees unbent, showing off his perfect calves. He did fifteen reps and rested for a moment. I pushed harder on the elliptical, pretending not to watch.

The TV screen in the corner broadcast a picture of the teenager who was shot by the police in Mosher.

A picture of Tyrique flashed in my mind. Was he safe? I didn't want to imagine anything bad. So, I distracted myself. What did he do for his workout routine? Maybe he swam or played tennis. But he definitely had to lift some weights for muscles like that.

The white boy descended from the leg press and stole another glance at Cliff. I was daydreaming about Tyrique when everyone in the gym was fantasizing about my man. How could I ever cheat on Cliff? Yes, he had a temper. But no one was perfect. I still marveled at why he was interested in me, even after living together for a few years. I'd never seen anyone checking *me* out. But everywhere we went, men and women stared at Cliff, licked their lips, or forgot that their mouth remained half-open. He looked like the perfect candidate for the cover of Men's Fitness. Or GQ. He had a temper but also had a good job that paid for our apartment in Highlandtown. He loved me and he wasn't the one to step out of our relationship. I pedaled faster, as if it could help me walk away from my mistake.

The fact that I still drooled over Tyrique bothered me even more. Was it my heart or my hormones? Or just the attention of a man other than Cliff, so I could imagine that I was desirable? But a one-off case didn't prove anything. I could find that in Kabul for a night. What was difficult was finding the one who would return the next day.

I remembered squatting on the side of a quiet dusty street near Mirwais Maidan, watching people. Men wore *pero-tanbo* in every color. A *krachiwan* leaned on his wheelbarrow and haggled with a female shopper who wanted him to push her load to her house. They argued back and forth for a few more rupiahs. The whole street smelled like pee, but at least my corner was dry.

My thighs hurt but if I had sat on the ground, the cold would have permeated my body faster. I'd had a hard day. No matter how much I asked for a chance to sweep the street, or carry someone's load, or just asked someone to find pity for my condition and give me something to eat, I had failed. I remembered looking at my feet, my toes showing in my dirty plastic slippers. I wasn't in a much better condition than my clothes, dirty and unwanted. My hair felt like steel wool that my mother used to wash pots and pans. I'd lost my family. I hadn't deserved any better. My fate had followed me to Kabul and there I was, sitting alone, hungry and about to shiver in the cold.

I would do anything to never feel that kind of heart wrenching loneliness. Why was I thinking of Kabul at all? Cliff wanted me. His temper was just part of the package. He finished raising his leg in the air and dismounted the equipment. The knee-breaker guy was now sitting on a bench, with a much better view of Cliff.

Feeling warmer, I slowed down to pat my cheek with the towel. I doubted that the carpet burn on my face was still an open wound. But I didn't want to test that theory by seeing if it burned with the salt of my own sweat.

If I'd made some flash cards with SAT words, I wouldn't have had the time to think about all this. The bruise on my face. My homeless nights in Kabul. Tyrique. In a perfect world, I would've been done with college a couple of years ago. But if I were to achieve my dream of getting a degree, I had to improve my language skills. Otherwise, I'd never be able to pass any other subjects. Math being the only subject I excelled at. I didn't have to speak much English to solve the problems.

I jerked, as someone dropped some free weights on the floor. I hated when guys did that. *If you could lift them, why can't you just put them on the floor like a normal person?* Or did he just want to make sure the whole gym found out that he'd lifted some dumbbells?

Cliff began wiping the handles with Clorox. That meant he was ready to go. I slowed down further, happy to be done with this. He walked up to me.

"Ready?"

"Yeah." As I casually looked away to take my towel, I saw the knee-breaker eyeing Cliff, surprised that Cliff was waiting for me.

"You gonna catch up?" he asked me.

"Yeah."

After Cliff walked away, I peeked at the guy. He looked at me with disgust, as if I had taken away *his* man. Maybe, I was a pile of dirt. Who else would cheat on the man that everybody wanted? But Tyrique…

I had to stop thinking. I had to go, so Cliff wouldn't have to wait too long.

I quickly wiped the handles and the buttons of the elliptical and paced toward the lockers. Cliff was already wearing his jeans and holding his jacket. He told me we'd wash up at home. This way, we didn't have to worry about the guy following us into the showers.

I opened my locker and took out my street shoes.

"You're awfully quiet tonight," Cliff observed. "Is everything OK?"

"Yeah." I untied my sneakers as quickly as I could and put on my black trainers. Cliff's neon sneakers were still on the floor. I put them in the bag and packed up my stuff.

I saw Cliff standing in front of a full-length mirror just outside the locker room. I followed the delicious trace of pheromones with a hint of his Yves Saint Laurent antiperspirant. He noticed me and turned around. "Thanks." His arms wrapped around me. The warmth of his body felt good on my wet T-shirt. "You look like a ruffian. It's hot," he whispered in my ear.

"We have an audience."

He knew whom I was talking about. "Let's put on a show then. Drop the bags."

I did. The sound echoed in the hallway.

He playfully shoved me against the wall and held my hands above my head and started making out. He tasted sweet like his energy drink. "Mmm."

Getting closer to feel his scent, I kissed his bicep.

That turned him on. "Not so shy anymore. I like it."

"There's a lot more where that came from." Just then, I realized I *was* a flirt.

He laughed. "You talk like that and you're gonna get something extra in the shower tonight."

"What if I pick a different lover from the gym tonight?" I tried my best to make it sound playful.

"You wanna cheat on me?" He sounded frisky, though a bit deflated. "If I wanted a cheater, I could've picked any gay boy from the catalogue."

And he would have certainly been better looking than me.

"He's coming." Cliff grabbed my chin then kissed me passionately on the lips.

The knee-breaker was walking toward us, but having noticed the public display of affection, he averted his eyes, pretending he'd found something fascinating about the texture of the wall paint.

"My heart beats only for you," Cliff said exactly as the knee-breaker passed us by.

I gave him a smile.

"You still think I'll be jumping in bed with any idiot like that?" He paused for a second and then picked up the bag. "You got all your stuff, baby?" He called out, making sure our observer noticed we shared the same gym bag.

I wrapped my hand around his waist. Cliff's hand glided downward and slipped into my pants back pocket.

I felt privileged to walk out of there with Cliff. I shouldn't do anything to jeopardize what we had. We walked north on Bouldin Street. An enormous dog ran toward Cliff, barking. It looked like the dog from the cartoon Belle and Sebastian.

"Aren't you gorgeous?" Cliff squatted and patted the dog, whose leash was dragging behind him. It licked his hand. "That's a good boy." Cliff patted the animal with enthusiasm.

"Good girl, actually." A woman appeared out of the dark, panting a little. "Sorry. I lost hold of the leash."

"No problem," he reassured her. "What's her name?"

"Polly."

"She's awesome."

"She likes you. She's not that friendly with most people."

Soon after I moved in with him, Cliff wanted to get a dog. I hated the idea, so I feigned being afraid of dogs. He never brought up the topic again.

"You guys look so cute together," the woman remarked.

"Thank you."

She took Polly's leash and walked away.

When we reached home, Cliff took off his shoes. I was lucky to have convinced a white American to not wear shoes in the apartment. "Anything for my boy," he had responded when I asked him. He stood there, waiting for me at the foyer.

I wanted him to stop looking at me, fearing he might see the guilt on my face. In my haste, I had re-knotted my shoelaces. "I'll be right there." I hoped he would wash off the dog's saliva off his hands in the meanwhile.

He didn't. Instead, he went to the living room and threw himself on the sofa. "Could you do me a favor and get me my phone charger? It's on the nightstand in the bedroom."

"Of course," I went to the bedroom and flicked the light switch. I gasped at what I saw on the bed. A burgundy velvet blazer was wrapped around a shiny black button-down shirt. A pair of black trousers with faint paisley pattern was positioned underneath. The trouser legs were placed just above black boots with extra zippers on the side. The clothes suited a fancy cocktail party.

"My way of saying I'm sorry." Cliff appeared behind me.

"Oh my God, these are gorgeous. Is this all for me?"

"You like them?" He sounded excited.

"Of course. That blazer," I picked it up and put it on my chest, "this is royal."

Cliff put his arm around my chest and pulled me close.

I felt so spoiled. "You didn't have to do that."

"I know. But I wanted to."

I kissed him. "Thank you. Thank you so much."

"You're welcome. Now go put them on, so I can take them off," he winked.

I pressed myself onto his stiff pecs. Cliff wrapped his arms around me.

Permeate

/ˈpɜːrmieɪt/ verb

Slowing my pace as I walked past Morning in Beirut, I looked inside. I used to memorize my SAT words sitting on the bar stool with the street view. Now, a young mother had placed two of her three bags on the stool as she fed the baby inside the stroller. A tray containing *zaatar* pinwheels, coffee cups, and an orange juice bottle sat on the table next to her third bag. I wondered where Tyrique purchased his coffee today. In front of me, the good-looking guy with locs was chatting with a customer. His nametag said "Derrick." A stack of The Baltimore Sun newspaper sat in front of the counter. The headline read "Officer Mistook Cellphone for Gun." Below was the already familiar picture of the 18-year-old who lost his life to this so-called mistake. The shooting that took place on Mosher Street. An infuriating headline that resembled too many others.

A cold breeze brushed against my face. Would anyone remember me from last week, visiting the coffee shop with Tyrique? I shouldn't have risked what I had with Cliff for a fleeting chance encounter. Stepping away, I zipped my jacket all the way up. I didn't want the taste of their coffee to remind me of him. On the way to the inn, I bought a cheaper type from Dunkin Donuts. I should be saving for college anyway.

By the time I got to work, the coffee was cold and tasteless. Nothing like the sensation of drinking cardamom coffee with a hint of local honey. The sediment would settle at the bottom of the cup, ready for a fortune teller to appear out of nowhere and declare something unavoidable like "you'll go on a trip" or "you'll meet someone."

Is it Tyrique?

Rebecca was taking a cigarette break and now the lobby was entirely deserted. I opened the internet browser on my phone. A blank page appeared, enticing me to type something. I locked the phone and put it aside. I took another sip and regretted it immediately. Then I threw the cup into the garbage bin.

Cliff liked French press coffee. What would he do if he ever found out what I'd done? He could have had anyone he wanted, but he chose me. He had been acting so lovingly before flying to Louisville for Thanksgiving. Had he been around, he might have noticed that I was quieter than usual. I rubbed the wound on my face to feel the hurt from our last fight. But it had already turned into a painless scab.

Rebecca rolled into the lobby. "Hey, Abdul. I noticed you still haven't picked up the note from your mailbox."

"What note?"

"Someone brought you something. A few days ago."

"Who?"

"Didn't leave a name. Or maybe he did. I don't remember." She shrugged and went to the office.

I followed her and noticed the envelope in my mailbox.

"Tyrone, Terrell, something like that," she was trying to recall who'd left me the note.

"Tyrique?"

"Yeah?" She wasn't sure.

I picked it up and went back to the front desk. I slid the envelope opener into the fold, trying to preserve it as best I could. Hoping it would smell like Tyrique, I brought it to my nose. It would've been too romantic if he'd sprayed it with his sea breeze cologne. He hadn't. The paper in my hand didn't contain any romantic gesture at all. It was from a block note with the Patapsco Paradise logo. Not the right type of stationery for a love letter.

At least there was no one to see my disappointment. Such is fate. "You don't have to suffer through it alone." Below the sentence, there was a phone number, described as "Domestic Violence Help Line for MSM."

Tyrique hadn't signed it as if I didn't deserve to see his name.

The only help I needed was him.

Tyrique had the wrong impression of me and Cliff. He wasn't a violent abuser. He just got angry once in a while. Last week, I had pushed him. It was me who started the whole fiasco. I had to get my jealousy under control. Cliff was hot. Boys were constantly trying to get with him. I just had to get used to it. That was the price you paid for having a boyfriend way out of your league. There was no domestic violence to seek support from. If anything, I deserved a good beating for cheating on my boyfriend. The desire still pounded in my chest when I thought of Tyrique and made me feel even guiltier.

I didn't want Tyrique to have this impression of me. I had to see him. Rebecca allowed me to take a quick break to go to the Patapsco Paradise.

The same young woman I almost collided into when I stormed out of the hotel last weekend was sitting at the reception desk. Trilce. She looked so familiar. She ran her fingers through her hair. "Good morning. How can I help you?"

"Hi. How are you doing?"

"Good. How are you?"

Now that I stood in front of her, I felt stupid for having showed up like that. She looked at me expectantly, smiling.

"I am looking for one of your guests."

"Sure. What's their name?"

I told her. She typed something and stared at her computer. "I'm afraid he's checked out already."

I knew she couldn't give me his contact information. I saw no point in asking.

"Have we met?"

Did she remember from last week?

"I've seen you before."

"I don't think so," I mumbled, sounding like I was hiding something.

"DC Pride," she exclaimed. "Right?"

"Ummm…"

We'd taken pictures with several random spectators at the parade.

She grabbed her phone and started scrolling. "Look!" She showed me a picture of her with me and Cliff. "This is my favorite picture from pride. I look good, no?"

In the picture, she was wearing butterfly wings. It was starting to come back to me. We even had talked about living in Baltimore and hoping to hang out at some point.

"And you came here last weekend. Oh my God, with our most good-looking customer, whose name, I think, was Tyrique Williams." Her volume increased as her excitement grew. "A tedious day just got interesting."

I looked around to see if anyone else was witnessing my embarrassment.

"We should grab coffee some time. And you can tell me all about it. You were supposed to get in touch last June. It's about time."

When I came to the US eight years ago, I thought I'd never get used to how closely men and woman interacted here. I felt shy talking to girls. But that slowly changed. In high school, a few girl classmates took my side when boys bullied me. I was an easy target, as a gay Muslim immigrant who didn't speak English well. Here, girls and gay boys were natural allies.

But now in front of Trilce, I still felt shy. I was caught in a love affair, and, in a lie about contacting her several months ago. I also wanted to ask why she was so interested. That would have been rude.

"Last Saturday, you acted like you were on cloud nine. Now you look like your favorite aunt just died. I can cheer you up. And if you start a long-distance relationship with this guy, you will need someone who's good at giving romantic advice." She pointed at herself.

She seemed nice, but I wanted to leave and forget about this whole thing. I shouldn't have come here at all.

"OK, don't be so enthusiastic," she teased, noting my silence.

"I'm sorry. I just..."

"How come you guys didn't exchange numbers? Well, I'm sure you'll find him on Grindr or something." She covered her mouth, perhaps realizing she was getting too personal. "Sorry. My mom always says I have no filter. What do I look like? An HVAC?" She started to grow on me.

"I'd love to have coffee some time."

"There you go. You look a lot more adorable when you smile."

Did she just call me adorable?

"What's your number? Obviously, giving you my number wouldn't do the trick!" She handed me the phone.

I typed my name and number.

"Well, OK then," she straightened her hair again. "Let me know how it goes with your future boyfriend."

"I already have a boyfriend." *Oh Gosh, I just admitted to being a cheater.*

"Oh wow! This keeps getting more and more interesting. In that case, you definitely need a good friend. You can never have too many of those!"

Too many friends? I didn't have any. Not since coming to Baltimore and losing touch with Rakesh and Niloofar. "I'd like that."

"I'll introduce you to another friend of mine. Shane. He's really cool. He does drag at Hippo. You should come see her."

Whenever we go out, everyone in the club wanted to dance with Cliff. Meanwhile, I stood alone, drinking at the bar and watching one thirsty boy after another hitting on him.

"Don't be a stranger." She signaled I should go. "I'll call you."

I nodded and walked away. A gush of freezing wind blew in as I opened the door and stepped outside.

"See you," she managed to say before the door shut behind me.

Back at the inn, I opened my phone. Something occurred to me. The blank browser page came up. A mild case of cyber-stalking wouldn't hurt him. I wanted to satisfy my curiosity, allowing my desires to undermine my morals. Again.

I typed Tyrique Williams. Out of all the results, how was I going to find mine? I clicked on the image filter. A football player. His face covered under the helmet so I couldn't know for sure. I scrolled down. A teenager with both thumbs up. A young man smiling under his graduate cap. An older man in a military uniform. Someone who'd decided to make his dog the profile picture. A picture of someone, hiking in the mountains, wearing sunglasses. I kept going.

I shuddered when I saw it. A black and white picture of Tyrique, looking at the camera. A halo of light marked the silhouette of his body, making him look like an angel. So beautiful that it couldn't fit this world. The other half of his face was dark, his gaze piercing, even through the phone screen.

I looked around to see if anyone could see me. Rebecca was in the office, typing something on her computer. Ms. Grace was off for the Thanksgiving break. I clicked on his picture. A website opened. His website. Under his picture, there were two links: on the interior, on the exterior. I tapped on the latter. Under the heading "biographical actuations," I read, "Born into a professional household in New Orleans in 1987..." *He's 27, three years older than me.* I hadn't prepared emotionally to dive into his life. I looked for another heading, "poetic expressions." I clicked. The next page showed me the titles of his poems and the literary journals where they'd been published.

The first link directed me to one of them. The poem didn't make any sense to me. Maybe I'd read it too fast. I read it again. The poem was a whole SAT vocabulary book. I didn't know the meaning of many words. Even those I knew didn't make sense to me in that particular constellation. Of the new words, "permeate" sounded the nicest. I looked it up.

"You busy?" Rebecca was back.

"No, not really. Just reading a poem."

"I didn't know you liked poetry."

Everybody in my culture liked poetry. "It just occurred to me that I can learn vocabulary from poetry."

"Sounds like a great idea. Who are you reading?"

"Umm... this young contemporary poet."

"I can recommend a few poets if you're interested."

"Thanks."

"Sure."

She could be kind like this, except when it interfered with the inn's "business needs." It took me a while to learn that in America, not everyone who is kind is your friend.

I opened my phone and went back to Tyrique's page. My chest turned into a fireplace as I stared at his picture. Yet, a layer of cold sweat formed over my body. Just last week, I was in his arms. And now, he was gone to some unknown place. Leaving me a note, empty of any sentimental message. Just a dry matter-of-fact phone number I didn't intend to use. I closed the app, my hand trembling.

The fire from the inner filaments of my core fought the cold that was permeating my skin. If only pain would vaporize like sweat. But pain nested somewhere deep in my guts. I stored it there, next to all my other aches.

The first word in his poem that I didn't understand was "tilt."

"Rebecca? What does 'tilt' mean?"

She explained.

I attempted making a sentence: "If my heart were a jar, I'd tilt it to pour out the emotions I feel for you."

Perhaps, I could use his poetry like a map to his head. To his heart. I could love and admire him from afar without cheating, without anyone finding out.

Tryst
/trɪst/ *noun*

Sunday afternoon, I was counting the minutes to the end of my shift. Cliff was supposed to be coming back from Louisville later at night, and I still hadn't planned dinner. Perhaps a fresh salad to serve with chicken breast to compensate for all the starchy Thanksgiving food he'd had. Just then, the door opened, and he walked into the lobby. He was wearing a tight suit with a pink floral tie, looking good.

"Cliff, you're back."

"Surprise!" He was carrying a bouquet of lilies and chrysanthemums.

"These are gorgeous."

Ms. Grace came over. "Clifford, so good to see you. I didn't know you're back in town."

"Came back early to surprise my better half."

"Oh I see." She turned to me and said, "He's a keeper."

"These are for you. Happy belated Thanksgiving."

"Oh my! Thank you, sugar. Same to you." She smelled the flowers.

I thought I was "sugar."

"Can I take him home now? Or do we have to wait for the clock to tick?"

"You guys go home," she approved. "I'll be fine. And watch him so he doesn't trip again dancing on the carpet."

Cliff stared at her, confused.

I had to interrupt before she put two and two together. "Thanks so much, Ms. Grace. I'll see you tomorrow."

"Have a great evening." Cliff stepped to the door, leading the way.

"You do the same," she answered.

It could have been my imagination, but she sounded... dry. I hoped she hadn't noticed the awkward silence about my carpet burn. We stepped out.

"I can't believe you came back early to see me."

"It's Thanksgiving weekend. I can only tolerate my brothers and their families for so long." He sat behind the driver seat.

I climbed into his silver Mini.

"Guess what? Jacob's marriage is likely ending."

"Jeez. What happened?"

"Millie told me, 'I wish he was more like you!' Right there, in front of everybody. I wouldn't be surprised if she divorces his ass by the fourth of July."

"Oh. What happens to their—?"

"I was like 'who's the loser faggot now'?"

"You didn't."

"He left the table. Meanwhile, Clyde was cleaning baby vomit off his shoulder the whole time. Life is taking my revenge for me."

His two brothers had tormented him when they were growing up. Physical fights and never-ending insults were the norm. One of the reasons Cliff got upset whenever he felt he was being disrespected.

Driving on Eastern Avenue, Cliff moved to the left lane to bypass a police car, parked at an angle. Two African American young boys were sitting on the curb. Their father was being questioned under the flood lights of the police car. The kids were about eight and ten.

I was eight when I'd had my first interaction with the Armed Forces, which was still better than the Revolutionary Guards or the Basij. Karim and I were playing hide and seek in *Bagh-e Melli*. I was hiding behind a bench for a long time. When I noticed Karim was getting close, I ran to the pole we'd used for *cheshm-gozari*. All of a sudden, someone yelled out "Stop!" I kept running, thinking that other people were playing a different game. There was no "stop" in the rules of hide and seek.

But then, I noticed that the man was wearing a uniform. Another officer yelled out, "Don't shoot, it's a child." They were about to let us go when my father showed up. As soon as they realized we were from Afghanistan, they said they have "cause for arrest" since drug dealers frequented the park. In their eyes, all of us were selling opium at all times. My father begged the police to let Karim and me go home. They eventually did, but that didn't prevent Karim from hitting me repeatedly on the way home, for getting our father arrested.

"What are you thinking about?" Cliff pulled me out of the memory. "You're so quiet."

It broke my heart to watch the two young boys sitting on the curb, looking petrified. But Cliff wouldn't understand my disdain for the police.

Back home, Cliff had the food ready: *kebab-e barg*, grilled tomatoes, a small piece of butter on the saffron rice, served with sumac and my favorite wine, Apothic Red. After dinner, we took our wine glasses to bed to snuggle and watch a movie I picked, *Humpty Sharma Ki Dulhania*.

A bit intoxicated, Cliff wanted to dance to the songs, which he did while stripping. Afterward, his naked body next to mine made both the movie and the wine more enjoyable.

Two hours later, he turned off the TV. "That was some movie. Very unlikely and… kinda long, no?"

"Isn't she beautiful? I love her."

"I highly doubt you picked this movie for her. You picked it for *him*." He referred to Varun Dhawan.

"A nice romantic comedy," I refused to admit I found the actor irresistible.

"Love conquers all. What an original idea," he mocked. "I would have never watched this if it weren't for you."

"So I guess love does conquer all." I kissed his cheek.

"I guess."

I put my head on his chest and lay on my back. "Cliff, why do you love me?"

"Are you still feeling insecure after all this?"

"I just wanna know."

"You serious?" he paused. "OK. Well, there's not one single reason. You're… deep, Abdul. I mean, in my twenties, I wanted to explore as much as possible. I was so promiscuous it was awesome. But I'd only get these super shallow guys. All they cared about was my abs. They had no real interest in me. I don't wanna toot my own horn that I'm hot and handsome."

"Which you are."

"But I'm more than just a pretty face. I'm smart too. I need grown-up conversation, not just celebrities and gossip about who's sleeping with whom. Also, guys who jump in your bed because you're hot will also jump in the bed of the next one. I'm a traditional guy. If I am in a relationship, I commit. I don't cheat. But ask any gay couple, they're all in an open relationship. What's the point? Just be roommates, then. And you know, you're from a country with more traditional values. So I guess I love that about you also."

Cliff was the only man who wanted me for something more than a one-night stand. Me, on the other hand… I felt dirty and cheap. "What else?" I was eager to be distracted from this last thought, now that he was more talkative than usual, thanks to the wine.

"You're beautiful, thoughtful, compassionate, considerate." He took his time to look for other attributes to point out. "You have strong beliefs." He added, his voice now animated, "The first time you saw me wearing shoes in the apartment, you looked at me like I'd just murdered a kitten."

I did appreciate that he hadn't fought me on that.

Cliff continued, "You're resilient. You've gone through so much in your life. But nothing could break you. Despite everything, you're proud and together."

"I'm one of the lucky ones. Nothing super bad really happened to me. I survived. Most people don't get away unscathed."

"Still," he insisted. "You're independent and strong. Like, I make enough money for you to be a 'trophy boy,' sitting on your ass all day doing nothing. But you insist you want to work and contribute. You're ambitious." He chuckled and caressed my hair. "Even right now, I bet that stupid SAT book is somewhere nearby."

It was on the nightstand next to my empty wine glass. I suddenly felt seen. And exposed.

"You always strive to improve yourself. Should I stop or should I continue stroking your ego?"

"Continue stroking," I teased.

"You have a killer smile that gives you dimples."

I kissed the end of his nose.

"Why do *you* love *me*?" he inquired.

Many reasons rushed to my head, competing with each other. He gave my life stability. He didn't ask me a million questions about my past to make me relive the difficulties. He could have had anyone, but he picked me and never stepped out of our relationship. He found me my first good job.

"Does it really take that long to think why you love me?" He interrupted my thoughts.

"No."

"So… what is it?"

"You have a nice dick!" I couldn't resist teasing him. It was too easy. He basically had asked for it.

He laughed so heartily that I had to lift my head off his chest. "That's reductionist! I just said you're better than that."

"It's the gist!" I lectured, also laughing now. "Summarizing what I like about you!"

"So I'm just your boy toy!"

"Pretty much."

"Well, I guess I'd better prove my worth then," he kissed my lips.

I lifted my hands so he could take off my T-shirt.

Malefic

/məˈlefɪk/ adj.

My phone had become dearer to me, knowing that somewhere on my browser, Tyrique's page had remained open. I put my SAT book on the coffee table, sat on the couch, and scrolled down all the way to the bottom of the poem to read the ending once again.

Yet over the years,
The papyrus unfurls,
Dispersing the pappi of the sage's lore
And the saga whirls.

Since I'd found his site and read all its content, I started calling him "Ty" in my mind. I thought we were too close to call him by his full name. He knew me as just Abdul. So, it was only fair. I imagined him reciting his poems. His voice would be masculine and intentional, yet tender. The vocabulary in his poems seemed much more useful than SAT words. Who would use "surreptitious" and "scrupulous" in a normal conversation? You couldn't really say these words without sounding pretentious. But a word like "unfurl"? Now that just sounded beautiful.

My phone screen lit up. A text message from Cliff. "We're coming home to brainstorm. Get dinner."

"We? Pizza OK?" I asked. No response. I suspected Malefic Mason would be coming. He reminded me of the Two Little Terrors, combined into one. The SAT work "malefic" summarized his entire personality. He carried a bad omen everywhere he went.

I should have been around ten years old in Mashhad when I noticed the Two Little Terrors: a couple of adolescent neighborhood boys, with small bodies and evil minds. They broke tree branches, terrorized the birds, and harassed me, particularly in the summer afternoons when they had nothing better to do. The first time they started making fun of me, I'd been trying to feed an alley cat. I complained to my older brother Karim about the two of them. He scolded me and said, if I stopped acting like a girl, the neighborhood boys would stop bullying me. "Why are you feeding the cat anyway? What are you? The old fairy from Cinderella?" Never again did I ask Karim to protect me. He knew I was gay before I did, and he didn't shy away from expressing his disdain.

I had to face the Two Little Terrors on my own. Whenever they felt like it, they'd get their instruments of death and aim at birds. But not at doves. The teenage boy across the street kept doves. The Two Little Terrors wouldn't dare even look at his doves when carrying their slingshots. That meant the only possible victims of their weapons would be sparrows. Sparrows. Who would harm sparrows? How lowly do you have to be to harm tiny defenseless little creatures like sparrows?

Whenever I saw the Two Little Terrors with their slingshots, I kept watch from afar to make sure they didn't succeed in hurting the birds. Thankfully, they had horrible aim. If they aimed at a sparrow, they'd hit the lightbulb above a neighbor's door. Something that earned them a bad beating once. I watched and basked in their punishment. But they soon resumed. They would spread breadcrumbs on the sidewalk as bait. To save the birds, I would throw a stone into the air, or cough loudly, or stomp my feet to scare them away.

Mason carried enough evil in him to fill up both of the Two Little Terrors. He was Cliff's best friend and hung out with him all the time. Now, I had to tolerate his face all night, and I didn't look forward to that.

I put the phone on the coffee table and got the phone number of the pizza place from the fridge door. I ordered four half pizzas: meat lover and pepperoni, veggie, and cheese. I walked a couple of blocks on South Ellwood Avenue by the Patterson Park to pick up the order. When I got back, no one was home yet. I turned on the oven on low and put the pizza inside. Not knowing how many people were coming, I put six plates on the table. I sat on the couch and opened my phone internet app again. "Unfurl."

Then I heard footsteps in the hallway. Cliff unlocked the door. He looked at me but didn't interrupt his conversation. Mason walked in behind him. He didn't even look at me. A third guy showed up next. His boots shined. None of them took off their shoes. I'd have to vacuum when they left.

"How are you doing?" The stranger extended his hand, one of the few African Americans that I ever remembered visiting us.

"I'm Abdul."

"Ben."

"Nice to meet you, Ben." I waited for the other two to acknowledge me.

Cliff snapped his fingers. "Get the food ready. We're starving."

"Yeah, it's ready."

Mason dropped his jacket on the floor and threw himself on the couch. He had long eyelashes and a small nose. If you saw only his face in a picture, you would consider him good-looking. But no physical attribute could compensate for his personality. His short and skinny body stretched on the couch as he put up his feet on my SAT book.

I reached out for the book. He didn't move.

"Lift your feet."

"In this country, we say 'please,'" he barked. "Cliff, haven't you taught her manners yet? So rude."

I yanked the book from under his foot.

"Yo, get the dinner already."

The worst thing about Malefic Mason was that Cliff acted up in his presence.

"What are we having?" Mason asked him.

Cliff looked at me, waiting for me to answer a question that wasn't directed at me.

"Pizza. With a few different toppings."

Mason complained to Cliff. "You told us not to get Chinese. Now we have to have *pizza*?"

"We got other things too." Cliff replied, waiting for me to elaborate.

"There's some soup from earlier. I can make some sandwiches. We also got ravioli and salad with beans." I had to weather the storm that was bubbling up in Cliff.

"What the hell is a beans salad?" Mason looked me up and down. "Nah, from what I remember, you can't cook." He looked at Cliff and suggested, "You should put her in some cooking class or something."

I would have pissed in his bowl if he did want the soup.

"And get me a drink," Cliff ordered.

I brought out the pizzas in two large trays and placed empty plates in front of each of them on the coffee table.

"She left the pizza in the oven for too long. It's dry as hell," Mason remarked.

Cliff yelled out, "Yo, bitch. Get me a Jack. I had a shit day." He wouldn't have called me that, without Mason egging him on.

I hated that it happened in front of Ben. I decided to act dignified regardless of Cliff's behavior. "What would you like?" I asked Ben.

He shook his head, silently disapproving of how Cliff was talking to me. "I'll have the same. Thanks, man."

"Some of us are faithful to our hometown," Mason teased Cliff. "Jim Beam for me," he told me.

Cliff liked his whiskey on the rocks. I brought three small glasses with the bottles of Jack Daniels and Jim Beam.

"What about Jack and Jim?" Cliff asked them, continuing their previous conversation.

"That's catchy, sort of." Ben clicked his glass with the other two.

"I don't like it. Sorry." Mason replied.

I left them in the living room. The smell of fresh pizza tickled my nose, but I had no desire to sit and dine with Mason and company.

"What the heck is this? Yo, bitch!" Mason yelled out.

I ignored him.

"Hey. Don't be disrespectful," my boyfriend-turned-monster replied.

He was warning *me*, not Mason. I returned to the living room. Mason didn't look at me.

Sometimes I felt like a stranger in this apartment. In this city, this country. I didn't know anyone with whom I could speak my language. People in Afghanistan would probably make fun of my "Iranian" accent. Iranians would see me as a foreigner. Here, no one knew anything about my background. People misplaced me based on my looks.

If they'd had a subscription to National Geographic, I'd be Uyghur. Otherwise, Chinese. They even truncated my name. Apparently, saying the full four syllables was too much effort. I could've picked a new name when I came to the US. But too much had been already taken away from me. My name was the last thing that was truly mine. So, I kept it.

Cliff snapped his fingers again, pulling me out of my thoughts. "Get your ass over here."

Did these two *have to* act like that in front of Ben? I wasn't new to their shenanigans, but I would have preferred to be treated like a human in front of their coworker. Ben was looking at me. I dropped my head so I wouldn't see the shocked look on his face.

"Come here," Cliff gestured.

I walked to Cliff and squatted.

"Show him, Mase," he told Mason.

"There's a bug in my drink." He passed his glass to Cliff, who showed it to me.

"I don't see anything."

"What did I tell you?" Cliff pointed his index finger at my face. "Rinse the glasses before making drinks."

"You told him to do that last time," Mason noted. "It's a fruit fly or something."

"But I—"

Before I could get the word out, a slap echoed in the room, making me lose my balance. What had just happened? In private, Cliff could get cranky sometimes. But in public, he was always the perfect loving boyfriend. I couldn't believe he'd just hit me in front of guests.

"Calm down, man," Ben interfered. "You're just angry because Owen was a dick today. Don't—"

"It's OK, Ben," Cliff cut him off. "We shouldn't have to explain a thousand times that we had," he turned to me and yelled, "a really bad day."

Mason changed positions and knocked over Ben's glass, spilling the drink onto the floor.

"It's not a big deal, just some whiskey." Ben spread several napkins on the table to absorb the spilled drink.

Meanwhile, I patted the rug with some napkins.

"If she was a dog, I'd say you should put her in a competitive obedience class." Mason was aware that Cliff loved dogs and I hated them.

"My man, just chill for a second," Ben intervened.

"She should apologize for being disrespectful," Mason replied. He knew exactly what to say to provoke Cliff. Lack of respect was Cliff's pet peeve. The Kentucky boy knew that with a bit of encouragement, Cliff would detonate. I had to calm him down before he got even angrier or lashed out at Ben.

"I'll help you get the drinks," Ben told me as he got up from the couch.

"The glasses are above the sink," I told him. "Sorry, I'm not feeling well. I think I'll go to bed."

"Sure thing. We'll try to keep it down," he reassured me.

From the bedroom, I heard the clacking of glasses a bit later. They resumed their discussion.

"What about Alpha?" Mason suggested.

"For a *dating app*?" Ben questioned.

So, they were trying to come up with a name for their app.

"I thought we wanted to have a broad appeal. Alpha sounds… kinda S&M-like," Ben observed.

"Fine, you come up with a name then."

I lay on the bed on top of my SAT book. My phone vibrated. I had no desire to look at it.

Undulate

/ˈʌndjuleɪt/ *verb*

The text was from Trilce, the front desk receptionist at the Patapsco Paradise. She remembered from a previous conversation that I liked coffee. She invited me to her apartment to try different types of it. I took a packet of Arabic coffee with me. Shane, her friend who performed drag, brought a stovetop espresso coffee maker. And she had a French press. We tried the drinks and discussed Shane's upcoming performance to a Meghan Trainer song. He was excited about the details of the dress and his dance moves. I'd seen clips of RuPaul's Drag Race before but witnessing a performer up-close was a more enjoyable experience. Plus, the various types of coffee tasted amazing.

As much as I didn't want to go home that evening, I couldn't overstay my welcome in Trilce's apartment. I had to go home and face Cliff. He was already there when I arrived. I guessed my expression betrayed my feelings, because he said, "Hey, you look frightened."

Of course, I was. If he struck me in front of company because of an imaginary insect in Mason's glass, he'd act much worse if I came home late, after hanging out with my new friends. He'd blow up if he ever found out about Ty.

Cliff approached me and gently played with my hair. "Baby, are you scared of me now?"

I went to the bedroom and sat down.

"Are you OK? You're sulking." He sat next to me.

Contemplating my options, I picked up the SAT book and opened a random page.

"Talk to me. What's going on?" He said in a low voice, as though comforting a child.

"What if I don't? Will you beat me again?"

"Awww… Beat you? When did I beat you?"

I turned the page. "Diligence" was the first word I saw.

"Oh, you mean last night? That wasn't a beating, stupid." He pressed his nose on my cheek and then kissed me. Back to his loving self.

A notification popped on my phone screen. Trilce just texted. "Hey. You wanna do mani pedi on Tuesday? Should we say at seven?" The screen went dark.

"That was just a slap," Cliff corrected me. "A little tap on the face really."

"Aha," I didn't look up. Technically, I had told him that he could beat me if he wanted to. I didn't mean it literally. It just felt like something nice to say at the time.

"You know some people slap and pinch their own cheeks just to get a little color on their face? A natural sort of makeup," he pulled on his cheek. "But you don't really need that. You're already beautiful. And you captured my heart a few years ago and, occasionally, you stomp on it." He wrapped his arms around my shoulders. His warmth felt good on my body. "Well, I'm happy you survived the violent beating. I'm such a monster," he kissed me on the cheek several times.

"Your beard feels itchy." A smile forced its way onto my face.

"Damn this beard," he pulled back and play-slapped himself. "It scratches my baby's smooth skin." He slapped himself again. "Oh no, I'm being brutal again. What a monster!" He joked. "Abdul, please put me out of my misery. Just do it. You must kill me." He put his hand on mine and made my hand form the shape of a gun.

"You're such a goof," I criticized.

"I'm trying to get a smile out of my boyfriend. You look even more beautiful when you smile."

I touched his beard. "You were so mean last night."

"You were being disrespectful." His voice was calm but firm.

"No, I wasn't."

"You were being disrespectful," Cliff pulled my hand away from his face. "You shouldn't have pushed my buttons. I was having a bad day. I told you that several times. McNair was such a pain. He hated every app name we came up with. We came here to loosen up and brainstorm. But you started having an attitude, and arguing, and being rude."

"*Mason* was rude. To me. And you just watched it. You didn't say anything to him. Why didn't you defend me? Why did you let him treat me like that?"

"I shouldn't have. I'm sorry. We already had a few drinks before we came home. I was… You know me. I would never behave like that if I was sober."

"Cliff, he called me a 'bitch.' Right in front of you."

"He did? Jeez, I'm sorry. I don't even remember. That's how drunk I was. We cursed at everybody. Mason was having a terrible day too. He just broke up with his boyfriend."

"Again? The new one?"

"Yes, the new one. We all know he's a whore," Cliff raised his voice. "He was still our guest. I thought Afghans are supposed to be hospitable."

Being hospitable doesn't mean the guest can call me names.

"We came home because I told them we could just relax and brainstorm. Coming from a loud and dingy bar, I wanted to show off what a great host you are. But then you started being disrespectful to me, in my own apartment, in front of my colleagues. I'm more senior than both of them." He pulled his arm from my shoulder and faced me. "I'm really trying here. I bust my ass at work to be able to afford this lifestyle. Living in this apartment. Eating well. Dressing nicely. But it's not good enough. I work out every day to look good for you. So that at night you feel proud of laying down next to me. But that's not good enough. My gym schedule has to be approved. My friends have to be approved. And if I bring my friends home, I have to pray that you're not in one of your moods. Because when you're cranky, you are disrespectful. And I won't have that."

"Cliff, I didn't mean to be disrespectful. But you can't let him treat me that way."

"OK. I'm sorry on his behalf." He sounded frustrated.

What else could I ask for, now that he'd apologized? I had to meet him halfway. "I'm sorry too." I tightened my armed around his waist. "You know I love you."

"You used to. When we started dating, you'd worship the ground I walked on. But now…" he exhaled. "You're not the same anymore. Something's changed."

Could he feel it that I had a crush on Ty? I had to take care of that. "I still worship you."

"Yeah?" He gazed into my eyes.

I nodded.

He began playing with my hair again. "OK. Then, apology accepted." He pulled me over as he lay down. I put my head on his chest. His heartbeat calmed me down. Like the pendulum of an antique clock.

"What did you end up naming the app?" I inquired.

"Actually, we have a good option that McNair is gonna put forward to the investors."

"Nice."

"Mason has started running the final tests before it can be released to beta users."

"He's such an ass."

"He can be," Cliff conceded. "But he's my best friend. We grew up together."

"In Kentucky, right?"

"We go way back."

"But he's evil."

"He's my friend. He's loyal. He's covered for me at work. And when he acts up, you should remain nice. Be twice as nice. Don't give him any excuse. Do it for me? Am I not enough of an incentive?"

"I'd do anything for you." *I should really do anything to make him happy. Especially, considering my indiscretion.*

Caressing his body gave me joy. His muscle definition palpable under my touch. His strength reassuring. If I were in danger, he could fight anyone to protect me. I couldn't fight to save my life. A couple of months ago, a drag queen was attacked in SoHo. If New York City wasn't safe, then nowhere was.

He kissed my hair, "That's my boy."

I tightened my hug around his chest. His heart rate was strong and peaceful. *How did he ever think he wasn't good enough for me? If anything, it was the opposite. What do I bring to the table? He could replace me by the weekend if he wanted to.*

"Do you think we fight a lot?" Cliff wondered aloud.

I took a deep breath and lay by his side. The blankness of the ceiling was calming. With Ty, I never had a chance to just lay down and... I had to stop this infatuation. Cliff stretched his body and crossed his leg over mine. I loved the weight of him.

"You have an older brother," he said.

Karim. I don't want to think about him. The way he kicked me in the chest as he threw me out of the pickup truck. Not that I blamed him for it.

"Me and my brothers, we were always fighting. I think at any given time, at least one of us had bruises from our fights. That went on until we were like… I don't know, twenty? Did you and your brother fight a lot?"

"Not really," I answered. But of course, we had. Nevertheless, I wasn't about to give him more excuses for acting like a fool. With Karim, our fights had consisted of him hitting me or calling me a girl. Or just random punches for no reason. "We would just—"

"Boys fight. *Men* fight. It's normal. We got all this testosterone bubbling up. And we all want to prove our strength. That's what happens when you get men in a relationship. All gay relationships are like this. Men have this natural need for proving themselves. Physically."

I scrunched up my body, my knee touching his calf muscle. Even though it wasn't flexed, I loved the touch of it.

He continued, "But physical strength is something both parties have. It's not like a straight relationship where the woman can't defend herself and can easily be overpowered. When two men fight, it's just business as usual. Just a natural expression of masculinity. It's the same male strength that attracted them to each other in the first place."

Easy for him to say. I couldn't hurt him even if I tried. Maybe I *should* go to the gym like he wanted me to.

"You beat me, too. *You* started whacking me that night after the gym. Remember?"

I remembered. But Cliff wasn't the one who ended up with a bruise on his face.

"You were going ballistic. You punched and hit me and everything."

I hadn't punched him to hurt him. I only wanted to get his attention somehow, to make a point. Though technically I guessed I *had* started it. "I'm sorry, Cliff. It'll never happen again. I—"

"You get jealous. But I've never cheated on you. And I never will. That's not how I was raised. I may flirt with boys just to prove to myself I still got it. But I'll never take it very far. Besides, I'd be scared of cheating. You would beat me down bad. Look at these muscles." He grabbed my bicep. That was his way of encouraging me to continue to work out.

"It's not funny," I objected, smiling. But as I pulled his hand away, my bicep flexed.

"Damn. Feels like a rock. I'm afraid of pissing you off. Just can't think of those punches raining down on me again."

I giggled. A welcome exaggeration. "Would you stop that already?"

"I'm too pretty to be disfigured. But even if you did go berserk and beat me up, it's not such a big deal. Men fight. I can take it. Then we'd make up again. Just the normal ups and downs of life."

I didn't quite believe his lame excuse. But you can't fight fire with fire.

Aberrant

/æbˈerənt/ *adj.*

Over the next few days, no matter how much I tried, I couldn't concentrate on the SAT book. I saw the words, but I couldn't even read them. They seemed like a random series of letters that didn't fit together, like staring at a bowl of soup with alphabet-shaped pasta.

My other source of new vocabulary, Ty's poems, had given rise to crazy thoughts of trying to contact him. The whole message had even been typed up. I had revised it several times to not sound too desperate. "Dear Ty, I'm not sure if you remember me. We met in Baltimore a couple of weeks ago and had Arabic coffee. Just wondering how you're doing. Best, Abdul." Initially, I wanted to add a postscript saying, "Thanks for the note." But I didn't want to give the impression that I was going to use it. He had misunderstood the situation. Although since then, Cliff humiliated me in front of Ben and Mason. I could easily imagine him high-fiving Cliff after he hit me that night.

I wished I could be near Ty. Would an email constitute cheating? I couldn't *do* anything over email, but maybe it would strengthen my emotional ties to him. Although, if

Cliff got to hit me in front of others, I got to email someone I liked. That was only fair. I re-read the draft again last night but couldn't push myself to press send.

To resume learning vocabulary, I had to open some mental space, without the obsessive need to revise this message or imagine Ty's every possible reaction.

What would be the worst reaction from him? Silence? No, that would keep hope alive. The worst would be him rejecting me.

I was sitting on the bed last night, considering various outcomes, feeling anxious. A nice bowl of *kashkew* would help me feel better. With some dough from Neima Store, I should be able to make some. It would be suitable for this cold weather. I kept reading my draft message to Ty and thinking about how much I craved some *kashkew*.

Cliff startled me as he entered the bedroom. "You studying?"

My hand shook. The phone made the swish sound of "sending" an email. Before I could research how to possibly unsend an email, Trilce messaged me, inviting me to get a pedicure in the salon where Shane worked.

Only people too lazy to cut their own toenails needed a pedicure. But I was afraid if I declined Trilce's invitation, she wouldn't invite me anywhere again. Our friendship was just beginning to take shape. After losing touch with Rakesh and Niloofar, I really wanted to hold onto this friendship.

I walked up and down the block, not wanting to go in without her. I'd skipped dinner to be there on time and I was getting cold just wandering on the street. At 7:12, I noticed a navy-blue Camry that hadn't had a new car shine in several years. She waved at me as she parked past the bus stop in front of the salon. With a grin on her face, she tiptoed to the parking meter in green flip flops as if we were going to the beach.

Her bag strap was slowly gliding off her shoulder. "Hi, Abdul. Sorry I'm late," she adjusted her bag.

Should I hug her? Shouldn't she initiate that? What if she didn't want to hug me?

"You should have waited inside. It's cold." She opened the glass door.

The bells above the door jingled and Shane walked towards us. He had colored his hair light brown à la Justin Bieber's mugshot. And today he was wearing eyeliner. "Well, hello stranger," he opened his arms to greet her.

"Hey." She hugged him.

Then he put his arms around me. I apparently had an apprehensive expression since he went on to say, "Oh, don't be scared. My colleagues don't bite." His tone was endearing.

"I can't wait," Trilce announced. "I brought something," she pulled a bottle of sparkling wine out of her bag.

"Time to party," Shane fake-clapped. "Let me get some cups."

"Here," Trilce pointed to a seat next to the door. "Take off your boots and socks. And place them there."

Several pairs of women's shoes were sitting on a wooden rack.

"I can't believe you wore boots to a nail salon. Next time, wear something easy to slip off."

I nodded.

"Take your time," Shane materialized, holding two plastic cups.

"You're the best," Trilce took one.

"Can we share a cup?" Shane looked at me. "Theoretically," he emphasized, "I'm not supposed to drink in the salon, even though I'm not even working."

"Of course. No problem."

"How do you feel about being the guinea pig today?" She popped open the bottle and poured some into the two cups still in Shane's hands.

I was still fidgeting with my shoelaces when I noticed he was also in flipflops. His toenails shone, reflecting the florescent lights in the ceiling.

"Somebody has to sacrifice their body for the sake of training."

"Pshhh," she waved her hand, dismissing the complaint. "This hardly makes you Marie Curie."

I concluded he was getting a pedicure from an apprentice who was still learning the tricks of the craft.

"Cheers." She lightly bumped her cup onto Shane's.

"Cheers," he took a sip and gave me the cup. He looked around, making sure no one saw him drinking, then grabbed the cup from me and took another gulp. "I just finished working on this diva who was trying my every nerve."

A middle-aged woman with pounds of makeup walked toward the door, wiggling her wrists. Her toes stood apart with the help of a set of separators. She gave him a half-hearted hug. "Oh, Champagne? How come I don't get treatment like that?"

Trilce stroked her hair out of her face. "Would you like some? I brought it myself."

Shane added, "We don't have a liquor license."

"That's a great idea. I'll bring my own Prosecco next time. Bye, sweetie. Good luck," she said to him as she stepped out.

He rolled his eyes and guzzled the rest of the wine. "Madonna, give me the strength."

I felt like I was stalling them. "You guys go ahead. I'll be there in a sec."

"You sure?" Trilce asked as she walked away.

"Your beverage will be waiting for you," Shane followed her. "Just walk up when you're ready. The flip-flops are right there," he pointed to the bottom shelf of the shoe rack.

I pulled off my socks quickly and stuffed them into my boots. There were stacks of thin plastic flipflops. The different colors and sizes. I picked a large pair.

Steam was rising from the three basins at the bottom of the large leather seats, getting filled with warm water. Froth was forming on top of each basin. The smell of roses filled the air.

The two cups were full again. Shane was already stretched on his seat. "Don't worry. My drinking has nothing to do with my fear of getting cut by a novice," he teased his new colleague.

"I'm sure it won't lead to amputation," she shot back.

Shane convulsed in an exaggerated fake laugh. "You're funny," he said sarcastically as his face turned dead serious.

I let out a chuckle, despite my efforts to not laugh at the trainee.

Trilce rolled up her pants. I did the same, feeling uncomfortable that I didn't know what to do here.

Shane pointed like a ballerina to a seat next to Trilce. "Have a seat. Lisa will be with you shortly."

I sat down.

"You can use this to get a back massage," she showed me a corded gadget, resembling a TV remote control.

The mild movement felt good on my back. I stretched my body to take in more of the sensation. The sparkling wine on an empty stomach had already relaxed me. The lukewarm water felt nice on my feet. It smelled like a rose garden.

Trilce let out a long exhale. "I needed this."

A woman who I assumed was Lisa showed up and asked me if I was ready.

"Lisa, this is Abdul," Shane introduced.

"How are you doing?" The R rolled out on my tongue. The wine was impacting my speech.

She put a towel on her lap and began to massage my foot.

"I love this new soap, Lisa. It smells better than Garett Neff's neck," Shane joked.

"Who?" I asked.

Lisa pointed at the five-foot black and white poster of a topless beautiful man, a Calvin Klein fragrance ad.

Trilce leaned forward. "Have you heard from that Tyrique guy? Our hottest guest of the season?"

Now that the conversation didn't revolve around Shane's drag performance, she'd remembered my romantic episode at her workplace.

Before I had a chance to reply, Shane turned to me and smiled, "Scandalous! I love it."

"The guy left him a love letter at his work," Trilce added with new enthusiasm.

"You go, honey," he approved. "So what happened?"

I sipped my wine. "Nothing. He just went back to Chicago." I'd read that on his website.

"It's OK," Trilce interjected. "It's raining men, right Shane?"

"I'm not really looking. I have a boyfriend." I didn't mean to say that out loud. The wine made me speak too much.

"I like this one. My type of people," he told her.

"So, is it an open relationship?" she queried, sipping from her cup.

"Something like that." I drank my wine just so I wouldn't have to speak.

"Wait, your man doesn't even know?" Shane leaned forward. His jaw dropped and he made a dramatic gesture of holding his hand in front of his mouth.

"Excuse *me*," the apprentice complained.

Shane had inadvertently pulled his foot, dropping the towel into the basin. "So sorry, honey. I just didn't expect that." Then he pointed to me and narrowed his eyes. "I like you. A proud slut. Just like me."

"I'm not a slut."

"Don't be offended. In my book, that's a compliment. You have to be attractive to attract."

"Let's see a picture of this boyfriend," Trilce requested.

I took out my phone and found one of my favorite pictures of Cliff: He's standing in the Patterson Park swimming pool, his hair dripping wet, drops of water shining on his chest like diamonds.

"*This* is your boyfriend?" She showed the phone to Shane on her other side. "That's the same hottie you were with at the DC Pride parade."

"Honey," he elongated the word. "Let me not lust after your man, though."

"Let me find a picture where he's wearing clothes." I was thinking of a picture by the Pagoda observatory.

"We want a picture with less clothes, not more," Shane pointed out.

Trilce broke into laughter.

"No, no. I don't wanna lust after your man," Shane repeated. "Don't show me nothing else. We're just becoming friends."

"Why are you cheating on the hot boyfriend?" she questioned.

"It just happened. I wasn't planning on it."

"Would you ever tell him though?" Her sense of curiosity had fully awakened.

"Be careful there," Shane warned.

They didn't have to know all the details.

Trilce's nail technician began to drain the water in her basin and lifted her foot.

"What if *he* was with someone else?" Trilce went on, undistracted.

I laughed nervously. "Then, I'd beat the hell out of him," I reached for my cup. It was empty.

"He's spicy, this one!" Shane snapped his fingers several times, in a low-key applause gesture. "But violence is not the answer."

"You're not serious, right?" She wanted to verify.

I wished I could get out of this conversation. Could I find an excuse and leave? My foot was in Lisa's hands as she was digging with a scary instrument around my toenails. "You know. Gay relationships are like that," I said, doing my best to sound like I was kidding. "You get two men together, they're gonna fight."

"Yeah, right." Shane brushed off my argument. "I've literally had *thousands* of relationships," he struggled to keep a straight face. "None of them violent."

Trilce shook her head. "Oh my gosh! Men always act like they're ten years younger than their real age."

"I prefer to call it young at heart," Shane added.

Trilce, who had finally exhausted her questions, began telling a story of a date. She noticed the guy checking out other girls during their dinner. I couldn't pay much attention.

The TV on the wall showed commercials for some medicine: a woman sauntering barefoot on the beach as the closed captioning warned of "strokes in rare cases."

Cliff has a temper. But that doesn't justify my disloyalty.

"A form of child trafficking common in Afghanistan," read the text on TV. The trailer of a documentary. The picture showed a *bacha birish* dancing with a lace scarf on his face. The words "abused and raped" appeared on the screen.

I shifted in my seat, holding tightly to its arms to not tremble. I pressed my free foot to the bottom of the basin. Was Rakesh still following this topic? Was he involved in the making of this documentary? Goose bumps covered my body. I clenched the seat arms. The topic needed attention, but I didn't want it to be the only thing Americans associated with Afghanistan. This and war.

Lisa looked up. "Is everything OK?"

I nodded and looked at my phone.

"So what did you do?" Shane asked, still engrossed in Trilce's story.

"What do you think? I wasn't gonna just watch him as he checked out every girl in eyesight. I said I needed to use the bathroom but also took my bag and jacket."

"Did he notice?"

"He said, 'you can leave your jacket here.' I was like, 'I'm gonna use the bathroom in my apartment.'"

Shane burst into laughter. "For real? Good for you!"

My two new friends were too invested in their conversation to have glanced at the TV. I tuned out of their conversation again. Lisa was applying some cream on my cuticles.

I needed to think of something else. The first thing that came to my mind was Tyrique's note. *What if I do call that help line? What are they gonna say? That I deserve better than getting beaten up? But I was the one who cheated. Do I really deserve better? What will I do if I leave him? Where would I even go? I don't make enough money to live on my own. The money I've saved is for college.*

"We'll be doing another round of soaking," Lisa interrupted my thoughts. She dropped a few drops of essential oils into the basin. "This is a fusion of peppermint and lavender. It helps relieve inflammation and stress."

Shane said something.

"I'm sorry?" I wasn't listening.

"Talk to us. Put your phone down," he insisted.

"What are you doing on your phone anyway? Stalking that guy, Tyrique?"

I felt a rush of heat on my face.

"Trilce," he scolded, "stop embarrassing my sister here."

I'd never thought of myself as a sister to a white boy. But Shane's affinity felt sincere.

"Fine," she laughed, sounding buzzed. "I promise I won't ask you any more personal questions. Just stop pouting. We came here to relax and have fun."

Shane turned to me and said, "One thing you'll notice is that there's an infinite number of unusual ideas in her head. She'll invite you to tons of strange things. You don't have to accept them all."

"How was ice skating with the guy?" she changed the topic.

"That one was pretty fun, I have to admit," he replied. "But blueberry picking?"

"The weather was good," she defended herself.

"And so was the already-baked blueberry pie that we bought on the way back from the farm. I wonder what your next great idea is gonna be. A cat yoga?"

She rubbed her chin, apparently considering that as a possibility.

Lisa instructed me to put my feet back into the water. They had to soak for about five minutes for the skin to absorb the oil.

"The best part is the wax massage at the end." Trilce was excited. "Your feet are gonna be softer than a baby's butt."

"That's true," Shane confirmed. "And your toenails gonna be shiny. You'll be sorry you have to wear shoes."

"Really?" I wasn't convinced.

"That man of yours will surely notice," he added. "It's all about self-care. When you're happy in your skin, you'll be happier in your life."

Americans didn't realize how ridiculous things like this sounded to immigrants. Did he think I wouldn't become a refugee if my toenails were filed more often?

"And your boyfriend will treat you like a prince," Trilce predicted.

"Or better yet, a princess," Shane joked.

Trilce filled up her cup, finishing the bottle. She then leaned back and closed her eyes. "Feels so good. I could do this every day."

It did feel good. I hoped Cliff would be in a good mood tonight. Maybe I should rub his feet to help him stay calm, prevent him from blowing up for any random reason.

The Tragedy of Child Sexual Exploitation in Afghanistan

By Rakesh Luthra

Kabul (Compass News) — Nineteen-year-old Samim lights a cigarette, his hands trembling as he talks about his younger brother Nazif. When Nazif was thirteen, a man came to their village of Bagram and offered him an apprenticeship as a car mechanic in Kabul, some thirty kilometers away. The money would help provide for the family.

"That was a lie. But I didn't know it back then," Samim says and covers his face with his hands.

The man came back to their house a few times and brought some money that Nazif had earned. However, Nazif never accompanied him in these few visits. The man assured Samim his brother was doing well.

Nazif liked math and found pride in his ability to solve arithmetic problems. "He wanted to be a teacher. For him, being good at math meant he had the intellectual faculties necessary to become a teacher," Samim explains.

Several months after the last visit, Samim came to Kabul to look for Nazif but he couldn't locate the car mechanic shop. Desperate, Samim showed his picture to random passers-by on the streets, hoping to find a trace of his younger brother. But Samim never saw him again.

After searching a few days, a middle-aged man recognized the picture and told Samim that Nazif danced well. "You have to pay a lot if you wanna spend some time with him," he concluded.

"I was so angry, but I thought he's talking nonsense because he'd smoked *chars*," Samim explains. "I didn't even hit him."

Soon, he realized that his brother had been forced into *bacha bazi*: a practice in which teenage boys dress in women's clothing and dance to entertain male audiences in parties. Afterwards, they're subjected to sexual exploitation, at times by the highest bidder. This illegal practice is taboo in the conservative society, making it difficult to track down, much less punish.

Determined to find his brother, Samim kept asking around until he found out Nazif had been killed during an attempt to escape. To safeguard Nazif's and his own reputation, he told the family that Nazif had died in a car accident in Kabul.

Samim inhales the smoke from his cigarette. "I fed my siblings with the money the man had brought." His fingers are pressing hard on the picture of Nazif. "I didn't know it was my brother's blood money."

Names in this article have been changed to protect the identity of individuals.

Recidivism

/rɪˈsɪdɪvɪzəm/ *noun*

The apartment didn't know peace. Even when Cliff was at work, I still felt this coarseness. As if any piece of furniture was going to betray me. The coffee table made me trip and the corners of the walls closed in on me. The open concept left me nowhere to hide, nowhere to block the visual reminders of what happened here. Sometimes, I enjoyed that. Like, when Cliff made me coffee in the morning, sat by my side and played with my hair to wake me up. Or when he took me in his arms to savor me like a handful of fresh mulberries. But sometimes, I couldn't deny the brutality of this place. When he crashed down, enraged by whatever I'd done or failed to do. *He has a temper.* He could get amused by an indiscretion of mine, but he could also get infuriated by something I thought was negligible. I hated the unpredictability. Cliff was volatile like Soviet landmines placed in unknown locations in the heart of Afghanistan. If I told him I'd made a mistake, would he kiss me wet or punch me in the face? The fear of blows that never came still left a dent in my spirit.

After breakfast, I packed my SAT book in my bag. The clock showed only 9:21. My shift would start at noon. But

I didn't want to stay home. So, I headed out. The CityLink bus was late. I didn't mind. Without prior planning, I found myself standing outside Morning in Beirut.

Derrick, the guy behind the counter, had his locs tied in a bundle behind his head. His facial hair had grown since I'd seen him last, a couple of weeks ago. He now had thin hair on his chin and a pencil moustache. As he wiped the counter, he said something to his colleague who laughed and went to the storage room. Derrick noticed me and nodded. I had to go in.

"Good morning. Haven't seen you in a while."

"Hi. How are you?"

I felt special that he smiled at me, a personal welcome message. Hopefully, he didn't mind me staying here for the next couple of hours until my shift started. Someone had left their empty cup and plate at my usual table with the view of the street. I put down my bag and placed the dishes on the tray above the garbage bin.

"Sorry about that," Derrick noticed me cleaning up.

"No problem." I turned to walk to my table when someone crashed into me, almost knocking me over.

"I'm sorry," he said, grabbing my hand to prevent me from falling down.

"I'm so sorry," I gained back my balance. I felt my shirt stick to my body. As I looked down, I realized that he'd spilled coffee all over my shirt.

The guy who looked like Rhydian Vaughan.

"You alright? You burn yourself?" Derrick was still watching.

"No, it wasn't hot."

"It was already cold." The guy added and then apologized again.

"It's OK. Just an accident."

He seemed concerned, although he'd just told Derrick that the coffee was already cold. He apologized a third time.

Everyone was looking at me. The guy was taller than me and had short black hair that spilled over the side of his forehead.

Now I have to go back home and change. But at least, the extra headache was caused by a gorgeous guy.

He introduced himself as Alex and asked for forgiveness so many times that it mortified me more. I tried my best to reassure him everything was fine. There was time for me to go home and change before my shift started. But he kept expressing regrets. I wanted to say, "You're too beautiful to be this upset." I walked to my table to grab my bag. But Alex took my bag and opened the door for me. He offered to switch shirts with me. I refused to take his shirt off his back. Then he offered to do a quick laundry in his Airbnb. In the end, I surrendered. Anything to make him stop apologizing and insisting that he should make it up to me.

He led me to his place. We made small talk. I took off my shirt to put it in the washing machine. Then, he immediately took off his own, saying that he'd perspired too much due to embarrassment earlier and needed a clean shirt too. He saw me admire his physique and called me "beautiful."

Who flirts like that so early in the day? I thought about giving up my shirt and running out of there. But I enjoyed his attention. *Give me more.*

He wrapped his arms around me and rubbed his nose against my ear, making an "mmm" sound, like he was tasting me, and I was orange blossom jam.

My having a boyfriend didn't bother him. He stood in front of me. His clavicle protruded from his shoulder, begging to be touched. A magnetic power pulled me to him. His skin was soft. He kissed me. I couldn't resist with his bed right there, waiting for us to enjoy each other's company. From then on, he switched between being rough and tender. He pushed me to my limits. And as soon as I was about to stop him from acting aggressively, a gentle touch would change my mind. I wanted him so badly.

Give me more.

Later, he ironed my shirt while I stayed on his bed, under his sheets. It felt so foreign to have someone else doing my chores.

He can be my savior, take me out of this town. "I want to see you." I said, hoping he would touch me again, to prove he still cared for me, even after the act.

"Yeah? Look," he flexed both biceps. "Oh, what about this?" He turned a bit, giving me the side bodybuilder pose.

No, I meant I want to see you *again. After today.*

"You should come to Long Beach. There are tons of picture-perfect boys."

Not a trace of romance in his voice. He wasn't interested in me anymore. Not after the morning wood had dissipated.

"Fix your tie. It's loose."

I obeyed.

"I think I made you late for work."

I stepped out the door.

"Bye." He closed the door as I was considering blowing him a kiss.

And there I was. Behind a closed door. Again. I was empty. Hallowed. Could everybody see it?

Maybe that's what Commander Aseel had seen in me: That I'd be willing. I felt a wrenching pain in my belly. It seemed like every passerby in the street stared at me. They all knew what I'd done. They knew who I was.

It was my own fault to be enthralled so easily. Even though I was the local and he the traveler, it felt the opposite. He was in his element. He was an American. From dreamy California. His name sounded like any other name. His features didn't make him foreign, they made him exotic. Desirable. He could become a bodybuilder, or a pianist, or a professor. Whatever he chose to be.

Me? My name confused people and my accent offended them. People would misplace me on a map. And if they knew better, they'd associate me with a never-ending war, with poverty, with desperation. And if they knew me, they'd know that my countrymen did their best to prevent my growth, to dam my flow. And if they knew me personally, they'd notice that something deep inside me always attracted such behavior. An enchanting seduction, until I submitted. And then, they disposed of me, when I no longer served a purpose. Maybe my knowledge of my own misdeeds made me realize I wasn't worth a better treatment. I had caused too much destruction to be able to recover. Karma doesn't forgive. Such was my fate.

When I got to Patapsco Inn, Ms. Grace exclaimed, "Abdul, are you OK?"

"Yeah," I answered, surprised by the concern.

"Do you know what time it is?"

I looked at my phone. 12:38.

"I tried to cover for you, but Rebecca is here now. She wants you to go see her as soon as you arrive."

I went to her office. She was going to reprimand me. That much was obvious. But I didn't care. Nothing she said would make me feel any worse than I already did. I couldn't even concentrate on what she said as she wrote me up. A written warning. This whole thing happened because I'd acted on my animal instincts. Again. I'd cheated on Cliff. And I got myself a second warning. And I lost my self-respect in front of a playboy from California.

After Ms. Grace went on her lunch break, I checked my phone. I had a new email message. My hands started to shake when I saw the name of the sender. Tyrique Williams.

"Abdul. I was surprised to see your message. Hope you had a chance to use the phone number. In my humble opinion, it can help you address the situation at hand. It's not my place to tell you how you should move forward in your relationship. Abdul, although I hate to sound overly critical, I have a suspicion that you weren't fully honest with me. Our encounter, though sweet and delightful, was still quite short. I don't want to become a home-wrecker cliché. 'The other woman' as the saying goes. You have to be truthful with yourself and choose the life you desire. Please believe me when I say that I wish you all the peace and joy. Always, Tyrique."

The screen looked blurry as tears formed in my eyes, my hands trembling. *The other woman? Who's the other woman?* I turned off the screen as if that would negate the message. *Am I the other woman because I'm not manly enough?* Everyone from my father to Karim to the Two Little Terrors told me I was too gentle. In their own way, they all attempted to toughen me up. But I'd survived on my own. How was I too feminine? It wasn't like I shopped in the women's department or wore eyeliner. I was masculine enough for Cliff.

I tasted the salt of my tears. My voice shook as I called Rebecca for help, "Could you please watch the reception desk? I need to use the bathroom."

She rolled her wheelchair toward me, probably still upset. But I couldn't pay her any mind. I had to wash my face before I started crying in the lobby.

In the bathroom, the Glade dispenser sprayed chemical lavender into the air. I stared at my reflection in the mirror. I saw none of the cuteness Alex had talked about. Not even *he* saw it anymore after he was done. The same with Ty. I was nothing but a temporary pastime.

The pain didn't startle me because I expected it. It was familiar. It just squirmed inside, growing from my stomach and expanding to my lungs, stretching into my arms and legs. Without a noticeable shock, I began to sink. I began to solidify and contract.

What I wanted most was to forget this pain. This specific pain that Ty just inflicted. His business-like email. The distance in it. I wanted to forget this specific pain.

Tonight, I decided, I was going to provoke Cliff. He had a temper, and I knew how to work it. And when he exploded, perhaps the physical hurt would drown out this emotional ache.

Remedy

/ˈremədi/ *noun, verb*

That night, as if he knew my plan, Cliff texted me that he'd be late. "Don't get mad. There's just a lot of work for pre-release."

I complained, "There's always something."

He didn't take the bait. "I'll make it up to you," he replied with a winking emoji.

The thought of Tyrique bruised me. As did the thought of how easily Alex closed the door on me. I was in a mood for a fight. Cliff never disappointed in that department. But I had to wait for him to come home.

I couldn't bring myself to open Ty's website and study vocabulary from his poems. I wished we'd never met. His smile, his kindness, his attentiveness... all of that, just to get me to sleep with him. He had no other interest in me.

My SAT book was missing, and I didn't feel like looking for it. Instead, I turned on the TV. A news story about the right to transparency in a complaint against police was packed in between thick slices of random commercials for razors, anti-depressants, and cars. I distanced myself from the obsession to buy objects that were supposed to bring you happiness. Soon, it felt like I was watching TV from behind a curtain of fog. The commercials didn't entice me, the weather forecast didn't interest me, and the jokes of the anchors didn't make me laugh.

Cliff came home around eleven. It took me a moment to bring myself out of my thoughts and back into the living room.

"Here's my baby."

"Now you remember me." I attempted to carry out my plan.

"You're so cute when you sulk."

"Obviously not as cute as the boys on your—"

"Abdul, I know I'm late. I'm sorry. I had a long day. But a good one. Can we try and not ruin it?" He took off his shoes and came over to the couch to hug me. "If we must, we can fight tomorrow, ha? Around seven? You hit me, I hit you, we have hot make-up sex, the whole shebang. But can we just have a quiet celebration tonight? This was a major milestone for me." He kissed me on the lips. "Here." He walked to the glass liquor cabinet and took out the bottle of cognac. "To us," he handed me a glass and clanked his against mine.

I relented. I had to try and live a good life. I was one of the lucky ones. I owed it to those who hadn't survived. To Jabbar. "Congrats on your app, Cliff." I raised my glass and took a sip.

Cliff threw himself on the couch next to me and put his feet on the coffee table. "This was a crazy day." He took another sip, "Remember Ben's marketing idea to have admirers who can only post comments but they can't have a full profile?"

No, I don't remember. "Uh-huh," I tried to appease him.

"He, of course, didn't know how to actually do it. But you know who did?" He pointed to himself. "Basically, we need to have two different types of profiles, a full profile, and a limited one. And you should be able to..."

I tuned out. When pretending to listen, I just had to make an occasional sound to feign interest in whatever he was saying. Meanwhile, I could remove myself from the never-ending banter about his work: his own brilliance and everybody else's inferiority. Ben ended up being the receiver of a lot of blame, because he specialized in marketing, not programming.

My phone screen lit up. A text from Trilce said, "How's the college student?" I clicked on the side button to turn off the screen. Then it lit up again. "Haven't heard from you in a while. Just wanted to..." I had to open the messaging app to see the rest of the text.

Her persistence reminded me of Rakesh. At first, Rakesh also seemed like a nuisance when I met him in Kabul so many years ago. I was hungry and trying to sleep on the corner. He had gotten rid of a bunch of boys who wanted to sell him gum or plastic bags or whatever. Then he approached me. Another guy who turned out to be his translator followed. They asked me why I was on the street and what I had seen there. I thought they were looking for opium. Or maybe they thought I was a sex worker. For a moment, it didn't seem like such a bad idea. I imagined it would hurt, but it could make me enough money to eat for a few days. I didn't do it. But I considered it for a second. I answered his questions. His Indian accent sounded melodic. It reignited my interest in Bollywood movies.

Later on, with my help, his report caught the attention of the whole country, and more importantly the so-called international community. His girlfriend, a Hazara NGO worker who lived in the US, helped find me lodging in Kabul. But she eventually realized that the only real hope was to get me out of Afghanistan. They both helped me come to the US. We lost touch after some time. I planned on reconnecting with them after I enrolled in a college in a few years.

Would they regret bringing me here if they saw me like this? A liar and a cheat, working in a hotel lobby?

"Can you imagine that?" Cliff's rant brought me back to the present.

"That's ummm," I had to pretend I was listening, "that's crazy."

"And we still had no idea why the data wouldn't transfer to the expanded profile." He put down his glass.

He poured himself more cognac and offered me some. I shook my head.

"Come on, Abdul. Yes, I'm late. But I was working. Not like I was having fun with random boys. Be happy for me. Smile."

I tried.

"Otherwise, I'll tickle you."

"No need." I smiled wider and took another drink.

"That's my boy." He kissed me on the lips and hugged me.

I was lucky to be with him. I wrapped my arms around him. He didn't spend his time gallivanting and sleeping around. He was working hard on this app to prove his value to the company, to allow me to dream of college. If I could get a high enough SAT score.

Anonymous

/əˈnɑːnɪməs/ *adj.*

F earing another rupture of jealous attacks from me, Cliff alerted me that his profile was one of the first twenty to become public. Since it was a dating app, he had to pretend he was single. "Like an ad to attract new users," he'd told me. From the pool of admirers, the initial twenty would each invite five guys to join the app, who would be able to invite two more, who in turn would be able to invite only one. Other new users could only "admire" and "comment," but couldn't have a profile unless invited. "Exclusivity creates demand," Cliff had pointed out. But I guessed that he'd learned that from Ben, the marketing lead. Of course, the public didn't know the app would become available to anybody within a few months, after the idea of exclusivity had created enough hype. Cliff wanted to let me know in advance so that I wouldn't be "throwing tantrums."

I helped him select a profile picture and a "pickup line" to caption it. We chose a picture of him shirtless in the gym, with his fist in the air, winking, his tongue sticking out. We'd change the photo and the pickup line regularly. He came up with romantic things to do and showered me with flirtatious attention, and I gave him as many compliments as I could, from which he'd fine-tune his pickup lines. It was similar to the first few months of us dating. We cuddled in bed, soaked in the tub blowing foam to each other, drank red wine and read sex stories out loud. From the twenty initial users, he wanted to have the highest number of admirers, which meant we constantly had to update the pickup line to attract more people: "Need someone to spot me" appeared next to a picture of him, lifting weights. "Wanna lick something sweet" captioned a picture of him with an ice cream cone. "Who wants a sniff?" He showed his biceps, fist above his head. Within weeks, Cliff collected over a thousand admirers and counting.

Mason also had a profile, but he lagged behind in admirers. The desire to see him lose to Cliff motivated me to come up with more ideas on promoting my man and let random strangers salivate over his pictures.

Yet, the popularity of his profile made me feel even worse about cheating on him. I compensated by admiring him more than anyone else could. I had to compete with all the virtual boys who kept coming up with creative ways to show how much they wanted him. From their comments, we created new taglines. A simple "dehydrated" led to many offers of bringing him water, coffee, and juice.

Aside from taking photos and brainstorming about marketing my boyfriend, I also had a wine and painting evening with Trilce and Shane. The art instructor had already sketched melting clocks on the canvases in the style of Dalí. Not something I could turn into a profile of Cliff, probably a good break. But I decided to surprise him with some cute new underwear for his next picture.

After half an hour searching online, I finally clicked on "purchase" on a bedazzled yellow and maroon brief. Once the order was complete, I went back on the Admire app.

Cliff had a new tagline, "Had a bad day. Wanna hit somebody." Under that, twenty-three admirers messaged: "I'd be your punching bag," "Anything to help you work out those biceps," "To be slapped around and beat up… That's hot." Boys were dying to experience Cliff's rage that sometimes descended on me. And I had complained about that. I, the cheater.

Cliff had already invited four admirers to join the app. I clicked on the first one. A Caucasian guy with a backward baseball cap and a blue tank top. The caption read, "In your dreams." I continued to read. For the "I admire" portion, where the user expressed what type of guy they were looking for, he'd written: "No spice. No rice." He went on to indicate he liked to work out and eat at new restaurants.

I clicked on another profile. Another Caucasian guy, shirtless, in front of a private pool. "I admire: All welcomed, especially Latinos. No Asians, sorry. Not racist, just a personal preference. Isn't that what a 'type' is?"

My stomach was burning holes in itself. Hugging my knees, I considered this reality check. My encounters with Ty and Alex had given me the false impression that I could be desirable. But Admire users reminded me those were the exceptions, not the norm. A sick trick of fate. It reminded me of the summer in Mashhad some fifteen years ago.

That day, I was hiding behind the street corner and watching the Two Little Terrors with their slingshots. They hid behind a tree trunk. One of them had a pebble behind the elastic band, ready to shoot. The other gave him directions. I saw him pull but I couldn't see their target. The other praised his timing. Then a loud clap of hands startled me and a whole flock of sparrows flew away. The shooter's pebble flew up, hit a branch, and fell on the ground.

I laughed and turned around to see who'd clapped his hand. I saw a boy, with blond hair and blue eyes, wearing bright yellow sneakers. He smiled at me. But the Two Little Terrors had noticed us.

"Who was that?"

"You want a beating? Who told you to clap your dumb hands?"

"Who did it? The Afghan boy or the pretty boy?"

"It was me," the blond guy replied.

"Well, you're about to get a good beating," the shooter threatened.

"Ashkan, what's going on?" I heard a woman's voice. Instead of a *chador*, she was wearing a white *manteau* and a floral headscarf that was almost falling off of her head. They were definitely not from this part of town. They looked like Tehrani people.

"Nothing, mom," said the blond guy, Ashkan.

"What do they want?" She looked at the two boys with slingshots.

"Nothing, ma'am. We were just kidding around," the shooter managed to blurt out.

"Mhmm." She took Ashkan's hand. "Go play inside. I already said you can't be on the street."

Ashkan walked away with his mom. What a royal name he had. We'd learned its meaning in our literature class a few months before. Somehow from all the vocabulary, I remembered that one. The rest were too difficult for the fourth grade.

He wore royal clothes too. A sky-blue t-shirt and burgundy shorts. I looked down to remember what I was wearing. A green shirt and khaki long pants. And plastic sandals. It reminded me of the cartoon The Prince and The Pauper.

"I don't wanna go home. I have no one to play with," Ashkan complained.

"Who's your new friend?" His mom looked back at me.

He waved at me to follow them. I didn't move.

"Come, come! Don't be afraid," his mom called out.

I walked behind them through their house gate and into the yard. I knew the house belonged to an older couple, probably his grandparents.

In front of us was the house building. Seven steps led up to a large balcony. A rug was rolled against the wall. Ashkan's mom walked up the steps and took off her *manteau*. Now that we were inside the house, she didn't have to abide by the strict dress code. She was wearing a sleeveless purple shirt and long white pants. My mom wore a nondescript black *manteau* outside the house, and cheap blouses and skirts inside. Her hair always remained covered. A little bit embarrassing compared to Ashkan's mother.

"Are you boys sure you wanna play outside?" She took off her scarf too. Her blond highlights reflected the sunlight, just like Ashkan's hair. "It's so hot."

"We're good. Right?" He asked me.

I nodded.

"OK, but I don't wanna see a nosebleed." She walked into the house.

Ashkan led me to the unpaved portion of the yard, to the left of the house. The soil was brown and dry and stretched all the way to the back wall of the house. Near the wall, I noticed a pile of bricks, the remnants of the house construction. A water-hose ran from the back to the front of the yard, next to a round flowerbed of cosmos flowers: white, pink, and purple.

"I wanna build a walkway to the flowers and a border for the flowerbed," Ashkan informed me.

"I'll bring bricks," I offered.

"We'll both take bricks and lay them on the ground." He led me to the back of the yard.

He picked two. I three.

"Show off."

A layer of dust rose above the ground as he walked. "Your sneakers will get dirty," I warned.

"It's OK."

We went back and forth, back and forth. Bringing bricks from the back and laying them in a circle around the flowerbed. We spoke scattered sentences. He laughed when I said that I'd named the neighborhood boys Two Little Terrors. He said it suited them well.

We constructed our pathway and lost track of time. We had completed the circle of bricks around the flowers and the walkway, by the time Ashkan's mom came back and rolled out the rug on the balcony.

"OK, Ashkan. You worked enough for today. What a lovely layout. Go wash your hands and get ready for the afternoon snack. Grandma is making tea."

I ran to the tap, and I held the hose so Ashkan could wash his hands. They might have allowed me into their yard, but they would not invite me into their house. That was why she told only Ashkan to wash his hands.

His grandma came to the balcony with a tray of teacups, a teapot, and a sugar bowl.

"My hero, my champion. Look what he made in one afternoon. He's already a civil engineer. Look at what he built!"

"You like it?" Ashkan ran up the stairs to the balcony.

"I love it, my champion. It's beautiful," she rubbed his hair.

Nobody invited me. "I have to go," I announced.

The grandmother looked at me and said, "Dear son, leave the tap open so the hose drips a little. And leave it by the flowerbed. It's really hot today."

I did.

"Bravo. Bravo, it looks so good," she continued to praise Ashkan.

As I walked to the gate, Ashkan yelled out, "Hey, what's your name?"

"Abdul Ali."

"Bye, Ali."

I walked out and didn't correct him. He was already biting into the homemade cake that his mom brought out.

I rubbed my hands on my pants and walked to our house. The layout of our construction was mostly my idea. But I didn't care that they only credited Ashkan. I even added a curve to the walkway to make it look better. Either way, I had a new friend. And *he* valued my work. Or so I thought.

The next afternoon, I was wearing jeans, my school shoes, and a white polo shirt, ready to construct whatever else Ashkan wanted to build. The Two Little Terrors were nowhere to be seen. But neither was my new friend. I remembered his mom had told him that he couldn't play outside. So, we probably had to play in their yard again. I rang the bell on their intercom.

"Who is it?" I recognized his mother's voice.

"Abdul Ali."

"Who?"

"Abdul Ali. Is Ashkan there?"

I heard the click as she hung up the receiver. Then another click. This time, Ashkan spoke. "Who is this?"

"Abdul Ali. You wanna play?"

"Oh, Afghan boy, is it you? Hold on, I'm coming."

He didn't even bother to remember my name. I felt a lump in my throat. "Afghan boy." The Two Little Terrors called me that.

I walked away and picked up pace as I heard Ashkan's footsteps jumping down the balcony steps. By the time he made it to the gate, I was already hiding behind the corner wall.

After a pause, he shouted, "Hey! Where are you?"

I walked away.

"Where did you go?" Ashkan yelled.

I'd lost my friend.

Some things never change. All these years later, all the way from Mashhad to Baltimore, my name still didn't matter. No one cared to know me.

At least, Trilce and Shane were good prospects.

I looked at the Admire app on my phone. Another profile said "White Masc only."

Cliff was an anomaly. I had to do everything in my power to hold onto him. To prove worthy of him. He had unlimited options. But I had only him.

There was no time for self-pity. I had to go and cook something nice for Cliff, show that I admired him more than the users of this app. Fried chicken thighs with a side of green salad.

Spectacle
/ˈspektəkl/ *noun*

Before another short trip to Louisville for Christmas, Cliff was talking to his mom on the phone, joking that a gun would be too much trouble to take on a plane. She had to think of another gift. She'd watched the news one night and had made up her mind that Baltimore was a dangerous place to live. It didn't make much sense to me. The police didn't threaten Cliff's life, the way they'd shot the unarmed teenager last month. I hoped Cliff had convinced his mom. With his temper, the last thing we needed in the apartment was a gun. He was back from his trip now, taking a shower. I used the spare moment to stare at Tyrique's picture on his website.

"What are you doing?" Cliff appeared at the door, nude, drying his hair with a small towel.

"Nothing," I put the phone aside, my face hot. *I really have to stop stalking Tyrique on the web. Just be in the moment and adore my Cliff.* "You look stunning." I got up from the bed.

"Aww, you missed me." He playfully spanked me with his towel.

"How is everyone back home?"

"Jacob was there. You should have seen him." He plugged in the hairdryer, which didn't work. He fidgeted with the safety button on the outlet. It sometimes malfunctioned. "His hair is receding. He looks worse than he did over Thanksgiving. Millie didn't even pretend to care. She's gonna leave him. I love to watch him suffer." He switched on the dryer, which began blowing hot air and making noise.

His older brother, Jacob, used to bully him as a child for acting "girly," which could mean anything, even smiling. Jacob would teach their younger brother, Clyde, homophobic slurs to use against Cliff. They were constantly fighting. Now Cliff enjoyed his ultimate revenge. And he didn't have to do anything for it. Just let time do its thing. He worked out so much that no one could accuse him of femininity, perhaps still making a point.

Karim used to criticize me for the same offense of acting girly. I never understood what I did that irritated him so much. I liked watching movies in a quiet room. He liked to play soccer outside. I would never see him again.

Cliff turned off the hairdryer, touched the edge of his spiked-up hair. "I casually brought up my salary, and his jaw dropped. I loved tormenting him all evening. Merry Christmas, brother." Checking himself out in the mirror, he rubbed some anti-wrinkle cream on his forehead. "What time are you off tomorrow?"

"Six."

"Get off at five."

"Is everything OK?"

"Yeah. Everything is great. McNair is inviting everyone to Bayadère tomorrow."

"What's that?"

"And he's inviting everyone's plus-ones. He said he really wants to see you."

"How does he even know me?"

"I've been using your picture as one of the test profiles. You're famous."

"Is it a celebration for the launch of—?"

"And a pre-celebration for one lucky person who's gonna be promoted." Cliff straightened his back and pushed out his chest.

"Oh my God, are you being promoted?" I asked, excited.

"No, no, not yet. That's why you have to be on your best behavior tomorrow. Wear your burgundy velvet blazer I bought for you."

"You don't think it's too tight?"

He gave me a questioning look.

"Wait, what exactly do you want me to do?"

"Nothing, just charm the old perv. Flirt with him a little. Like you did to me the first time. I don't know. He asked to see you at the exact time I'm up for a promotion. So don't mess it up."

"I don't know how to do it." *Did I somehow seduce Tyrique? What exactly did I do?*

"It's not like I'm asking you to sell your body. When we met, I immediately knew I wanted to spend some time with you. Even if I had to pay!"

Does he think I used to be a sex worker? He never listened. I stopped correcting him a long time ago.

"I don't blame you. Living in abject poverty is hard."

When did I give that impression?

"Just randomly touch his knee," he continued. "Accidentally drop something on the floor," Cliff dropped his towel on the floor, "and then take your sweet time picking it up." He simulated how it should look. "Remember, this is a case of bend-your-back, not-your-knees." As he stretched to pick up his towel, he fell over me, forcing both of us to tumble against the wall. "See it's not that difficult."

"You're terrible."

"Just go with the flow. If you please the old fool, he'll send me to New York. That can *really* open doors," he kissed me on the lips. "And when I get promoted, I'll buy you a pair of velvet pants. Make that rump shine. So the whole world will notice I own that ass."

"And you wanted to share me with your boss?" I couldn't believe he wanted to sell me out.

"Why you gotta be so crude, stupid? Just lead him on. *If* it comes to that. I don't even know. Just don't mess it up for me."

"You want me as a bargaining chip. Maybe I can be a—"

"Look who's been learning some metaphors," he grinned and pulled me to the bed. "Maybe all this studying is helping after all. Where did you learn that, Mr. Bargaining Chip? That's hardly an SAT word."

"I have been studying. And saving for college." *My* wishes also mattered.

"If I get the promotion, I'll pay for your college. I'd already planned on it. Which is why I work so hard. I don't want you to worry about money. Ever. All of your attention should be on me." He lay on top of me. His skin smelled like the sandalwood soap.

"Get off me."

"Come on, Abdul. Please," he begged. "My job is on the line here. Just be nice to the old fart. Out of everything I've ever asked you to do, this is the most important. Do it for me."

Maybe I did owe him that. Before I moved in with him, I'd always felt unsafe. Always a stranger. Always in precarious living conditions. No papers in Iran. Homeless back home. A series of temporary residences here in the US. But Cliff brought stability and safety to my life. He brought me to live with him in this luxury apartment complex. He bought me so many presents when we started dating. I couldn't afford to buy him expensive gifts. He had the power and the will to protect me. He helped me with my naturalization paperwork. Helped me find a job. His stiff muscles that hugged me represented a layer of defense that he wrapped around me. He was worth a couple of hours of discomfort. "Fine," I conceded.

"Yes!" He waved his fist in a winner gesture.

To leave work early the next day, I had to lie to Ms. Grace that I had a stomachache. I wore the burgundy velvet blazer as he asked.

When I showed up, Cliff and someone who I assumed was Mr. McNair, were waiting at the entrance of the Hippodrome Theatre. Cliff was wearing a bowtie. I imagined us looking good together.

Then I saw Malefic Mason as he held onto his date for the night, speaking with a straight couple. Ben, who had come to our apartment a few weeks ago, was missing.

"Here's my better half." Cliff put his arm around my waist, and I instantly felt at ease.

"Oh, the famous Abdul," Mr. McNair extended his hand. "From Afghanistan."

"Born and raised," Cliff remarked.

I was born in Iran, and he knew it. He probably just didn't want to correct his boss. "Nice to meet you, Mr. McNair." I shook his hand and lowered my head.

"You can call me Owen," he smiled. Even his name sounded ancient. He had salt and pepper hair. A bit chubby, dressed in an expensive black suit.

Mr. McNair showed the tickets to the attendant who scanned their barcodes and welcomed us. Our group was led to the side. A server brought us Champagne in plastic cups.

We all ended up sitting in the same row. The fifth row to be exact. The hall smelled like polished wood. The plaster work and the lights were exquisite. I sat between Mr. McNair and Cliff. Until the show started, Mason's date for the night kept talking and making him laugh. He was such a cliché that I thought he was faking it. Like a caricature of Shane on steroids: fluttering his limp wrists, constantly clutching his imaginary pearls, and making incessant comments about everyone's looks. He had something to say about every single person's outfit. Hearing him was exhausting.

Mr. McNair talked about the history of the building. I pretended his stories fascinated me, so perhaps I was as big a fraud as Mason's date.

As Cliff was listening to another one of their unfunny jokes, his phone fell on the floor. He either didn't notice or wanted *me* to pick it up.

"Excuse me, Owen." I pretended I couldn't miss a single detail about how this former movie theatre had closed in the 90s. "I'm sorry. Just one second." I got up and looked over the row in front of us. It mortified me that I had to bend over the seat to fetch the phone. Cliff laughed at something and tapped on his thigh, oblivious to my ordeal.

"You need help there?" Noticing the Champagne cup still in my hand, Mr. McNair offered to hold it for me.

"Thank you, Owen. So kind of you." I bent over and paused one second too long to "show off the goods," hoping this was flirtatious enough. Instead, it felt cheap. "I'm sorry you had to hold the cup."

"Oh, shoosh. It's your lover's fault for being so clumsy."

I handed Cliff the phone and pulled down my blazer. He gave me a strange frown I couldn't decipher.

"Have you read the program yet? I don't mean to interrupt the conversation but you'd understand the ballet better. It was quite unorthodox for its time."

I didn't know what "unorthodox" meant. "Would it be too imposing if I ask you to tell me? I don't read fast in English and I'm afraid my vocabulary isn't good enough."

"Don't underestimate yourself, young man. Your vocabulary seems up to par. But I can give you the CliffsNotes."

What did it have to do with Cliff? I couldn't quite focus on the story, not sure if I was playing my role well, the way Cliff expected.

"Are you OK, Abdul? You seem a bit tense. I'm starting to think the Champagne may not be authentic if it's giving you a headache."

"I'm fine, sir. I'm—"

"Would you like some more to drink?" Cliff asked him. "I was gonna go anyway." He made a hand gesture like he was cutting his throat.

What's up with him? I don't know how else to flirt with his boss. "I can get it. Would Mason and…" I'd forgotten his date's name.

"Let's just get drinks for all of us." Mr. McNair offered. "I'll go with Abdul. You stay and listen to Mason's story."

"Are you sure?" My boyfriend sounded hesitant.

"You worked hard these past few weeks. We'll get the drinks. I need to stretch my legs a bit. The design of these seats leaves something to be desired."

How much do they charge for drinks in a place like this? Should I offer to pay?

Mr. McNair started telling me an anecdote about the first ballet he'd seen. He had been shocked that men's costumes showcased their "derrières" so much. He didn't sound creepy, just making small talk with a stranger. I wished Cliff hung out more with him and less with Mason. He paid for the drinks and offered to help carry the tray.

When we came back, Mr. McNair told Cliff, "Your lover is a delight. I know you think you're a catch, but so is he."

Cliff smiled. "Yes, boss."

Act I soon started. Now I understood what Mr. McNair had meant. The male dancers wore shiny tops and white leggings for pants. You could see their glutes bouncing.

Was I objectifying the performers by watching them dance? I closed my eyes to just enjoy the music for a bit. Why were people obsessed with always dancing to music? Wasn't just listening good enough? One of the reasons I liked Ramesh so much was that she never danced. I had seen a few of her music videos. She never danced as though it would violate her dignity as a singer. Her song with *Raqs Sharqi* beats was called *Afsous*. No one dared dance to *those* lyrics.

I felt a motion and opened my eyes. Cliff crossed his legs. I placed my hand on his calf, trying to feel anchored to him. He held my hand and whispered something to my ear, "You need to behave." I felt I was somehow failing him. He probably wanted me to put my hand on Mr. McNair's knee.

During the intermission, Mr. McNair told me a story about his youth when he worked as a pool boy and had a secret crush on the husband of the household. Meanwhile the wife tried to seduce him.

Soon after, Cliff wanted to follow Mason to the bar. He turned to me and asked if I wanted to go with him. I got up, "accidentally" putting my hand on Mr. McNair's forearm. But his story wasn't over, and I didn't want to be rude. Cliff noticed that I was trying to be nice to his boss, as he'd asked.

The night passed without incidents. Mason didn't throw any insults my way and Mr. McNair didn't show any inappropriate interest in me. He just shook my hand and said it was a pleasure to meet me. He then reminded Cliff that I was a gentleman. I thought it was more a complement, rather than an expression of disappointment.

Back home, Cliff wasn't happy. "Do you have no social skills? What the hell was that spectacle you put up?"

"I'm sorry. I *tried* to lead him on. But he had no interest in me."

"That was obvious from the first second you said hi. You still spent the whole evening drooling over him."

"But you told me to do that. Remember last night? You begged me to—"

"I don't beg," he yelled. "I kept trying to signal to you to stop. Twice I tried to get you to come with me to the bar so we could talk. I even gestured 'abort, abort.'" He gesticulated cutting his throat. "I literally told you to behave."

"I'm sorry. I didn't understand what—"

He stomped toward me. "How dumb do you have to be to not know what this means?" He began making the same signal of cutting his throat. Then, he made a fist and lifted his hand.

"Cliff, stop. You're my safety. It's really unsettling when you get violent." I was in no mood to get beaten up, having done what he'd wanted.

"Violent?" He shouted. "Is that what you think of me? Until five minutes ago, you'd punch me every time your jealousy flared up."

"Cliff, please." Now, I was the one begging.

He shook his head. "It's OK. I guess Mason will hate you less since you contributed to his upcoming promotion."

"Was it that bad? I'm so sorry."

"It's OK," he walked to the bedroom. "I'll start looking for another job. Let's just go to bed."

"Cliff?" I took his hand. "You forgive me?"

He gazed at me. "Yeah, stupid. What's done is done."

We may fight sometimes. But our love is too strong to waver.

Aperture

/ˈæpətʃər/ *noun*

Ever since I'd lost my SAT book, my main pastime had been taken away from me. Viewing Tyrique's page just depressed me now. I didn't want to give him more chances to hurt me. But with Cliff gone again, I had little to distract me. Despite his belief that I hadn't left a good impression on Mr. McNair, ruining his chances for promotion, it turned out that his boss did like me. A couple of days later, he chose Cliff to accompany him to a New York trip.

Cliff was excited about spending New Year's Eve at Times Square. I could hardly tolerate the crowd in a night club, much less being surrounded by thousands of people who had gathered to watch the ball drop. Not that it dropped to explode into beautiful fireworks. The ball of light slowly descended as if on an old elevator and then... nothing. What was the big fuss about?

As soon as she found out that Cliff was out of town, Trilce suggested to have a "girls' night" at the Four Seasons. She got a large discount for the first Friday of the year. We were practically spending the night there for free.

"She always has some creative idea to do something new," Shane pointed out. "She sent me to a nude camp in the summer. It was amazing. I felt like a literal fairy. I was wearing so much glittery makeup."

"Of course, you did. You should show Abdul the pictures. Of the upper body only," she corrected herself. "You looked good."

The three of us wore the white robes and slippers with the Four Seasons logo and headed to the hot tub. Trilce was carrying a Champagne bottle again, Shane the ice bucket, and I the glasses. A staff member smiled at us on the way. "Happy New Year."

"Same to you," she replied.

We bypassed the locker room and went to the hot tub. She opened the bottled and poured for us all, placing the bottle in the ice bucket.

I hesitantly took off my robe, feeling shy.

"Look at you," Shane whistled. "Now I understand what keeps your boyfriend around. You look like a professional swimmer."

I wished I was wearing more clothes. Then, he took off his robe, showing off the smallest bikini I'd seen.

Trilce turned on the jets and stepped in. "Could you possibly wear any less?"

"I didn't wear a thong out of respect for *you*," he answered. "You know how straight guys wear capri pants instead of swimsuits? I always wanna say, 'Your dick doesn't reach your knee. Who are you kidding?'"

I laughed and followed him into the hot tub. "Cheers," I clinked my glass against theirs. "Did anything interesting happen in the nude camp?"

"Mmmm." He replied, either to my question or to the Champagne.

"You were very happy when you came back," she remarked.

"I might have sampled some appetizers if you know what I mean!"

"And the main course?" I teased.

"How dare you, sir? A lady doesn't kiss and tell." He took another sip. "Not in front of another lady."

Trilce splashed water on him.

He shielded his mouth with his hand and looked at me. "I'll tell you all about it later. You should absolutely do it."

"He has a boyfriend," she reminded.

"You know what you guys should do?" Shane exclaimed at me, apparently loving his own idea. "You should make a sex tape!"

I covered my face, embarrassed.

"I'm surprised Ms. Original hasn't suggested it yet."

"That's all you. I'm not saying nothing!" She winked.

"What do you think?" His excitement still at its peak.

"No way. Why don't *you* do that?"

"I'm sure there are clips of me online. Once, I was with this guy in a hotel room when his roommate walked in and... let's just say he enjoyed the show."

"Don't overshare," she warned him. "I'm afraid you'd scare off Abdul. Not everyone is a—"

"Are you a prude, honey?" He asked me.

"I'm... not drunk yet."

"There's no excuse for that." Shane picked up the bottle.

I took another sip and held out the glass for him to fill up.

"How did you meet your boyfriend?" Trilce changed the topic.

"We met in a bar."

"Oooh, grinding on the dancefloor, sweaty and shirtless?" Shane remained animated.

"No, more like, having a drink and then going home when the bar got so loud and crowded that we couldn't hear each other anymore."

"I *told* you," he pointed his finger at Trilce. "Just because you sleep with someone on the first date doesn't mean your relationship is doomed."

"Well, technically the first date came after." The sparkling wine was already doing its magic on me.

When the bottle finished, we went back to the room to drink more and watch a movie.

"We should watch Sex Tape," Shane proposed. "That's like the theme of the night."

"Hardly," she corrected.

"I like Bollywood movies."

"So what I'm hearing you say is: you love Bollywood movies so much that you've already seen them all. And you're looking for a romantic comedy with the beautiful blond Cameron Diaz!" Shane insisted.

Trilce shrugged and looked at me.

"I mean, if *that's* what you heard me say," I consented.

We started the movie and got room service: hamburgers and French fries and a third bottle of sparkling wine. We enjoyed the movie, which bolstered Shane's confidence in his own taste. He then suggested that we watch *A Haunted House 2*. We were too wasted to argue. Also, who wouldn't want to see Marlon Wayans?

After the movies were over, Trilce asked, "Are you guys OK sleeping on the same bed?"

"We're fine, honey. Two bottoms don't make a top," Shane grinned.

We all slept like babies.

Repercussion
/ ˌriːpərˈkʌʃn/ *noun*

On the way to work in the morning, I was listening to Sajid Jannaty's song "Nawai-e Ishq" on repeat. The singer looked royal in the video, sitting on his throne. He was my favorite in all of Afghan Star contestants. I was ecstatic when he won a couple of years ago. Sitting on the bus, I closed my eyes to enjoy the music more.

"Hey. I haven't seen you in a minute," a beautiful guy with locs that fell to his shoulders was smiling at me. I thought I'd seen him before, but couldn't remember where. "You used to come to the coffee shop all the time."

That was why he looked familiar. He was the barista from Morning in Beirut. "Hi." I tried to remember his name.

"Derrick."

"I remember," I tried to be polite. "Abdul."

"May I?" he pointed to the empty seat next to me.

"Please."

His presence felt warm. "What are you listening to?"

"A song by the winner of Afghan Star. It's a singing show like American Idol."

"Let me listen." He took my earphones. "Nice. Sounds like Indian music a bit. How have you been? Haven't seen you since home boy spilled his coffee on you."

"I can't believe you remember that," I cringed.

"A playboy like that bothering my cute customer? Yeah, I remember."

I covered my mouth with my fingers, as if smiling would be taking away from the cuteness that he'd just observed.

"Are you going out with him?"

He had never talked to me this much. He was always friendly, but we never got a chance to really chat.

"No. It just took a minute to part ways that day. He was very determined." I omitted the details.

"Good," he smiled. "I thought you were trying to make me jealous."

What does that mean? Is he...

"Can I take you out then?"

I remembered the profiles on the Admire app saying things like "No spice, no rice." A chance like this wouldn't come again.

"We can grab a bite. For lunch. Or dinner," he interrupted my thoughts. "You can't survive on coffee and pastries alone."

Cliff was out of town. I still had to get over Tyrique. This would be the last time I stepped out of my relationship with Cliff. Just a lunch. We wouldn't even have to do anything.

"Come on," he persisted. "Don't leave me hanging."

I loved the way he spoke, his voice deep and soothing. "OK." *I should have said something classy like "I'd love to."*

"Cool."

I gave him my number.

"Hey, you like Mexican?"

"Yeah, definitely."

"You'll love the place I'm taking you."

The way he took control pleased me. It made me feel led, but not yanked. I would go anywhere he wanted. And of course, I did love the place he took me for dinner later that day, after my shift at the inn. A burrito for me that I ate with a knife and fork, and hard tacos for him that he masterfully bit into without making a mess. When a tiny bit of guacamole was left on his lip, I was so tempted to use it as an excuse to kiss him. But this was Derrick so I couldn't act cheap.

My temptation only increased when my phone vibrated with a message from Cliff. Things were going well, and he might come back with good news. I quickly put the phone aside. We had a whole lifetime to spend together. My moments with Derrick however were limited.

"You got somewhere to be?" Derrick had noticed me checking the phone.

"Right here with you," I smiled.

He chuckled and brought his chair closer, putting his hand on the back of mine. "I wanted to kiss you but then, I thought, my onion breath mixed with your hot sauce would make an entirely new kind of dish."

I took a pack of Ice Breakers chewing gum out of my bag.

"Thanks, you wanna get out of here?"

We ended up in his living room. A couch sat in front of the TV and an armchair on the corner. A light with paper shade arched down over the coffee table, where books of various sizes were scattered. The first one I noticed was titled Introduction to Psychology.

"You go to school?"

"Only part time. I usually have classes in the evening, but this is my lucky night," he announced as he kicked off his sneakers. "Have a seat. I'll get drinks."

I took off my red Converse shoes and put them at the door. I then picked up his bulky sneakers and lined them up by the wall.

"You didn't have to take off yours." He came with a bottle of Crown Royal that he poured into two empty glasses. "Cheers." He took a sip.

"Where I'm from, everyone takes off their shoes at the door."

"Sorry. Remind me again where that is."

"Afghanistan."

He sat down on the couch. I next to him.

"My feet hurt." He placed his hand on my knee to balance himself as he put his feet on the table.

"I can rub them for you." I did that for Cliff sometimes.

"No. I got a better idea." He leaned toward me and put his lips on mine.

I closed my eyes and let him take me over. His Chapstick tasted like mint and honey, making me salivate. He leaned on me more and moved his legs to get closer. Then he let out a whimper.

"What's wrong?"

"Nah, it's just my foot. I had an encounter with the gentlemen of BPD. One of them stomped on my foot."

"Bastard." I assumed it was just a "stop and frisk" type of interaction. "Randomly, of course," if anyone was stupid enough to believe that.

"They can do whatever they want. Qualified immunity."

"I know what that is. The Afghan police is like that too."

"Damn," he shook his head. "A couple of my friends are cops but they can't protect you a hundred percent, you know. The guy jumped me for no reason. And emptied my bag on the street. Stomped on me and then let me go."

"This evening?"

"Before going to the Mexican restaurant."

"I'm so sorry. That sucks. Are you sure it's not broken?"

"Yeah. That would hurt much worse. And my sneakers have a good layer of padding. Did you see what they tried to pull in the Mosher case? I'm going to a rally this weekend. We demand the footage of the shooting be released to the public. We have to fight every step of the way."

Dealing with law enforcement was a never-ending battle. They did whatever they pleased. They stomped on Derrick's foot with no reason. "Let me massage it with some Icy Hot. You can't be in pain the whole evening."

"OK, fine. Not gonna say no twice." He caved in.

"Do you have Icy Hot?"

"In the bathroom. You're such a sweetheart."

I moved to the door I assumed was the bathroom.

"In the cabinet," he yelled out from the living room.

I turned on the light and found the tube. Several containers of hair products sat around the sink. In the mirror, I noticed a pair of red underwear that was now drying on the towel rack. Then I saw my reflection in the mirror. Maybe it was the lighting in his bathroom, but in his mirror, I didn't look ugly. Derrick had called me a cutie earlier. I touched my angular chin. Rubbed my finger on my eyebrows. My black hair was shining under the light. Did I always look like this? I was presentable! Possibly even cute. I smiled at the thought. Dimples dug into my cheeks. Maybe it was a blessing that I couldn't grow a beard to cover up the dimples. My teeth resembled a picture from a dentist advertisement. That only widened my smile.

"Found it?" Derrick called out.

"Ah… yes." After a last glance at the mirror, I walked out of the bathroom.

He was stretched out on the couch. "Thank you."

I moved the armchair closer. "OK, put your foot on my knee."

"I kinda feel shy now."

"Where does it hurt?" I ignored him.

"Right on the metatarsals."

I had no idea what that meant.

"Right above the toes. I'm also taking Anatomy."

"Are you pre-med?"

"Kinda. Keeping my options open."

I put some ointment on his foot. I remembered having read that medical professionals are less likely to take it seriously when African American patients complained of pain. I rubbed gently to make sure I changed that norm.

"That feels good. Thanks," he took another sip of his drink. He untied his locs, laid back his head and closed his eyes.

"I love your hair. It's so beautiful."

"You wanna touch it?"

I shook my head.

"Usually, if I'm with anyone who's not Black, he wants to touch my locs. It's OK, though. I plan on touching a lot more than your hair."

I laughed, looking forward to that.

"I like your smile. It… like… lights up the whole room. Oh, that feels good. Where did you learn that?"

"I haven't." *Just practiced on Cliff when he was tired.*

"You self-taught? You're good. You should be a *masseur*."

"What's that?"

"A male massage person or something like that. Isn't that French?"

I had no idea.

"You can make a lot of money doing massage. White gays love that. Not that I'm complaining. What do *you* wanna study?"

I didn't respond. Because I had no idea. Cliff wanted me to do Business Administration but that seemed extremely boring.

"You'll figure it out. By the time you take all the required courses, you'll know."

"I haven't even taken the SAT yet. Not to speak of even passing it."

"You'll be OK. If you're so dedicated that you study randomly in a coffee shop... Have you thought about starting from a community college? You may not even have to take the SAT."

"I've heard of that. Is it true? I'm kinda afraid of taking classes and not understanding the books. My English isn't very good."

"You speak English better than some Americans. You just need some self-confidence."

"You're too kind."

"I *am* kind. But this is not an example of it. I mean it. If you ever need any help, you can ask me."

"Thank you."

"Especially if you do that when I'm helping." He extended his hand and gave me my glass. "You're brave offering a foot massage to a stranger. Weren't you afraid of me having some callused feet, stinky, with dirt piling up under cracked toenails?"

"Eww."

"Exactly."

"Still, I don't want you to be in pain." The whiskey warmed my throat and stomach as it went down.

"As much as that feels good, I have something else in mind. Something I enjoy even more." He stood up. "Now it's my turn to make you feel good." He took my hand and led me to his bedroom. He was still wearing a sock when he laid me on his bed and undressed me. His skin felt soft as pistachio blossoms.

Derrick bent over me. His locs poured over my face like a waterfall onto a lake. The oaky caramel taste of liquor felt wonderful on his lips and tongue. I wanted to give him all of me. I wanted to end, so that I wouldn't have to go back home. Maybe my love for Cliff had already faded. Being in someone else's bed for the third time. I wanted Derrick to use all of me so that I wouldn't be able to think these thoughts anymore.

When he fell asleep, he was lying on his side, and so was I. His arm was wrapped around my chest, and I held his hand in mind. As I kissed his fingers, he let out a moan and pulled me closer. His breath, soft and peaceful, caressed my neck. His chest expanded and retracted against my back.

I imagined how we looked from different angles. The best view would be from the ceiling, so Derrick's locs could be seen and adored. With the royal burgundy sheets covering us. I wondered what Cliff would do if he ever saw that image. A storm of punches and kicks would rain down on me.

Cliff wasn't a bad person. Yes, he had a temper. But his anger was just a masculine trait. A proper gay guy should find that masculine aggression attractive. On the Admire app, I had seen so many messages from boys who wished they could have what I had.

He'd never cheated on me. Sometimes I wish he had. That would help me feel less awful. Derrick pulled his arm, lying on his back now.

My glass of Crown Royal was on the nightstand, next to the condom wrapper. I took a sip and typed a quick message to Cliff, saying the bed was cold without him. Another sip of whiskey fogged my thoughts of him. To calm myself more, I started to listen to the inhales and exhales of the man lying next to me. Like peaceful waves on a beach.

When my eyes opened, sunshine was extending its hands through the windows.

"Good morning," Derrick said as he walked out of the bathroom, apparently straight from the shower. Drops of water on his skin sparkled in the sunlight and the towel that would have been around his waist was instead wrapped around his locs. All the hormones in my body awoke upon seeing that picture.

"I wish I could come back to bed, but I have to go to work," he said.

"What time is it?"

"A quarter to nine."

"What?" I jumped out of the bed. "I should have been at work fifteen minutes ago."

"Oh no! You should have told me to set the alarm. Can you call out sick or… I don't know, come up with an excuse?"

No, I already got written up twice. "I think I'll just run," I pulled on my pants. I texted Ms. Grace, saying my bus was stuck in traffic.

"There's OJ and croissants in the fridge."

"No, thanks. I have to go right away. I'm sorry I know it's rude to dash out like this." I put on my shirt, realizing I had to go home to change into my uniform.

"It's OK."

"I'm sorry." I put on my jacket and wore my shoes, sticking the laces inside.

I took a cab and reached the inn at 9:42. Ms. Grace just gave me a sad look.

"Abdul, I need to see you in my office." Rebecca greeted me. "Now."

I knew exactly what was coming. Her wheelchair never looked so mechanical before. She spoke about me being a helpful and friendly receptionist. Our guests had good things to say about me. But the first warning, the second warning. I had a habit of being late. "I'm sorry but I'll have to let you go." She then said something about my last paycheck and whatever health insurance.

I used all my energy to not cry in front of her, staring at

my black dress shoes. I had decided I wouldn't cry anymore.

She could probably guess that I hadn't slept at home. Could she detect the look of shame on my face?

As I walked out of her office, Ms. Grace called my name. "You're going to be all right," she emphasized.

I said goodbye. I even hated the sound of my voice.

Foreboding
/fɔːrˈboʊdɪŋ/ *noun*

I checked the water temperature in the tub. After what I did during his absence, the least I could do now was to pamper him, remind him that he was still my number one. I mixed the Epsom salt in the water. Then dropped some lavender essential oil. Finally, I added some bubble bath to make it froth. Cliff had really enjoyed blowing bubbles for his profile picture. I lit a couple of candles on the sides of the tub.

"It's ready," I announced as I went to get his KBS beer from the fridge.

He'd been cheerful since his return from New York yesterday. I didn't have the heart to tell him I got fired. No hurry to summon his rage.

He took off his clothes. "I thought you were making a salt bath."

"Yeah." I walked in with two bottles in my hand.

"What's up with the bubbles then?"

"I thought you liked it when we were taking pictures."

"You mixed Epson salt and soap?"

"Yeah?"

"You stupid," he messed up my hair as he took the beer. His touch reassuring and playful.

"I'm sorry. I shouldn't have mixed those?"

He lay down in the tub and took a sip. "The water feels good. Even though you ruined the positive effects of the minerals."

"I'm sorry. Do you want me to redo it?"

"To wait another half hour for the tub to fill? Nah, it's fine." His voice sounded calm. "You coming?"

"I was thinking I can wash your hair."

He dipped his head into the water. "With a nice head massage? Even better."

I sat on a stool by the tub. "Tell me about New York. Did you get to meet the people you wanted to?"

"New York is amazing. We went to the club one night and ended up dancing on a platform between two twink dancers. They were all over me. The number of my Admirers doubled overnight."

Thankfully, I hadn't been there to experience that. Dancing was the most awful activity I could imagine. "To what song?"

"I don't know. Some Britney or whatever. But the club aside, I got to shake a lot of hands and give out a lot of business cards."

The shampoo smelled like cucumber. I massaged his scalp slowly.

"You never know which connection is going to lead to the next opportunity. New York is where it's at. There's nothing keeping me in Baltimore."

"Keeping *us* in Baltimore," I corrected and wiped the froth from his forehead.

"Mason took some guy to his room, as I knew he would. Desperate as always."

I thought the whole point of me trying to appeal to Mr. McNair was to earn Cliff cookie points so that he would go to New York, without Malefic Mason. "I'm surprised anyone wanted to go with him. It's not like he—"

"You know what he did? He made his app profile super popular, using bots."

"What are bots?"

"Software, basically. Mason got thousands of these unreal social media users to boost his Admire profile. He's got many, *many* more Admirers than I do."

"But that's cheating."

"I'm just happy for my exclusivity idea."

Ben's idea.

"The fake users can't have profiles. But their number raises our visibility like crazy. McNair was happy."

"Mason just can't play by the rules, can he? I don't like him."

"Yeah, you've made that quite clear. Too clear at times. He's still my buddy."

"You deserve better friends." *And a better boyfriend too.*

"You should be happy he's a whore. You know he had a crush on me, right?"

"What?" A ball of foam dropped on his cheek.

"If he didn't go out with random guys, he'd be hitting on me."

"I didn't know he was after you."

"He might be over it by now. Of course, he got the hots for me. Who wouldn't? But... He's so bland. There's nothing that exciting about him."

Has he ever done anything with Mason? Even the thought of it was repulsive. I couldn't ask Cliff about his sex life before me, when I was secretly sleeping around.

"Hey, where did you go?" he snapped his fingers, unhappy that I was daydreaming. Cliff looked around and changed the subject. "I wish we had a Buddha statue for the background."

A Buddha. A couple of weeks before my eleventh birthday, the Taliban began their assault on the Buddhas in Bamiyan, a UNESCO World Heritage Site. The destruction took several days. They used mines and rockets to demolish the ancient monumental statues. I remember my parents were shocked, watching it on TV, our last year in Iran. Karim asked my father, "Shouldn't we be happy that the idols are gone? We're Shi'a after all." He replied that they had historical value.

When we moved to Bamiyan, we went to see the site. The empty spaces of the Buddhas were enormous. The statues must have been majestic. Now, there was just an overwhelming void. Our history had been silenced.

"Get me another beer," Cliff asked.

I did.

Posing for the pictures, Cliff leaned to the side and put one leg out of the tub. "OK, I have an idea. I'm gonna shake the beer bottle really hard and you take a picture as it erupts." He put his thumb on the top and pumped his arm back and forth. "Ready?" He held the bottle in a suggestive pose and lifted his finger.

The beer fizzed. A text from Trilce showed up on the screen and almost ruined the pictures. I pressed my finger on the volume button, taking a burst of shots. "These are amazing pictures." They were thirst traps, but I approved over my better judgment, hormones working against me as usual. "How do you come up with these—?"

"Sexiness comes to me naturally." He lowered his body back into the water, the beer bottle empty.

The doorbell rang.

"I'll be right back." I went to the door and looked through the peephole. Ms. Grace was standing behind the door. I opened the door. "Ms. Grace, hi."

"Hello, Abdul. How are you?"

"I'm fine."

"You are?"

Embarrassed, all I could say was: "My own fault." I knew she'd done everything to cover for me.

"Rebecca feels bad too. We all enjoyed working with you. Except for your..."

"I know. Thank you. I'll miss you so much."

"You didn't answer my texts."

I had been *trying* to avoid this conversation. "I'm sorry."

"It's alright. But I brought you this." She opened her bag and pulled out my SAT book. "You left it at the counter a while back. Didn't you miss it? It's been sitting in your box for weeks now."

I never checked my mailbox at work. "Thank you so much."

"You're welcome. If you need anything, like a reference for a job application—"

"Who's that?" Cliff yelled from the bathroom.

I wasn't ready to tell him yet. "I'm coming," I managed to say.

"He's home," Ms. Grace observed. "You better go before he gets angry."

I stared at her for a moment. She knew. When Cliff came to pick me up after Thanksgiving, she mentioned I'd fallen down while dancing. He, of course, didn't know what she was talking about. And she made the logical conclusion about the wound on my face. I felt ashamed. "Thank you. I'm so sorry you had to come all this way."

"I had to check on you. Make sure you're OK. Take care of yourself. You have my number. Reach out once in a while."

"Yeah, I will."

"Go. Go before he gets upset." Ms. Grace turned away but then faced me again. "You don't have to put up with any type of nonsense. Remember that."

I nodded.

"Let me know if you need anything," she repeated and walked down the stairs.

"Bye." I closed the door and went to the bathroom.

Cliff was standing by the mirror. "Who was that?"

"Ms. Grace. From work."

"What did she want?"

"She brought my SAT book."

"Why? Why couldn't you pick it up tomorrow?"

I hesitated.

"What's going on?"

"I… I got fired."

"What?"

"I'm sorry."

"What did you do?"

I looked at the floor. Water was dripping from his skin onto the tiles. If he hit me and I slip, I could break a bone.

"Answer me."

"I crashed the reservation software. We lost the data for several weeks." My voice was hardly audible.

"How did you manage that?"

"I opened a bunch of windows?"

He frowned. "It shouldn't be that easy to crash something. I can come and talk to them. I'm sure they have no idea how programs actually work. They can't fire you for their crappy computer system."

He had so much faith in me.

"You wanna fight this? We can even get a lawyer or something."

God, no. I don't want you asking about this ever again. "It's OK. I was getting bored with it anyway."

He hesitated for a second, then approached me with a serious face. "If you wanna stay at home and be a trophy boy, you need to look better than this." He lifted my T-shirt. "I want chiseled abs, biceps like balloons," he asserted. "Your ass can't be your *only* good feature."

"I thought you said I was beautiful."

"You can be." He was getting angry. He raised his hand, making me jump back. "Your cheeks get rouge and cute when I slap you," he dropped his hand and smirked. "What? You should *want* me to do it."

He was on the verge of exploding, and it seemed like even he himself didn't know if he could control his rage. "Show me the pictures." He took the phone from me. He swiped through. A big smile adorned his face. "Although it's easy on the photographer when the model is… me," he snickered.

"Yeah." I kissed him, then lowered my voice. "I'm sorry. I'll find another job."

"Like hell you will. And the money I allowed you to put aside for your college fund, I'll take it to cover a small portion of our living costs. I never signed up to be a sugar daddy. And this…" He paused. "You know what? I won't allow you to ruin this evening. I…" He took a breath. Then suddenly, he clapped his hands, stomped his foot on the floor, and shouted "boo."

I jerked back, startled.

"You're such a girl sometimes." Cliff started laughing. "Cut it out. I don't like that. But I do like it that you're afraid of me. You're getting too comfortable bringing home bad news." He grabbed my chin and gazed into my eyes. Then he took the beer bottle and smashed it on the floor. Glass splinters flew in every direction. We were both barefoot. It reminded me of Basanti dancing on glass shards in *Sholay*. In a certain emotional state, I would step on the broken glass for Cliff, but I would not dance.

Cliff's chest was red with anger despite his efforts to calm down. I could read from his expression that he needed to express his rage that spilled out of him. He took a couple of deep breaths, his chest losing the redness and slowly turning pink. He lifted his foot.

"Careful," I warned him softly. "Don't step on it."

"You make me so angry sometimes," he confessed.

"Forgive me, Cliff. Please. I'll get another job."

He exhaled noisily, like puffing out cigarette smoke. "I don't want to see you with that stupid SAT book again."

"OK," I nodded. "I'll do anything you want." I touched his chest, lightly. His heartbeat was only slightly higher than usual. "Making you happy is my number one…" I used to talk to him like this when we started going out. Nothing else had mattered to me back then. What had changed, and when?

"OK." He ruffled my hair.

With my help, he had succeeded in managing his anger. Maybe I should dedicate my life to making him happy. Like any love story. Wasn't his smile worth the world? "Go and rest a bit. I'll clean up and come. We can drink and post those pictures on your profile. Let the thirsty boys salivate."

"OK," he stepped out of the bathroom.

With a padding of toilet paper, I started picking up the pieces of broken glass and putting them into the garbage can, the light reflecting against the sharp edges.

All the cuteness aside, his smile wasn't *everything* to me. I wanted to make him happy but that wasn't my *only* goal.

It made me sad that most probably, I would never be able to go to college.

Pinpricks
/ˈpɪnprɪk/ noun

Raindrops permeated my jeans, creating wet spots. Cold and pointy, like a pincushion for sewing needles. My bag sat safely under the umbrella on the other side of the bench. A small puddle took shape at the corner of the curb. I could hear tiny streams gushing towards the gutters, accompanied by the staccato of rain drops on the umbrella. A gentle breeze brought a scent of fresh mud. Some fifty feet away, a snowman was slowly losing its form, the charcoal of its eyes already droopy, giving color to its cheeks, as though crying. I felt jealous of how it was slowly melting under the rain, becoming one with water and earth.

"I want whatever he's smoking," said a man's voice, making fun of me.

"Stay away. God knows what he's on," a female voice replied.

"Coming."

I imagined her pulling him away from me, the supposed frightening junkie. Their voices faded. I wasn't a threat. Not to them anyway.

In a way, I had to be thankful that here, no one paid much attention to me. I could go anywhere I wanted. If

I were still in Iran, my *amayesh* card would determine the city where I had to live and work. But in Baltimore, my employer wouldn't pay me less because of my ethnicity. I'd seen an Iranian documentary once online, where the amateur filmmaker interviewed the owner of a garment workshop who hired immigrant children from Afghanistan. "I feel bad for them, they should be in school," he confessed, before adding, "but they're so much cheaper than Iranian labor." The film was soon taken offline. Telling the truth endangered the Iranian filmmaker.

At least here, as I sat in the park under the rain, I was free. The Arabic coffee I had earlier no longer had any warming effect on my body. It was even branded as "Turkish coffee" in the only alternative coffee shop I could find: Turkish Delight. Morning in Beirut was no longer an option. No need to witness how Derrick would lose interest in me after that night.

A set of footsteps interrupted my thoughts. It sounded like women's boots, presumably with high heels. The sound got louder over the wet ground.

She got closer to me. "Well, hello stranger," she sounded familiar.

I looked up. "Trilce?"

"Why are you sitting in the rain?"

"How did you find me?"

"You're the first guy who ghosted me. D'you know that? And we weren't even dating."

I meant to apologize but I didn't. The rain got heavier, filling the silence between us.

"Sure, I'll sit down with you," she initiated. Her long jacket covered most of her leg.

She closed her umbrella and put it next to my bag. "What's going on?"

I let out a long exhale. "Not much." Without looking at her, I could feel she gave me a crooked look.

"Do you know what I had to go through to find you?"

I didn't. Had she talked to Ms. Grace? The most she could have gotten out of her was my home address. How did she… Trilce put a paper espresso cup on the bench. The logo said "Turkish Delight."

"You're resourceful." *And almost like a stalker.*

"I know we're not that close yet. But I also know when I smell trouble."

Is that how I smell?

"Abdul, I know something is off. Maybe I can help, maybe I can't. But I wanna at least be here for you."

"Why?" I wiped my face to prove I wasn't crying. Just raindrops on my face.

"Because life can be good, sometimes. And I'm gonna stay around until you realize that." She put her hand on my leg, pressing the cold jeans against my skin. It must have felt cold on her palm, but she didn't pull away. "And even after you do, I'll be there to take your hand."

Trying my best to sound normal I replied, "I'm fine."

"I was looking for a new hobby anyway."

"So *I'm* your hobby?"

She removed her hand. "The guy who works at your favorite coffee shop—"

"I don't go there anymore."

"The guy with the locs," she ignored me. "He looked weird when I asked about you. Did you sleep with him?"

Touché. I hated how she could put random facts together and see the big picture.

"You did, didn't you?" she sounded excited now. "I'm not judging. It just looks like you're not too happy with your boyfriend. Why is that? What's wrong with him?"

I felt relief that someone took the time to get to know me a bit. Something none of the four men I'd recently gone to bed with had bothered to do. "What makes you think something's wrong with him?"

"You said you don't have an open relationship, but you act like you do."

That was the problem when intelligent people started paying attention. They could sniff a lie. I thought about how to dissuade her from staying. But part of me wanted her to stay.

"What is some of the new SAT vocab you've been studying?"

Silence.

"Where is your book? Or do you use flash cards?"

I didn't reply.

"Here's a word: conversationalist."

Despite my resistance, a smile sparked on my face.

"Oh, you already know that one! What about... vivacious?"

"Stop," I said louder than I intended. "SAT is useless. I'll never go to college."

"Why not? You haven't learned the word persistence yet? Grit?"

I was in no mood for her jabs. "Cliff emptied my savings account, that's why. Ms. Observant."

"He can't do that."

Technically, it was a joint account. My salary was never entirely mine to begin with, and neither was my savings. "You don't know anything. My entire salary wouldn't even make a third of our expenses. Without him, I couldn't have saved a dime." I paused, letting my words sink in. "After I got fired, he got upset that I don't contribute enough." I lowered my voice, expecting her to blame me.

"You need to stop punishing yourself. Everyone has been fired at some point in their life. If he is a good person, he'll get over it. Maybe he already has."

Perhaps.

"Your value doesn't come from your paycheck. Whatever guilt you feel for being… in between jobs, or whatever shame you feel for being gay, it doesn't define you."

I did deserve the punishment.

"It's really getting cold. Let's get out of here."

A chill wrapped around my body with her reminder.

"I'm parked a couple of blocks away," she picked up her umbrella.

"I don't wanna wet your car."

"No one said you should pee there!"

I burst into laughter.

"Better a wet car seat than a sick friend."

I noticed a Black Lives Matter sticker on her bag. "What's this?"

"Oh, I went to a protest. Apparently the police is hiding more footage about how they shot that guy in Mosher last November."

"I hate cops," I got up from the bench.

"We're not gonna go down without a fight." She rubbed my shoulder.

At that moment, I wanted to hug her. I needed a friend. I picked up my umbrella and held it above our heads, following her to the car.

"They are no angels" — Victimizing child survivors of sexual exploitation

By Rakesh Luthra

Kandahar, Afghanistan (Compass News) — "The more powerful you are, the more beautiful your boys," declares a merchant on the condition of anonymity as he describes the practice of *bacha bazi*. "I enjoy the boys' company. I like to listen to the music and watch them dance," he admits openly.

When asked if he has sex with them, he replies, "If they want, I don't have the strength to deny them." Confronted with the fact that some of these boys turn to this practice out of economic desperation, he snickers and adds: "Money can be very convincing."

This is a taboo subject, making it difficult to research. A study by the Afghanistan Independent Human Rights Commission found, however, that cases of *bacha bazi* occur in virtually every province of the country. For powerful men such as police officers, warlords, and prominent businessmen, it's a sign of status to keep a *bacha birish,* or more.

"This is child exploitation. This is human trafficking. But whom can you turn to if the police are complicit?" asks the spokesperson of the Commission, Gulbahar Mirdadzai. "In some cases, the abusers are police officers themselves."

Ten years ago, Compass News began this ongoing series by reporting a case in which the victim attempted to report his abuse to the authorities in Kabul. Police officers sexually assaulted fifteen-year-old Jabbar, who died in peculiar circumstances. At least one of his friends believed he committed suicide.

The presence of children in police bases have been a subject of intense international controversy. Many fear that these children may be taking part in armed conflict.

The Police Chief of Kandahar Province, Farid Nazari states, "If there are any young boys on the bases—which I doubt—they only play support roles, such as cooking and driving, making tea." The latter category of the so-called chai boys also includes boys who are subjected to sexual exploitation in police bases. They are kept away from their families, all the while at heightened risk of armed attacks due to their location.

The Deputy Police Chief, Anwar Ramazani, expresses some sympathy, but for the perpetrators. "My men risk their lives every day. They work hard for a meager salary. You have to allow them a little room to blow off steam. They deserve a little release." He alludes to sexual exploitation of children and goes on to say, "Some of them have been chai boys themselves. Now it's their turn. If anything, they're collecting a debt," he casually refers to the teenagers' bodies as commodities.

The Penal Code of 1976 bans sex acts between males, which is considered aggravated if the victim is under eighteen. Likewise, the Law on Combatting Abduction and Human Trafficking of 2008 provides for heavier penalties if the victim is under eighteen. But these laws are generally not enforced. Chief Nazari cannot recall a single case in which a client was prosecuted for sexually abusing a young boy.

An official of the Ministry of the Interior speaks of prosecution, but again, of the wrong party. "These child prostitutes must be prosecuted to the fullest extent of the law. They are no angels," he asserts, ignoring that victims of crimes cannot be prosecuted for having committed the same crimes. According to international law, no one should be prosecuted for the crimes they committed as a direct result of being trafficked. But like local laws, international conventions mean little in everyday life in Afghanistan.

Rekindled

/ˌriːˈkɪndl/ *verb*

Ty had posted a new picture on his website. He was wearing a scarf and smiling in front of a piece of graffiti art, similar to those by Chris Brown. I didn't know how long I stared at his picture and daydreamed about him smiling at me. He would put his scarf around my neck to pull me closer, his lips would feel soft on mine. I had previously listened to the recordings of him reciting his poems. His voice had a grave and melancholic quality, sounding different from the flirtatious things he'd said to me. I tried my best to remember his voice from November. One particular sentence still echoed in my head. "A boyfriend that hits you is just a boy. He's not a friend."

I picked up my bag to retrieve my only physical reminder of him. As I pulled out his note of the domestic violence helpline, my hand touched a clump of papier-mâché, that smelled like fungus. I tried to unfold the paper, but it disintegrated to smaller lumps. *No, no, no! This is the only thing that he gave me, and it got destroyed when I sat under the rain. What if I never see him again? The only thing that reminded me of him is now gone.*

I tried to stop my brain from running into a state of despair. I wasn't going to cry. Not anymore. Maybe I could find that number on my own. So, I researched it. The first Google hit showed pictures of white women under banners, "Our stories" and "Donate." So did the second hit. I added "gay" to my search. This time, I got an organization in Massachusetts and another one in Britain. None of these was the one Ty had found me.

A text message from Derrick showed up. I hesitated for a second, then swiped it away.

How do you seek help if you're experiencing anger from a loved one? A thought flashed in my head. I picked up my bag and left the apartment. Twenty minutes later, I was in front of the store called Open Books.

"How are you doing?" said the woman behind the counter. "Can I help you find something?"

"No, thanks. Just browsing for now."

Scanning quickly through the signs, I found the self-help section. After going through titles on finances, leadership, spirituality, body language, and a stray German dictionary, I identified three books: *Men who beat woman: a psychological analysis, Narratives of Domestic Violence Survivors: an anthology of twelve women's triumphs,* and *Recovering from Abuse: How to stand by your man and move on.* My fingers rested on the last one. I already owed Cliff for having cheated on him. Perhaps I could pay him back by rebuilding my loyalty. *Isn't faithfulness one of the most important aspects of a relationship? To stand together through thick and thin?* If the gay community wanted to be allowed to legally marry, shouldn't we also live by its most basic principle?

"Abdul?" Someone called my name.

My hand shook and pulled out the book. I caught it in the air.

"Abdul! It *is* you," said the warm voice with Indian accent.

I couldn't believe my eyes, but I immediately felt a rush of warmth in my body when I recognized his chubby cheeks. He had the same long eyelashes that I'd seen in the streets of Kabul back in the day. I turned the book so he wouldn't see the cover.

"Rakesh. Oh my God." I bent down to touch his feet, the way I had seen in Bollywood movies.

He was wearing brown shoes with orange laces. But he pulled me up by the arms and embraced me tight. "What a fortunate coincidence." He looked as kind as always. "I'd recognize that face anywhere in the world. You've grown up to be such an amazing... strong young man."

"You look exactly like ten years ago."

"Oh, you should see my gray hair. I'm an old man now," he exaggerated.

"Rakesh... I don't even know what to say. So happy to see you." I shook my head, still not believing this, while feeling guilty for not having reached out.

"Me too, *yaar*. Me too." He hugged me again.

I closed my eyes to savor his squeeze.

"Sorry, were you looking for something?"

I shoved the book into the empty space on the shelf, spine to the back. "Not really. I was looking for this book about... living in the moment. But they don't seem to have it."

"Niloofar is not going to believe this. She'll be ecstatic to see you, Abdul. Let me quickly pay for these."

I noticed three books in his hands. "My treat," I offered.

"No. You're too generous, but thank you."

"Please. You've done so much for me and I never got a chance to really say thank you."

"Your wellbeing is the best gift I can get. No thanks necessary."

He put his hand on my shoulder. We joined the line.

"Is Niloofar here?"

"She's in DC. I'm here for the day. Took a day off."

"Are you still with Compass News?"

"Yes. Still going on missions here and there. I was in Paris after the Charlie Hebdo attack."

"Oh my God. Did you know anyone who...?"

He shook his head. "I'm so sorry we fell out of touch. We were both out of the country when you turned eighteen and by the time we returned..."

I was already gone. I hated the foster family. "I'm sorry too. With all the social media these days, there's no excuse."

We finally reached the counter where the woman processed the payment. We then went to the coffee shop next door. He allowed me to pay for his coffee.

"How is Niloofar doing?" I asked as we sat down.

"She's great. I insisted that she come with me to Baltimore. But she had some important meeting of some sort. I'm sure she's going to regret her decision now."

"Is she still at that NGO? Jawana, was it?"

"Sort of. She's now an outreach consultant for them."

"Do you guys have kids?"

"We're not married yet."

"I'm sorry. I just assumed..."

"No children. But soon, God willing. Our wedding is in February. Enough about us. Tell me about you. What do you do now? Work? School?"

The coffee tasted bland and watery, comparing to the Arabic coffee I was used to. "I'm studying for the SAT."

"Scholastic Aptitude Test, impressive."

I felt stupid that I had never looked up SAT to see what it stood for. "Meanwhile, working at the front desk at a small hotel." I didn't want to admit that I was unemployed.

"You always wanted to go to university. I remember that very well." He took a bite of his cheese Danish. "Are you seeing anyone?"

"Yeah. We've been together since 2011, actually."

"That's perfect. Can't wait to meet the lucky guy."

"Definitely," I chuckled. But I had to steer the conversation away from Cliff and our… situation. "I owe you guys my whole life. I'd be a… I don't know, a drug addict or a prostitute somewhere, possibly dead by now." The words sounded crass, but I wanted him to know how much I appreciated him and Niloofar.

"Stop it. I think you would be working on your education no matter what. Your determination was always solid. Destiny just put me and Niloofar on your path to give a helping hand." He smiled and took a sip of his coffee. "You're young. You'll have a lot of great achievements in your future."

"Still, I could never thank you enough."

"Just pay it forward. At some point, you're going to find yourself in a situation where someone else will need *your* help. That's how life goes." He stared into the space for a second and then exclaimed, "You know what? You should come to our wedding."

"What?"

"And bring your boyfriend." He paused, considering something, "I'll do my best to get you a proper invitation. We might be out. But please, this is an official invitation right here." He tapped on his heart.

"Are you sure? I'm certain you guys have finalized the seating chart months ago."

"Who cares about a seating chart? If it weren't for you, Niloofar and I might not have even met. Initially, we started hanging out while brainstorming on how to get you out."

"You were always so nice to me."

"It's final then. It's on February Fourteenth in DC. Valentine's Day, easy to remember. It's only a short train ride away. I'll text you the details. I'm already seeing you as the guest of honor."

"You're too kind. It'd be my pleasure."

"And bring your guy. What is his name you said?"

"Cliff."

"You both will be our guests of honor."

That would be the best way forward for Cliff and me. Showing up together to the wedding of my old friends. *I will have a chance to show him off.* The thought made me grin.

Parachutes

/ˈpærəʃuːt/ noun, verb

I hadn't had real friends for so long, I'd forgotten how amazing they feel. Trilce always radiated an unfamiliar sense of positivity, as if she had just swallowed a bowl of sunshine. Shane made me laugh. And now, finding Rakesh after such a long time warmed up my bones. If I somehow ended up in another pit and couldn't scramble my way out of it, I had friends who'd be looking out for me, willing to throw me a rope. From the first moment I saw him at the age of fourteen, Rakesh had been kind to me. We met in Kabul, in the summer of 2004.

Back then, my body betrayed me and protected me at the same time. My hair was dusty and coarse. When I touched it, I couldn't run my fingers through. It felt like steel wool, the cheap type that disintegrates as you scrubbed the burnt gravy off a frying pan. I could smell my own sweat from having worked all day.

That night, my stomach twisted as though I'd inhaled a snake. Stomachache accompanied me all the time. No matter how much I ate, it wouldn't go away. My wages of the day could earn me enough food for dinner. But I had to put money aside for the future.

The dust in the air hindered most of my sense of smell, so I could tolerate my own body odor. Dirt had covered my feet, my pants. If I looked bad, no man would find me attractive. So, he wouldn't hurt me. Looking bad benefited me and I wasn't planning on changing that. Working on a construction site exposed me to men all day. I feared people. The more men I encountered, the more my chances of getting hurt. But I also feared loneliness. If a man found me when I was all alone, no one would stop him from doing whatever he wanted to do to me. No one would care enough to look after a dirty fourteen-year-old, living on the street.

A breeze raised a fog of dust. People passed me by. No one bothered to see me. But no one bothered me either. I pulled my knees closer to my body and covered my head with my hands. Folding my body meant the snake in my stomach had less room to swirl. *Tomorrow, I'll work harder. I'll beg Karbalayi Sahib for a few more rupiahs. If I fed the snake, maybe it would calm down.*

Finding a job wasn't easy. But I tried my best. I shoved my fears deep inside my body and tried to expand my body as I walked, so I'd look strong enough to work in construction. Karbalayi Sahib had originally refused to hire me, calling me "scrawny." But after much pleading, he relented. He probably saw the desperation in my eyes. Still, he agreed to pay me a fraction of what he paid adult workers. "But don't sleep here," he warned. That was why I was sitting on the street, hearing a commotion.

Someone was speaking English. Somebody else replied in Persian. Soon a group of boys descended on them. One offering tissues, another trying to sell them chewing gum. Others just asking for a few rupiahs so they could buy some bread.

After some time, the boys realized that they weren't going to sell anything. I heard them move on to their next target. I could now try to relax and sleep a little. But then I heard heavier footsteps. Both men approached me. The foreigner squatted next to me and the other bent over.

The foreigner looked Indian, with dark skin and facial hair. "How are you?" he asked me.

"Fine, thanks." I only knew basic English, having newly arrived in Kabul.

The local man said. "Why are you sitting here on the street? You don't have a home?"

The Indian man said something I didn't understand. The other one translated. "He asks how come you didn't try to sell us something? A whole group of boys showed up."

I buried my face in my hand.

"You sit here a lot? You don't feel cold at night?" The Indian man wrapped his arms around his shoulder, gesturing the cold I should have been feeling.

"It's summer." I wanted them to leave me alone.

"Oh, you have thick skin. Very good." The local man tried to sound friendly.

The foreigner spoke again.

"He says, you should know a lot about what happens on the street. Are you here the whole day? Or just at night?"

They were probably looking for drugs. I didn't have any. Not because I knew better at the time, but because I didn't want to lose control under the influence and end up somewhere on my belly with my pants pulled down. Or would it be so bad if it earned me enough money to eat? I probably just hadn't been hungry enough. Maybe that was what these two men were looking for.

"My friend is a reporter. You know what that is? He writes for a newspaper."

I considered the two of them. Was *that* how reporters looked?

"We're trying to find a party. To write about. Do you know of parties with musicians and things?"

Why had they approached *me* of all the kids? I was just sitting there, not saying anything, not doing anything. But somehow, they could see it in me that I liked colorful clothes? That I liked music? I even liked Commander Aseel at first.

"I don't know of any parties. I don't dance."

"Not looking for dancers." The local man patted my shoulder as if to calm me down. "We know there are bad men who hurt dancing boys. We want to find them."

To do what? Take them to the police? They're part of the police. Or to take away the boys? And put them in prison?

The Indian man interrupted my thoughts as he showed me his card, written in English. It had his picture.

"Rakesh," he pointed to himself.

"His name is Rakesh." The local man felt the need to explain. "My name is Daoud. See, he's Indian. They don't do bad things in parties."

"Leave me alone. I don't know anything."

The translator spoke to Rakesh and stood up. "If you remember anything, find us. We come here to eat."

"Hunger?" Rakesh questioned in accented Persian.

"Are you hungry?" Daoud corrected him.

I looked at him, and then at Rakesh. He signaled to me to follow them and pointed to a small tea house on the corner.

"We're going to get something to eat. Right there." The translator stated.

Rakesh waved at me again. I didn't want to refuse food. If they wanted to kidnap me, I could run away. Or yell and attract attention.

"Come, eat. We don't want anything in return." The local man clarified.

I didn't move. They looked at each other and walked away. I slowly stood up and walked behind them.

At the tea house, I sat at a table close to them, but far enough to be able to escape if they jumped me. The smell of fresh kabob pranced around the place. The server boy brought them glasses of water and a small plate of bread and herbs. Rakesh passed me a piece of bread and some herbs. Then a glass of water. The server scowled at me. I would have to sleep farther away from here. I scarfed down the food and immediately realized that neither man had even touched their appetizer yet. Rakesh looked at me and gave me his own piece of bread too. Daoud did the same. I should have felt ashamed, but hunger didn't let me. I couldn't wait for the kabob to arrive. Would the boy bring more bread?

After I finished everything, Rakesh asked me if I wanted any more. I just looked at my dirty feet. Even though they had already fed me, they didn't ask for anything in return.

I went back to the tea house the next night to find them. They didn't show up. Then the following night and the one after that. I'd almost given up hope, when, on the fourth night, they appeared again. They bought me food and tea. Rakesh was kind. And this time the translator was less curt, perhaps to appease Rakesh.

I didn't know what it was in me that awakened so much compassion in him. Maybe as a foreigner, he couldn't guess that I'd brought shame and misery to my family. I didn't deserve his kindness. But his benevolence never faded.

To thank him, I found out some information that could be of use for him. He rescued me in return.

Respite
/ˈrespɪt/ *noun*

I knelt in front of one of the orchids with purple and brown petals. "These flowers look like the face of a monkey. Isn't that amazing?"

Cliff was standing next to me.

I touched his calf to attract his attention. "You see?"

"You get excited by the weirdest things."

"I love orchids. They're so magical." I got up and followed him through a door into what seemed like the tropical exhibit. I held on to his arm as we walked. *You see this guy who looks like a model? He's my boyfriend.* I wanted to enjoy every moment. Then I got distracted again.

"You see the birds of paradise? So strong and healthy."

Cliff put his hand around my waist. He looked at the flowers with feigned interest. "I mean, I'd be concerned if they *couldn't* keep their plants happy here. That's their job."

"It's still impressive." I pressed my body into his to acknowledge his attempt at looking interested. But also, I wanted to make it clear to the guy with glasses that just walked in, that we were together.

"Well, I'm happy you're enjoying this."

We hadn't gone out on a date in a while. He hadn't taken me to New York, but he said he would make it up to me. So here we were. Two of the very few people at the Botanical Gardens in DC, on a miserably cold Saturday. Hence the need to show off my boyfriend to whomever was around.

"I could sit here the whole day. Read a book or just—"

"I haven't seen you with your favorite SAT book lately. Did I miss your test or something?"

"No." *You told me you don't want to see it.* I walked to the next big plant. A banana tree, or maybe coconut.

"I've been so busy with the app release and everything. Been neglecting you a bit."

"It's OK. I—"

"When is your test?"

The question surprised me. "What?"

"The SAT test, stupid." He playfully shoved me to the side.

I was addicted to his strength and assertiveness. "I'm not taking the test. What's the point?"

"You think you're not gonna pass?"

"I know I won't." I tried not to say the obvious. "I never even checked out the—"

"Not with that attitude."

I walked on. "It's fine."

"I thought it was your dream to go to college."

"My dream is you," I switched topics.

The guy with the glasses showed up behind Cliff. He looked at us and smiled. "You guys are so cute."

Cliff thanked the guy and paused for him to walk by. Then he told me, "But I wanna help you achieve your smaller, less important dreams too." He winked.

"How can I afford college?"

"You don't have to go to Georgetown. I thought you had some savings. Did you spend it all?"

"I thought you were gonna..." I didn't know how to tactfully say it.

"I was gonna do what?"

"Like… use it for our expenses?" I lowered my voice.

"Why would I do that? The app has been quite successful. You act stupid sometimes."

He himself had told me that. Had I imagined it? Or did he just threaten it when he was angry? And now that he was in a good mood, the threat was gone. "I'll find another job. I already applied to a bunch of places." I wanted to remind him I wasn't a lazy bum.

He playfully pulled my head back and grabbed my waist, like he was about to kiss me. "What if I want you to go to college? If we wanna become trail blazing gay royalties, you're going to need some education. I can help you with the tuition and everything. We can be some high-society power couple."

"That sounds wonderful."

"So you'll resume studying?"

I nodded. "I'll do anything you want me to."

He kissed me a few times on the lips, like he was hungry for me. "That's what I like to hear."

I took his hand in mine and walked on. "Sometimes you're so sweet, I wanna pinch myself to make sure I'm awake."

"Oh there's a lot more than just pinching I wanna do to you," he ruffled my hair.

"You're terrible!" I teased.

"That's right." He leaned in and said softly, "The pervy guy with glasses is still hovering around. I think he wants us."

"I'm not sharing you."

"Well, then I suggest we get out of here."

I led the way out of the Gardens. I had to resume preparing for the SAT. The air outside smelled of some wild herbs.

We had dinner at an Indian restaurant called Le Mirch, and then visited the Kramers bookstore, since the gay one had gone out of business. Later, we ended up in the Ziegfeld nightclub to watch a drag show. After hanging out with Shane, I had developed a new appreciation for the art.

As it turned out, Ella Fitzgerald, the hostess, had been a DC icon since the 1970s. She took the microphone and asked random audience members embarrassing questions. I hadn't laughed so much in a while. It was a perfect club where I could watch the show and enjoy it without having to dance. Billie Ross, the most beautiful performer, danced to a Whitney Houston song. The crowd adored her. Finally, Kristina Kelly performed a slow song, a glittery hibiscus in her hair. The makeup was too much and absolutely perfect.

When the show was over, most people went upstairs. I asked Cliff whether we should follow.

"You may not like it there."

"Why? What's happening?"

"At first, I wanted it to be a surprise. But now that I think about it, I'm afraid it might be triggering for you."

I remained silent, waiting for him to go on.

"There are nude dancers up there. The patrons here love that. They put dollar bills in the dancers' socks. But I don't want it to remind you of… We don't have to go."

I had never seen such a thing. Would it be fun to witness?

Cliff noticed I was considering it. He added, "They're all adults who choose to do this. They all probably have day jobs. It's the only club with nude dancers that I know of. Even New York doesn't have them. But if it makes you feel uncomfortable, we stay down here. Or we leave. Whatever you want."

I didn't want the memory of Commander Aseel's evil habits to prevent me from enjoying a night out with my boyfriend. "Let's go up," I decided.

We went up to the second floor. I noticed the huge dancefloor, the disco ball, and the TV screens showing video clips. And then my jaw dropped. There were several dancers on various stages, dancing in the nude, with full hard-ons. They seem to be having a good time, talking to the spectators and dancing with them. If I'd learned anything from Shane, it was that some people liked to perform. I didn't want my past to stop me from enjoying the present.

"You ok?" Cliff asked. "I'll get you a drink to loosen up a bit."

It might have been the alcohol. But the dancers were magnificent. When my cup was empty, I finally gained the courage to approach my favorite dancer's sock. He put his calf on my shoulder and shook his goods above my head. I patted his calf and gave him the dollar. He blew me a kiss. Then Cliff's hands wrapped around my belly. He licked my ear and said, "You're doing so good."

My boyfriend brought me more drinks and more dollar bills. I felt as if I had died and had gone to paradise. "It's just an illusion," Ella reminded the crowd when we were leaving.

Back in the hotel room, Cliff laid me on the bed and took my clothes off. He pulled the petals off a red rose, one by one, and scattered them on my body. It was almost like having an out of body experience. He said he could tell I was enjoying it, because I curled my toes.

The next day, as he drove us back to Baltimore, I kept my hand on his thigh the entire time. Once we got to the apartment, he threw himself on the bed.

"I'm stinky but too tired to take a shower."

I lay next to him. "I love the scent of you."

"You're nasty," he teased and pulled me to himself.

"Cliff, remember I told you about Rakesh?"

"Ra-who?"

"The Indian journalist who saved me."

"Oh, yeah."

"He's getting married. To the same woman who helped me with my paperwork. They invited us to go to their wedding as guests of honor."

"I didn't realize you were that close. You don't even talk about them much."

"I know. But I was the reason they met in the first place."

"Really?"

"The wedding's on February Fourteenth."

"Is that how you wanna spend Valentine's Day? Instead of us doing bad things?" He lifted my body and fake-spanked me.

"We could do bad things in the hotel after the wedding. Like last night!"

He chuckled. "They're getting married in the middle of the winter? They want their love story to be dead from the start?"

Their major Hindu celebration was going to be in the summer in India. If I could go to that, I'd wear a shiny blue sherwani. I would wrap the red and gold turban around my head.

Cliff pulled his hand from under me, dragging me out of my daydream.

"Can we please go? Please." I pulled on his hand.

"OK, fine. We can't get married but we can be guests of honor in straight people's weddings. Where is it?"

"In DC."

"Hold on. You knew you wanted to go back to DC again in a couple of weeks?"

I should have planned it better.

He shook his head. "OK, if it's that important to my baby, we'll go."

He just called me baby. That's what Ty called me. Urgh, I'm such an idiot for thinking of Ty right now. I'm never gonna look at another man again.

"How did you meet this guy again?"

"He wanted to write a report and needed help in finding sources."

After paying for my dinner a few times, he asked for my help. He needed to establish trust with teenagers who were suffering sexual abuse. I didn't immediately tell him my own story, but I said I'd find some leads.

"You could find sources because you were familiar with the culture," Cliff gathered.

"In the market, I once saw this guy looking at ankle bells. I approached him and said, 'I love how they sound when you dance.' I asked him if he knew anyone who wanted someone like me."

Cliff was staring at me. He didn't interrupt or check his phone. He just waited.

"He told me his name is Shayan. He said his boss just recently got a new boy and probably didn't want anybody else for a while. I said I needed the money. He said the money was good. I asked if it hurt at night after the party was over. He said when he used opium or hashish, it didn't hurt too much. 'You shouldn't resist,' he told me. I remembered his exact words to this day." I patted Cliff's arm, wondering if I should continue.

"What happened?"

"Rakesh located the new boy that Shayan's boss had just recruited. But it turned out the boy, Jabbar, had been kidnapped. He was anxious to get out. Rakesh found an intermediary who went to some party and offered a lot of money for Jabbar for the night. He wanted to help him escape. The boy was infuriated about what he had suffered through. Despite Rakesh's warning, he went to the police to report his abuser. The police officers violated him and then threatened to charge him with sodomy if he told anyone. Things got dangerous."

"Then what?"

I saw Jabbar one last time. He was desperate. His hands were shaking as he smoked and said he couldn't live like this. He had nowhere to go. His family wouldn't take him back.

"The police and the criminals were working together. Jabbar committed suicide. He died in a car accident. He was only fifteen."

"Jeez, are you serious?"

"I ran into Shayan soon after. He said his boss wanted to take me on now. I said I'd changed my mind. But that didn't matter. Rakesh said I was in danger. He went to an NGO to find me a place to live, and hide. That's where he met Niloofar. His fiancée."

"That is really awful. I'm sorry. What happened to you after…" he caught himself before asking more questions. "Do you wanna talk about it?" Cliff caressed my face with the back of his hand.

I shook my head.

"OK." He hugged me tight. "You're safe now."

I took his hand. "It's because of you. I started to lose my fear of people only after… moving in with you."

"No one can hurt you now. I'm here." He squeezed my hand.

I could hear his heartbeat. I loved him so much.

Admonish
/ədˈmɑːnɪʃ/ verb

At the bar, I could easily become invisible. Everyone was used to the shy type, standing alone, not talking to anyone. I sipped my lemonade vodka and glanced at the pink hippo logo, laying down and smiling, one hand underneath its head. Still waiting for her own drink, Trilce leaned against the bar and watched the crowd as it grew larger. One of the drag queens stepped toward us. She was wearing a tiara and a silver dress that looked like a hundred seashells. The bartender handed her a green drink. She saw me staring and winked as she took a sip and walked away.

"She winked at me," I was surprised she even noticed me.

"Alondra?" Trilce asked. "Yeah, she's nice."

"You come here a lot?"

"Yeah. Here I don't have to shoo off every man in the vicinity. I heard this is the largest dance floor in the whole state. If only the bartender would *see* me," she raised her voice in another attempt to get his attention.

"Is Shane gonna perform tonight too?"

Ben showed up and put his empty glass on the bar. Wearing a sports jacket and button-down shirt, he stood out from the crowd of tees and see-through shirts.

"Would you like another drink?" he asked me.

"Thanks." I shook my head. "I can't believe they forced you to come to a gay club."

Ben didn't reply. He noticed Trilce standing next to me. "And what is the lady having?"

"The lady," Trilce sounded as if she was ready to bite his face off. But then she turned around, looked Ben up and down and finished her sentence, "Would have whatever you're having," her voice turning flirty.

"Gin and tonic it is," he smiled. "I'm Ben."

"Trilce."

His smile widened as he showed his index finger to the bartender. He took Ben's order immediately.

"He saw *you*," Trilce remarked loud enough for the bartender to hear. "As if by a miracle," she emphasized.

"I guess some people are just blind to perfection," Ben replied.

We clinked our glasses together. In a crowd of gay men, somehow the only straight guy and girl managed to find each other. They even took a liking in one another. Before we had a chance to say anything, the saxophone loop began to shake the floor in a melody we all recognized: Problem.

"Oh my God, I love this song," she announced.

It was Ariana Grande.

"Would you like to dance?" Ben asked her.

"Yeah." She pulled my hand.

"I don't dance," I yanked my hand out of hers, then realized I'd overreacted.

She looked at her drink that was about to topple. "What, never?"

I shook my head.

She paused for a second, deliberating if she should ask. But she realized the song wasn't going to stop for a discussion. "OK, Ben. It's just you and me then. Make it count." She gave me the side eye.

Ben started dancing with more swagger than any of the gay patrons. Trilce had moves too.

Not far away, Cliff was dancing next to Mason and his newest boyfriend: some twink with short blond hair, who was wearing, of all things, sunglasses. Pretentious. Some guy was trying to dance with Cliff. His t-shirt said: "Parental Advisory: Explicit Content." No originality.

As the song switched to J. Lo, I found a sexier thing to look at: the video clip was playing on the screen behind the bartender, showcasing a bunch of gorgeous guys in speedos, competing for the singer's attention. Then I heard Mason's voice ordering drinks. In my peripheral vision, I saw the Explicit Content guy standing next to him as well. The one who was after Cliff. Turning slightly, I could faintly hear their conversation.

"…the hot guy you were dancing with?"

"The cute boy in sunglasses? He's mine. You can take your paws off him," Mason answered.

"No, not your boy. The muscle guy in white."

Cliff was wearing a sleeveless white shirt with the collar unfolded.

The music got louder. I heard Mason say, "Boyfriend."

"Who?"

I assumed Mason pointed at me.

The guy replied, "The Chinese boy? What does he see in *him*?"

They got their drinks. I looked away to pretend I wasn't paying attention. Mason probably made a gesture. The Explicit Content guy whistled. I looked back unintentionally to see what they were talking about. They were both staring at my butt.

"The hot guy got a temper though. I wouldn't be too pushy if I were you," Mason played it cool as he walked away.

"He could beat me up any time he wants," replied Explicit Content, without any consideration that I could hear him. Alcohol made him lose his sense of shame, if he had any.

I ordered another lemonade vodka and busied myself watching the screen. But soon, the stage lights came on and the drag show began. Alondra, who had winked at me earlier, lip-synced and danced to a Shakira song in Spanish. Then another performer in a tan bodysuit performed to Chandelier.

Cliff came and ordered a brandy on the rocks, got me another drink, and two more for Mason and his date. Just as he was about to walk back to the dance floor, Mason showed up behind me.

"Abdul?" So, he knew my name wasn't *Yo, bitch*. "Come over to the dance floor. Let's have a good time."

"I *am* having a good time." *Without you,* I wanted to add.

"All these thirsty boys are trying to hit on your man."

"I know. I trust him," I squeezed Cliff's bicep. *And he trusts me... mistakenly*. I realized alcohol had begun to take effect.

"Come, dance with us. Don't you be such a party pooper. You haven't even talked to Chase yet," Mason insisted.

I didn't move. *Why can't he get lost?*

"I know we've had a rough time recently. Let's have a ceasefire. If we can't make peace in a gay club—"

"I don't dance," I cut him off.

Cliff put his hand on my shoulder, trying to calm me down. "He doesn't. He's not kidding."

"Why not?" Mason was probably drunk. "It's not that hard. Your mama gave you a great ass. Shake it a little."

"Mine is greater," Chase decided this was the time to announce his existence.

"Please go," I tried to control my nerves.

"We're gonna have to tolerate each other. Do it for Cliff."

"Stop it, Mason. He doesn't really dance," Cliff batted him off. "If anyone should ask him to dance, it's me. Not you."

"Not you and your monogamy speech again. We're gay. We don't have to…" Mason gave up on convincing Cliff. "Come on," he addressed me.

"Let him be," my boyfriend took my side.

Mason pulled my shirt. My glass only contained mostly ice and syrup at the bottom. I raised my hand and before I knew it, I'd thrown the rest of my drink on his face.

"Oh nooo," Chase dramatized.

A crowd began forming around me. The music stopped and the next drag queen started yelling "excuse me" in her microphone.

"He threw his drink at him," a spectator announced.

I should have apologized. But I was too shocked at my own action.

"*He* did it. *He* started it," a bystander told the bouncer who appeared out of nowhere, pointing repeatedly at me.

"Out," the bouncer had lost the seductive tone with which he had greeted me earlier. He took my arm.

"I can walk." I saw Trilce's face as I exited the club.

A couple, smoking by the entrance, looked at me funny as the bouncer accompanied me out to the street. I began to walk down West Eager Street, away from the club.

What got into me? For once, Mason wanted to turn down his malefic nature. Now, he'd despise me even more. And if getting kicked out of the club wasn't bad enough, I'd have Cliff to deal with. He might show up, all sympathetic that my fun night had taken a turn. Or he could turn into a monster and explode that I disrespected his friend, and hence, him. I never knew what to expect from him. I could already hear him getting close.

"I don't know why everyone always says that *I* have a temper. You're obviously much worse," Cliff caught up with me. He was now wearing his jacket and handed me mine.

I felt too hot to need it. "Why is he harassing me to dance? I told him—"

"Shhh. It's OK." Cliff interrupted.

"It was *his* fault," I said. "But they threw *me* out of the club. I was minding my own damn business. They should've thrown—"

"Don't worry about it. I was ready to go anyway."

"Aren't you gonna slap me for being disrespectful?" I mocked. Anger bubbled in me like water that was about to boil. I could happily engage in a fight right there on the street.

"I'm here," my boyfriend hugged me. "Let's just go home. I'm cold. You sure you don't wanna wear your jacket?"

"Why are you so nice to me?"

"I'm supposed to be, stupid." He ruffled my hair. "That's my job."

Prospect
/ˈprɑːspekt/ *noun, verb*

T rilce had given me the information. I walked into the
Hilton, ready to explain to the receptionist that I was
there for the job fair. But no one asked. With a quick
glance, I identified where the crowd was heading and noticed
huge signs on tripods with arrows pointing to the conference
hall. Tables lined up along the walls and in several rows. Some
tables had obnoxiously large banners. Like the US Army,
black on yellow. Next to them, Amnesty International with
the same color pattern but a very different mission. A smaller
sign said: "Volunteer opportunities."

A long time ago, I had shared with Cliff my hope to
someday work for an organization that helped people, like
Human Rights Watch. He pointed out I wouldn't want
to work in a sector that required unpaid internships, and
subsequent low salaries. He was right. If I was ever going to
save enough for college, I couldn't afford to volunteer. He
promised to put me through school, then denied it, then
reasserted it again. I couldn't put my faith in someone who
could change his mind so often. Or detonate for any reason.
Or no reason at all. Who could have faith in such a prospect?

I had to stand on my own. My own money, my own college, my own choice. I could take advice, but not direction. This job I was hoping to get would help me have an emergency fund. Just in case.

A white guy with stylishly disheveled hair that flowed onto his forehead attracted my attention. His velvet burgundy blazer looked like mine. *I should have worn the same blazer.* Maybe my checkered pink shirt looked distinct enough for him to recognize its brand. I stopped by the H&M sign where he was standing.

"Good morning," I greeted him.

"How are you doing?"

"Good." I hated when people replied "well." It sounded pretentious. "How are you?"

"Are we interested in applying to work here?"

I loved how he sounded like he was going to aid me in the process. "Yes. I always admired the garments." It sounded unnatural to use that term for "clothes," but he didn't seem to mind.

"Yeah? Any particular label?"

I thought H&M was the label. "I love the dressy style. It's chic but accessible for everyday use." I borrowed from Cliff's remarks about clothes.

"Black label! Modern classic," he concluded.

At the risk of looking stupid, I smiled.

"Nice shirt you're wearing."

He did recognize the brand. I still had nothing to say. My eyes lowered to avoid staring at him for too long. I saw his black shirt with the first button undone, showing a bit of his chest, but not too much.

"Phillip. I'm one of the managers," he extended his hand.

"Abdul."

"What's your availability, Abdul?"

"I can start any time."

"For a sales associate, we require 24/7 availability. Not that you need to work overnight, well not typically. But you might be needed for any shift between six a.m. to nine p.m. Is that something you would consider?"

Consider? I would work any time as long as they hired me. "Yes, sir."

"You make me feel old," he grinned. "You're not from the south, are you?"

I shook my head.

"I thought so." He'd noticed my accent. "Please don't call me 'sir.'"

"OK."

He knew he had the power in this interaction. But he still treated me with respect. In my head, I begged him to give me a chance.

"Here's what we're gonna do," he instructed. "Apply online. We only accept electronic applications. There's a questionnaire that will take about thirty to forty minutes. Take your time. Don't panic, and be consistent. You can say the sky is green as long as you say so every time the questionnaire asks about it. Which store are you interested in?"

"The one by the Inner Harbor. It's a short commute from where we live. But I can go to another store as well," I tried to leave the options open.

"The one on Light Street. That's my store."

"Perfect," I did my best to sound enthusiastic and professional.

"Be there at 9:30 Monday morning. The store opens at 10, so you'll have to knock on the side door."

"OK."

"Don't forget to bring your Social Security card. And your application number. Take a screenshot or something."

"Sure."

He paused for a moment, noticing an African American guy who was standing in front of the table. He was wearing tight jeans, a low V-neck, and a bulky colorful necklace with an ancient Egyptian look. His stubble was perfectly trimmed, making the women's necklace look masculine. Next to his sense of fashion, I probably looked like a butler.

"Thanks for stopping by, Abdul," Phillip said.

"Thank you. Thanks so much."

Phillip had already started a conversation with the other applicant.

As I walked away, I turned and saw him glance at me. I smiled, exiting the conference hall. I wanted him to see that I didn't stop by any other table. I visibly had put all of my proverbial eggs into this one basket.

"I think I got a job," I texted Trilce.

She sent me confetti emojis. "Where?"

"H&M."

Thumps up emoji.

"I have to apply online."

Three dots appeared on my screen. After a pause, the text finally came through. "You haven't applied yet? How do you know you already got the job?"

"The manager told me to go to the store on Monday."

Another thumps up emoji. "Where else did you apply?"

Should I have applied to more places? Nah. He's hiring me. I could sense it. My H&M shirt sealed the deal. I smiled as I typed, "He's nice."

I feared she was about to text "don't sleep with him." But in the end, she didn't reply. Everything worked out. Now, my salary would be deposited into my own account. When I saw Rakesh and Niloofar, I wouldn't have to lie or say that I was unemployed. They'd be happy for me. They'd see that all the troubles were worth it.

Niloofar was fierce and tender at the same time. When she heard a condensed version of my story, she did everything to make sure I was safe.

When I realized Shayan's boss wanted to recruit me to dance, I had to hide. In 2004, Kabul didn't have any shelters I could go to. Rakesh found the NGO where Niloofar worked. He helped me get a job, working part-time as a kitchen help at a restaurant near the UN green zone. Niloofar fought with him and complained about child labor. But Rakesh convinced her it was the least bad option. The more Rakesh researched his upcoming article, the more he worried about me. Boys like me risked their lives if they escaped or tried to. When his report was published, it caused an international uproar. Niloofar was worried that I could be linked to the story. She asked me if I wanted to come to the US. She and Rakesh had started dating by then, as much as people can really date in Kabul.

Niloofar found a conference on human trafficking in Washington DC. She reached out to the organizers and got me invited as a witness. Soon, I became familiar with the term "unaccompanied minor," which meant all processes were much more complicated, and took three times longer than usual. As a sixteen-year-old without parents or any documentation, I couldn't apply for a passport. I didn't know all the details, but I guessed Rakesh paid a bribe to get me a *tazkira*. My well-being didn't concern the bureaucrats. Only Rakesh and Niloofar cared about me. To this day, I didn't know how they managed to make it work. They gave me a ticket to New York, with a stop in London.

The Kabul airport didn't give me too much hassle. People in Afghanistan grow up quickly, so it wasn't strange for them to see me travel on my own. In London, however, I was stopped. The officer looked Indian, so I thought he'd be nice to me, like Rakesh. But he spoke with that weird English accent and took me out of the line and into another room. They searched me, took my passport, scanned my luggage. They asked me questions, then brought more officers to ask me more questions. I had two problems: Afghanistan passport, unaccompanied minor. The officers repeated these terms over and over. I faced these same obstacles at JFK, except the American officers didn't even feel bad for harassing me so much.

At the conference, I delivered the key witness testimony. Speaking about such a personal thing in front of hundreds of people freaked me out. I had no recollection of what I'd said. I nervously read out loud the statement written in very simple English.

What stood out to me was that everyone talked about "survivors." They thought it was more empowering than the word "victim." For me, the two terms had two different meanings. I had survived. I was one of the lucky ones. Not everyone did. Jabbar didn't. Relative to others, I hadn't even endured anything to have survived it. But I didn't object to their terminology. It wasn't my place.

The day after the conference, Niloofar got me a lawyer to apply for asylum. My speech at the conference became "supporting evidence," another term I quickly learned.

My phone vibrated. "Time to celebrate then," Trilce finally texted back.

I inhaled cool air, my chest expanding under my pink checkered shirt that had gotten me the job. Such a perfect morning.

This weekend, I'd attend Rakesh and Niloofar's wedding, and show them that their efforts had changed my life. That I was worth the effort. Although, Jabbar deserved it more, had he survived.

I clicked on my Instagram. Ty had posted a new picture with a tiny cup. "Love me some Arabic coffee." *I introduced him to that*. The tiniest contribution to his life I could make, but better than nothing. I wished I could talk to him.

I shook my head to physically force the thought of him out of my mind. Infatuation was no friend to stability.

Petulance

/ˈpetʃələns/ *noun*

My favorite burgundy velvet blazer was part of my outfit for the wedding tomorrow. For Cliff, I had picked a neckerchief that would go with my bowtie. Our clothes would complement each other without being too coordinated.

I still couldn't believe Rakesh had made me the guest of honor, and so close to the wedding. I didn't know for sure if the wedding consisted of the reception only or also the religious ceremony of *aqd*. Regardless of it being performed in private or in front of all the guests, the cleric had to be progressive, considering that Niloofar was Muslim and Rakesh Hindu. Perhaps that explained them welcoming us, a gay couple, with open arms.

Around nine in the evening, my phone beeped. A text from Cliff said, "The App download numbers are off the chart. Going to celebrate."

I poured myself some leftover Chardonnay from the fridge and had it with some *bolani*. Music videos from The Student of The Year provided the soundtrack to my dinner. At ten, I skimmed through random pages of my favorite book *Image of Emeralds and Chocolate*. By eleven, I started to worry. The wedding was at five. We had to be there at four. If we left by noon, we should be OK. That would leave us enough time for traffic and whatnot. The parking was limited so I didn't want to arrive later than two. Even if Cliff was drunk now, he should be fine by noon tomorrow.

By midnight, anger started to sink in. *Of all the nights Cliff could get drunk with his buddies, he chose tonight. He knows how much this means to me.* Rakesh had literally saved me from living on the street and Niloofar had risked her career for bringing me to the US. Being in their wedding was the least I could do to thank them.

After the episode at the club last weekend, I could understand he wanted to party without me. But carousing until late when we had to travel the next day got on my nerves. If anyone hit on me again, I would cheat. Even if only to get revenge. These thoughts attacked me for several hours as I continued to change positions in the bed. At some point, I heard people behind the door. I checked my phone. It was almost three in the morning.

The keys jingled and dropped.

"Got it," someone said and opened the door. A few people came in.

I got out of bed and went to the closet to find my robe.

"What's her name again?" Mason was back to his usual self. "Yo bitch," he yelled out.

What an ass. Throwing a drink in his face wasn't enough. I should have punched him too.

I walked into the living room. Ben and Mason were holding Cliff from each side, almost dragging him to the bedroom.

"Hey man," Ben greeted me.

"Is he OK?" I asked.

"I already did the hard part when he was throwing up," the Malefic boy barked. "Since you never happen to be around when he needs you."

"I'm fine. I didn't even throw up that much," Cliff slurred his words as he spoke. His eyes were blood shot. He attempted to take a step but tripped over his own foot. Mason pulled his arm and brought him back to his feet. I put my arm around his shoulder as I helped the Kentucky guy bring him to the bed.

Cliff squeezed my ass, "Look at this rump. He got ass for days." He kissed me on the cheek. His breath smelled of sour vodka, mixed with stomach acid. "That's one of the reasons I love you, you know."

"Shhh, just come to the bed," I felt embarrassed.

"That's what *he* said," Cliff replied.

I didn't know if he was kidding or if the Malefic boy had been making advances at him again.

Cliff threw himself on the bed. Ben showed up into the bedroom. At least I wasn't there alone with Mason and a drunk boyfriend.

"I've never seen him so faded," I observed. "You didn't give him anything, right?" I glared at Mason, hoping this wasn't the aftermath of molly or something.

"Just alcohol poisoning," Ben replied. "Nothing some water and sleep won't fix."

"Thanks for bringing him home."

"Give him an aspirin," Malefic Mason ordered.

But I was happy for the tip. I had to take care of him to ensure he could drive in a few hours.

"You're able to handle it from here?" Ben asked.

I nodded.

"I already did the hard part. You should pay me for doing your job, bitch. Maybe with that ass of yours."

"Get off my boyfriend, you dickhead," Cliff shouted.

Nothing revolted me more than the idea of having sex with Mason. My boyfriend knew that well.

"Come on, man. You're kinda drunk yourself," Ben grabbed his shoulder.

I walked them out the door. After they were gone, I took an aspirin for Cliff. The sight of a drunk Cliff in bed softened my heart a bit.

"Come cuddle with me. My head feels like it's full of cement."

"You're gonna be fine. Here, have this." I handed him the pill and gave him a tall glass of water.

"You trying to choke me?" he complained.

I untied his shoelaces and took off his shoes. Then I unbuckled his belt and pulled off his jeans.

"You're so rough. Am I your enemy or something?" he whimpered.

I slowed my pace as I unbuttoned his shirt and took it off. I imagined his soft chest hair, showing under the neckerchief I had picked for tomorrow. Actually, for later today.

"I'm upset with you," I told him.

"I know."

"We can't be late for the wedding."

"I'll be fine after sleeping a little." He sounded like a child who's been scolded.

"Why, Cliff? Is it because of last Friday?"

"Didn't you have a friend, a dancing boy, who committed suicide?"

Why was he thinking of Jabbar right now?

"I'll protect you, baby. I'll do better. I'm such a dickhead. My anger is overwhelming sometimes. Can't help it."

He was drunk and incoherent. I sat on the bed next to him.

"No one else would stick around with me. This one guy I was dating back in the day…" He wiped his mouth, considering if he should continue. But intoxication got the best of him. "He called the cops on me. Can you imagine?"

I didn't know that. Police only created more problems. They never solved any problem.

"I'm sorry. I promise I'll never hit you again. You've been the perfect boyfriend."

I hadn't been.

He pressed his body onto my thighs. His abs were pronounced and beautiful. Why would I need another man to make me happy? Was I as ungrateful as Mason thought?

His grip softened. He'd fallen asleep. Even in sleep I didn't dare tell him the truth. But making no sounds at all, I mouthed my confession: "I've cheated on you, Cliff. I'm sorry."

The reek of sour alcohol was no longer present. Instead, the pheromones caressed my nostrils. His chest raised and lowered as he began to breathe deeper in sleep.

He looked innocent and vulnerable. I lay next to him and kissed his chest, apologizing in my head.

At nine in the morning, I woke him up to give him more water and aspirin.

"My perfect boyfriend," he said as he fell back asleep.

At eleven, I gave him some coffee and a honey and butter sandwich. After a few bites, he said it made him sick.

I helped him take a lukewarm bath. His eyes even redder now than last night. I started to panic that he wasn't going to come to the wedding. I didn't know how to drive.

"I feel like shit," he said as he wrapped the towel around himself at noon.

"You're gonna be fine. Do you want some more coffee?"

"Nah," he growled. "Stop giving me all this crap."

"We have to leave. Did you forget? You can lay down for a bit before dressing up. I've already picked your outfit and everything."

"Oh you did, didn't you?" He drew the curtains and turned off the light. He wanted more than a short nap.

I pulled the curtains back. "Come on. You know how much they mean to me."

"Yes, Abdul. But what do *I* mean to you? Your man is sick and all you can think about is a wedding party?"

"Cliff, please. It's just a hangover. You're not sick or anything."

"My head feels like you're hitting it with a claw hammer. My stomach is twisting and you say I'm fine. Why don't you go alone?"

"They invited us both. As a couple." *And the train is on a Saturday schedule.* "I want you there with me. They've done a lot for me and this is all I can do to thank them."

"*I've* done a lot for you. I would still do anything for you, Abdul. And if I was in a condition that I could go, I would absolutely do it. But I'm just too sick."

"Please?" I begged.

"You go. I'll sleep and get better by the time you come back."

I texted Trilce, asking if there was any way she could take me to DC. Maybe I should take a cab. How would it look if I showed up alone? The clock by the bed said it was 1:37. I wouldn't be able to make it.

Half an hour later, Trilce replied and said she couldn't do it. She was in another rally, asking the district attorney to charge the police officer who shot the teenager in Mosher. I wore my shirt and the purple bowtie. I knotted it again and again. It looked crooked. I needed Cliff's help. His outfit matched my bowtie. We should be going as a couple. The time was 2:21. I still had to style my hair, find a taxi, confront Saturday's traffic… There was no time. I'd arrive late, with a crooked bowtie. Alone.

If I couldn't be there for Niloofar and Rakesh, I could at least be here for my own boyfriend.

He had scrunched up the sheet underneath himself and folded his body fetus-style to keep warm. I took off the bowtie and threw it on the ground, pulled the sheet, and covered him. "I'll text Rakesh and say we can't make it," I whispered.

"Really?" He moaned. "You do love me, stupid."

"You want a cold cloth for your forehead."

"Yeah."

I went to the bathroom and rinsed a face rag under the cold water. I looked at the mirror. My hair in disarray but my shirt looked immaculate, shining. *Nothing should look this good when I feel so bad.* I wrung the towel and crawled onto the bed, letting the shirt get wrinkled like the sheet. "I'll take care of you until you feel better," I said begrudgingly.

He felt better by seven in the evening.

Exuberance
/ɪɡˈzuːbərəns/ *noun*

Trilce felt bad that she couldn't take me to the wedding. So, she came up with a plan to make up for it. Another one of her ideas to do something fun and unusual: cat yoga. The smell of rubber attacked me as I unrolled the yoga mat. I thought it was probably mixed with the odor of sweat and chemical disinfectants too. With the seven cats the animal shelter had brought for the class, perhaps even more unpleasant scents would soon descend on us. Of all the people in the studio, only the instructor, Ben, had his own mat. His was made of straw, reminding me of woven bamboo shades that some people placed outside their windows in Mashhad to prevent the sun from warming up their houses in the summer.

I wished I could wrap myself in a straw mat to protect myself against pity that, I assumed, Ben sensed for me. Or even disdain. He had witnessed one of Cliff's outbursts while being encouraged by Malefic Mason. He worked with them, so he probably took their side. I glanced at him, sitting with his legs stretched out and his feet "activated," whatever that meant. *Hopefully, he'd be too Zen to think about me.*

He told us to inhale, lifting the arms above our heads, then exhale, lowering them. Trilce followed the directions with an invisible smile. When she invited me, I asked if I'd clutter their date. She laughed and said, "I didn't invite you to be a third wheel. In the yoga class, it would have to be a train with so many wheels." I didn't understand what she meant about the wheels. She then clarified, "Our dates are a lot more intimate. This is just for the three of us to hang out. And clear our heads."

"This time as you breathe out, bend forward and touch the floor," Ben instructed. "If you can't reach the floor, you can touch your feet, or grab your shins, or your thighs." His voice gave tranquility to the room.

As I reached out, my hands were nowhere close to my feet. I scanned the room to see if anybody could do this. Ben, of course, had folded his body as if he were made of paper. I had to find someone else to imitate so I wouldn't give the impression that I was checking him out the whole time. I chose the blond girl on the side to be my model.

Ben guided us to a deeper stretch, which I couldn't do. Then we had to reach out in a "downward dog" position. I looked around. Trilce smiled at me as we both noticed a black cat walking toward Ben. I wondered how he would react if the cat hissed at him. Or worse, scratched him. Would he remain so calm and peaceful?

The tree pose made me wobble. The blond girl placed her toes on her calf with the heel still on the ground. So did Trilce. But Ben had his leg folded all the way up, with his arms strong and pointing to the sky. His armpit hair had been trimmed short, not like the rain forest that many straight guys cultivated. And not shaved like some gay guys. A straight guy who did yoga and took care of himself. Trilce had found herself a good guy.

A tiny yellow kitten stepped on my foot and meowed. I lifted her up to my chest. She immediately started to purr and press on my chest, alternating her paws. I closed my eyes and started to rock my body slightly, like comforting a baby. I tried to sync my movements to her paws: four presses for inhale and six presses for exhale.

From then on, I tried to loosely follow the poses. But my attention was on comforting my little kitty that occasionally meowed and changed her position in my arms. *Would Cliff let me bring her home?*

Why couldn't he control his rage, like everybody else? I understood that boys fought all the time. Surely Karim and I did. But he was older, bigger, and stronger than me. So, our fights mostly consisted of him beating me up. And the final kick in the chest, when we parted for the last time.

Cliff and I were not boys anymore. But like Karim, he was stronger and taller than me. I couldn't really hurt him even if I tried. As grown-ups, we shouldn't have to fight at all. With my H&M job, I started to have an income. Cliff expected me to contribute to our living expenses. But he wouldn't have to know exactly how much I made, now that the money would be deposited into my own account, as opposed to our previous joint account. I would start saving money. I would walk out if Cliff did anything crazy. Also, thanks to H&M, I had taken possession of my Social Security card and passport. Perhaps getting fired *was* a blessing in disguise.

Someone sneezed. I looked up. Ben brought his hand to his mouth, and then stepped to the side to take a few tissues.

I did the Reverse Warrior with one arm folded, holding the kitty to my chest. Then, for no reason, she started clawing at me and moving around. I carefully pulled her claws out of the fabric of my T-shirt and put her down on the floor. She just walked off as if she hadn't been my baby.

"Now take a giant step back with your right foot and fold your left knee, taking a deep lunge position." Ben sneezed again. "Sorry. Seems like my allergy tablet wasn't strong enough."

Why would he agree to do a cat yoga if he's allergic?

I copied the blond girl as closely as I could. After doing the lunge, we lay on our mats to meditate. My brain kept going. I now *had* a contingency plan if things got too wild. I'd take my stuff and leave, rent a room somewhere near Trilce's apartment in Belaire Edison. Even better, I could become a roommate of a Baltimore University student, who could even advise me with the SAT and college applications.

My kitty was in the arms of a middle-aged woman with veiny hands. Ben pressed on my shoulders with some lavender essential oil. I wished I had some of that perfume on my own hands.

Soon after we said "namaste," Ben sneezed again and left the room. Trilce asked me to clean her mat as she checked on him. I looked at the blond girl. She sprayed her mat with something and then wiped it off.

"May I?" I asked when she was done. She smiled and gave me the bottle and a small towel. I cleaned my mat and Trilce's. My kitten was now running after someone's mat, jumping in the air and clapping her paws, as if she was trying to catch an invisible butterfly.

"Are you thinking of adopting her?" the woman from the animal shelter asked me.

"I'd love to. But I have to ask my boyfriend first."

"They're from the Loving Care Shelter. We have cards on the desk. I think she took a liking to you." She nodded and walked away.

Noting that Ben and Trilce were both outside, I went and rolled up Ben's mat. It smelled like he regularly used essential oils.

Outside, he was holding a paper cup.

"He's allergic to cats. And yet, he did this for me," Trilce told me.

"Claritin obviously didn't do the trick."

"You poor thing," Trilce kissed him. Then she picked up her slip-ons. "You guys wear your shoes. I'll be right back." She walked to the bathroom.

"Oh thanks." Ben noticed me carrying his mat.

I collected my boots and sat on the bench, "You're really good." I pulled my socks out of the boots.

He sat next to me. "I started yoga a while back. My job is one hundred percent sedentary. I needed something to keep my body from falling apart. There's only so much jogging you can do."

"Yeah." I started to tie my boot laces. My phone vibrated. Another text message from Derrick. I silenced the phone. I wanted to recommit to my relationship with Cliff.

"But more importantly," Ben added, "yoga helps me clear my head, stop the internal dialogue, you know."

The blond girl showed up and retrieved her sneakers.

I was ready to get away from Ben before he said anything else.

"Abdul, I..." He paused for a second.

In my head, I begged him to not bring it up. I looked around. All of a sudden, there was nobody to distract us. "Thanks for leading the class. At first, I was afraid it was a date," I switched topics, trying to prevent him from talking about Cliff's outbursts.

He cleared his throat, probably still considering if he should say something.

Please don't. I stared at my boots. The ones Cliff had bought for me.

"I know you and Trilce are close."

I smiled, flattered.

"Think of me as a friend too. We're here for you." He put his hand on my shoulder, still smelling like lavender.

Oh my God, what if he tells her? I don't want her to pity me.

"I have a fantastic idea," Trilce showed up. "We should go to a salsa class."

"You guys should definitely do that." I offered as a way of backing out.

Ben stared at her for a second. "We can do whatever you want."

"Isn't he a gem?" she asked me.

"Yes, he is," Ben replied as he took her hand, interlocking fingers. That was how Ty held my hand, a few months ago.

"You should come also," she told me.

"I don't dance, remember?"

"I thought you don't dance only when accosted by Malefic Mason."

"What now?" Ben noticed my nickname for his coworker.

"Fine," she capitulated. "We can all go on a picnic when the weather gets warm."

"Picnic?" Ben objected. "Not so sure about that one."

She gave him a crooked look. "And I called you a gem and all."

He lifted his open palm up in a "sorry" gesture.

"What fun thing can we do then?" She thought for one second before coming up with the next idea. "Abdul can teach us how to cook an Afghan meal. One of those rice dishes, ha?"

"Now *that* I can fully support," Ben concurred.

Vicissitude

/vɪˈsɪsɪtuːd/ *noun*

A cat was walking around the staircase. The door to the first-floor apartment was left ajar. "Look at the kitty cat." I carried a bag of groceries, one hand on the bottom, the other holding it against my chest. Cliff carried the two bags by the handle, unconcerned that they could tear before reaching home.

"What do you think about adopting a kitty?"

"That's a great idea. If you wanna vacuum every day," he dismissed my suggestion.

Years ago, he wanted to adopt a dog. I lied that dogs scared me. He was already scary enough when he got mad.

He put the bags on the floor and reached for the keys in his pocket. A faint hint of smoke hung in the air. We could hear a sharp beeping noise. As soon as he opened the door, the heat blew onto us, mixed with smoke and the smell of burnt food.

"Did you leave the stove on?" Cliff demanded.

I hadn't used the stove all day.

The kitchen seemed normal but foggy. The smoke detector was beeping with a vengeance. Cliff ran to the bathroom, where the smoke was much thicker. "Whoa," he yelled out. "Abdul, fire extinguisher."

I ran to the kitchen sink and pulled out the red cylinder. The fire made crackling sounds. Cliff started spraying foam.

The towels in the bathroom had already burned. Cliff hosed down the shower curtain that was quickly coming down. Each of its hooks now holding up a little flame. Pieces of burning shower curtain fell on the floor. Soot had covered the sink mirror and the walls around. Next to the sink, the hairdryer had melted.

"The power outlet always malfunctioned," I noted.

"Open all the windows. And the door," Cliff instructed. "Damn, I totally forgot…"

I propped the front door open, with a bag of groceries. A cross breeze was now blowing from the living room window and out of the front door.

Cliff was looking around the bathroom, making sure all flames had been put out. He turned on the vent.

I texted Trilce: "We had a fire in the bathroom." I looked to see if he was getting irritated, ready to blame me.

"We're lucky it didn't set off the sprinklers." His voice remained calm, even though a bit anxious. "Have you ever seen those things in action?"

I looked up, not getting the point yet.

"Mason once set off sprinklers in our middle school lab… the whole floor smelled like sewage."

I started fanning the smoke out of the bathroom with a towel.

Cliff had a mischievous smile. He snatched the towel from me and softly struck my butt with it.

I held his arm and exhaled in relief. At least, he wasn't mad. Maybe, he was getting his bad temper under control.

As freezing air gushed in, the smell started to fade. But within minutes, the apartment turned into a fridge.

In the bathroom, portions of the walls had turned black, paint now peeling off, as it had shrunk in the high temperature.

"I'll clean up," I offered.

"Tomorrow."

"Do we have to call the fire department and report it or whatever?"

"We need to call the home insurance company," he replied.

"I didn't even know we have home insurance. Maybe we could—"

"It's good *one of us* is smart," he interrupted. "Don't clean up until after the insurance people come and take pictures."

"OK."

"Shouldn't be that hard to clean this up." He wiped his finger on the mirror, his fingertip black with soot. Then he wiped his finger on his face in a straight line.

"Are you a football player now?" I chuckled.

"It's kinda hot. Come, let me do it to you."

I walked to him.

He tapped on my shoulder and made me turn around. Then pushed my face onto the wall from behind, "Why did you burn down the apartment? You want the insurance money? For your college?" he joked.

The wall was still warm against my face. I looked into the mirror, at a thin strip of my image, where Cliff had cleaned the soot with his finger. Half of my face was covered in black. Cliff wiped his finger on the mirror again and drew a line on my clean cheek as well. Like football players.

"You look hot. Who you trying to seduce?"

I bit my lips and pushed my body into his.

"Oh, I know. Hold on." He took his cellphone and held it in front of me. He clicked a few times. "Come here." He stood next to me and clicked a few selfies.

"Let's close the windows. It's got really cold." Then I heard the sound of sending a text. "You can text pictures to the insurance company?"

"No, stupid. I'm texting Mason."

"Why? Why to Malefic Mason." I surprised myself, insulting his best friend like that.

"Malefic? Well, look who's learning new vocabulary. Maybe we should put the insurance money toward your college."

"Really?" I tried not to sound too happy.

"You *do* know you have to apologize to him, right?"

He was probably right.

"He's good at his job though. Did you know you can use Bluetooth to communicate with strangers? Yet another trick up his sleeve. He keeps finding ways of enlarging our audience. I have to keep an eye on him. I'm the one who should be promoted and sent to New York."

I would miss Trilce so much. "Are we definitely moving?"

"We're lucky nothing else got damaged. I have a…" he seemed distracted. "Let me check on the safe. I have tons of USBs in there. Documents and everything."

He left the bathroom. I wiped the mirror with my hand. The mirror wasn't entirely damaged. But the corner had a burn stain that wouldn't come off no matter how much I rubbed it.

"The safe is fine," Cliff yelled from the bedroom. "But it's warm from the heat on the other side. Isn't that something?"

I went to the kitchen, closed the front door, and started packing the groceries.

"Where's your passport?" Cliff called out from the bedroom closet.

"In my bag."

"That's stupid. You wanna increase the chances they be lost? Or stolen?"

I didn't want to give up my papers. H&M provided the perfect excuse for me to hold onto them. And now Cliff wanted them back.

"You must keep it safe *in the safe*. Give me your Social Security card too."

The bathroom fire hadn't caused an eruption of rage. I didn't want to argue with him about my documents getting locked in the safe. He might still be edgy. No need to agitate him now.

"Abdul, chop-chop. If the safe is open for too long, it'll alert the security company."

I picked up my bag and gave him my passport and Social Security card. "Thanks. I didn't think of that."

"That's why they pay me the big bucks. For my brains." Cliff closed the safe and pressed the pound key. The electric lock clicked. The green light blinking.

At least, I no longer had the temptation of leaving my boyfriend. He had my documents locked up. But he also had completely controlled his anger, despite the fire in the bathroom. He was improving. Not like I deserved much better after cheating on him.

"You look hot like that. Go on. I'm ready to be seduced."

My face was still covered in soot. The marks on Cliff's face also looked good. I turned my back to him and lowered my jeans so he could see half of my pink briefs.

"That's what I'm talking about." He got up and followed me to the bedroom.

Ignominy

/ˈɪgnəmɪni/ *noun*

Standing behind one of the four tables in the baking class, I clicked on my phone to make sure I hadn't missed any texts from Trilce. Behind the other tables, two couples explored the ingredients: white flour, whole wheat flour, butter, sugar, cream cheese, and bowls of different sizes. If Trilce and Ben were going to occupy the fourth table, did I have to work on my own? Had she invited Shane? There was only one table left. The door opened and a white gay couple entered, holding hands.

"You made it," the teacher with red hair and oversized glasses exclaimed. Judging by her figure, she didn't eat a lot of her own pastries. I hoped she could teach us something, other than how to get sugar, glaze it with honey, and dip it into high fructose corn syrup. Which was how all American sweets tasted to me.

The couple spotted me right away. I smiled and nodded. Gays recognized gays.

I was going to share my table with Trilce and Ben, I concluded. Not that it bothered me. I could just relax and let the two of them do the work.

"Good evening," the teacher said. "I guess we'll start now. My name is Stephanie and we're all going to bake a delicious fruity swirl Bundt cake tonight. I see we have our couples here. Are you here on your own, sugar?"

Assuming I was the sugar, I replied, "Yeah."

"What's your name, honey?"

"Abdul."

"Oh fun. Like Paula Abdul?"

"Yeah."

"Don't you just love her? 'Straight up' ha?" Her enthusiasm scratched me.

The gay couple sang "oh, oh, oh," making the girl in the middle table smile.

"Let me check to make sure everybody is in the right class. We have Devon and Tiffany, Matt and Marina, and of course, Anthony and Tony."

You must be kidding me.

"And Abdul is on his own—"

"He's with me," Trilce barged in and stood next to me. "Ben can't make it though," she told me in a low voice.

"Let's start then. The first thing I do is to wash my hands," Stephanie announced. "Feel free to use the sink if you haven't already."

"But the cake is gonna bake at a high temperature," probably-Anthony observed.

Probably-Tony agreed.

"I know. I guess I have OCD. But speaking of temperature, you wanna pre-heat your oven. Put it at 350."

"I don't wanna eat whatever *they're* making," Trilce mumbled and went to the sink.

"I was worried you may not show up." I admitted.

She took off her black jacket. Underneath, she was wearing a white T-shirt with a graphic of a few kittens playing on a Xerox machine. The shirt said "copycat."

"Is everyone ready?" Stephanie asked a few minutes later. "The first thing we wanna do is to mix the cream cheese, butter, and sugar and beat them up until they get fluffy. You'll notice that you can choose the amount of sugar. Remember, we're gonna add fruit preserve later on. Keep that in mind as you decide how much sugar you'd like to add. I don't like my cake too, too sweet. Half a cup is what I like. But if you really got a sweet tooth, you may wanna double it. Even one and a half cups if you *really* want to make it sweet."

"I like it sweet," said Anthony.

"Yeah," Tony pronounced as if "yeah" had two syllables.

"What do you think?" Trilce asked me.

"Maybe half?"

"I'm in no rush to get diabetes," she concurred.

We then added vanilla to the mixture. It smelled warm.

"I already know what our next adventure is gonna be," Trilce announced, mixing dairy products.

"Beat it up good," encouraged Stephanie.

For a second, I wished my boyfriend was here with me. Ben could have accompanied Trilce. What if Ty was here? *I've got to stop thinking about him.* Cliff had been so good recently. His angry phase was over. Maybe he used to get mad before, because of some problem at work.

Some flour particles hung in the air and landed on Trilce's thigh through the patches in her jeans.

"Now here is the fun part," Stephanie declared. "You wanna sprinkle some flour to make a thin film on the oil. This way your cake won't stick to the pan. But don't overdo it."

"I got it." My friend dusted some flour on the pan. But her hand shook a little too much, and fistful of flour went flying in the air, landing on our clothes.

Matt and Marina were showing each other how to oil the pan properly. Tony had stuck his finger in the bowl of flour and left a white fingerprint on Anthony's nose. Stephanie then gave us a choice of fruit preserve. I picked fig.

"Now swirl that onto the top. Stay clear of the pan. The preserve is heavier than the mix. It'll naturally settle as we bake it in the oven. You just don't want to have it all at the bottom."

"Swirl, swirl," Trilce joked as she moved the plastic spatula.

Tony was swirling like a ballet dancer.

I shook my head. "Cheesy," I whispered.

"They're cute," Trilce offered.

As much as they acted like clichés, it put me at ease to see a gay couple.

We soon put the pans into the ovens. Stephanie gave us a choice of red or white wine to enjoy as we waited for the cakes to rise.

I checked on the cake. When I turned around, Trilce was looking at her phone.

"Hey, Abdul. Can you look at this for a sec?" She showed me her phone. I saw a picture of me, in our burnt-out bathroom. But a significant detail was added to the picture. The wine glass slipped from my hand and shattered on the floor. The picture showed my entire face covered in soot.

That can't be. Cliff just wiped one finger on my face to make me look like a football player. He didn't do all of this. I looked up at her.

"What is this?" she questioned.

Anthony was also looking at his phone. He showed it to Tony. He waved his index finger at me, "no, no, no."

"How did you get it?"

More phones beeped.

"I got a Bluetooth alert and then this popped up," she was confused. Shocked.

I thought for a second. It must have been Mason. Cliff had told me Mason used Bluetooth to contact strangers.

I pulled out my phone and checked my Twitter. The picture of me in blackface had been retweeted thousands of times. It mentioned my handle. I remembered how Mason had used bots to gain many more admirers than Cliff.

I held onto the table to steady myself. All eyes glared at me as more of them looked at each other's phones and then at me. My chest contracted. I took my coat and ran out before Stephanie had a chance to kick me out of her class.

Abate

/əˈbeɪt/ verb

I was so angry I almost punched a guy when my carryout order at the restaurant was delayed. I wanted to hide my face, before more people saw the blackface picture Mason was disseminating.

When I got home, Cliff was changing his clothes, probably had just arrived from work.

"Hey. I brought Chicken Pad Thai from PF Chang," I greeted him.

He looked at me as though my face disgusted him. "This time you've really outdone yourself, haven't you?"

I didn't know what he meant. It wasn't as if I had a trail of other racist gestures to have outdone myself now.

"What came to your stupid little brain to think you have to make this and then send it out to the world?"

"Cliff, I didn't—"

Before I could finish my sentence, he smacked me across the face. My ears buzzed from its sound.

"Do not interrupt me," he yelled, with his face red and his nostrils engorged. "Didn't you think about backlash? Was this some crazy joke? Didn't you think it would jeopardize my career?"

I stood in silence. He hated it when I talked back in his moments of rage.

"Do you have anything to say for yourself?"

Hesitant, I could only whimper, "You're so angry your chest is red."

He grabbed my hair and pulled back. "You took a blackface picture and now you're worried about my chest?"

I didn't know what to do other than let his fury erupt.

"Look, your cheek is red. I think I should make the other one match." He slapped me hard on the other side.

Maybe I should just leave tonight. He still has my Social Security card and passport in his safe. I didn't have enough money to last me even a month. Where should I go tonight? I needed Cliff to convince Mason to take this picture offline. I needed him.

"I don't know why I keep your stupid ass around." He grumbled as he pulled on a T-shirt.

"May I speak now?" I hated how meek I sounded.

He frowned and jerked his head, perhaps surprised I asked for permission. "Go ahead."

"I would never do anything like that. Why would I? It jeopardizes my job too."

"As much as folding clothes is a career," he mocked. "But you can forget about going to college now."

"Cliff, please. I don't even have this picture on my phone," I reached out in my pocket and gave him the phone. "Here. Look. I don't have any pictures from that night."

He took the phone but paused, thinking.

"Remember, we were just playing around. You made one single line on my cheek. We thought it made me look like a football player, remember? I had some soot on my ear, but nothing like this."

"You put your face on the wall and smudged your face with soot," he recalled.

He had pushed my face onto the wall. He tapped on something on my phone. I panicked, wondering if he was about to discover the pictures of Ty.

"So you didn't take that picture?"

I shook my head.

"OK. I believe you." Cliff took out his own phone and checked something. Keeping both phones in his hand, he clicked off his screen. "Set up the table. I'm starving." He sounded calmer. I wasn't going to escalate and ask him anything. He kept my phone.

In silence, I brought plates, forks, and two bottles of Loose Cannon, the beer too fitting for his mood tonight.

"Who is this Tyrique Williams?" He looked up from across the table.

I almost choked on my noodles. "Who?"

"Don't play stupid with me or I'll make you swallow your own blood. You have his website open and you're following him on Instagram."

"He's no one. Just a poet. I use his poetry to learn vocabulary. For the SAT."

"You'll never go to college, stupid," he mumbled chewing his food. "Where does he live?"

How could I distract him from asking too many questions about Tyrique? "I don't know. I know nothing about him other than a couple of his poems."

"You've been on his site a lot."

How did he know that? "I'd completely forgotten I had his page open."

"You know what's gonna happen to you if you so much as look at another man." Holding the phone, he made a fist, his bicep flexing. "I'll remember his name. He'd better never show up in Baltimore. Or I'll make you both regret it."

I shook my head. "I have no reason to cheat, Cliff. Sometimes, I have to pinch myself to believe that I'm with *you*."

"That's true," he ate the next forkful. "Not a bad looking boy, though. I could bang him for dessert."

I felt the sourness of my stomach acid just imagining that picture. "You are *my* man," I said, even as I thought, *Ty is mine.*

"Look at you." Cliff slapped his hand on the table. "You're practically drooling just looking at me. That's how you used to look at me all the time. You used to worship the ground I walked on."

My face got hot. I looked at my plate.

He switched phones and clicked for some time.

"Didn't you tell me that Mason could artificially increase the number of times something is shared online? I was with Trilce when she got the same picture through Bluetooth." I patted his forearm, begging in my mind that he find a way of taking down the photo.

"You think he did this?"

"Why else would people retweet a picture of me thousands of times? It's not like I'm famous or anything? Why would anyone care?" I clutched his forearm harder, trying to prevent my hand from trembling.

He squinted. "You say people got the picture through Bluetooth? You have to be nearby to do that."

"You think maybe he asked Ben what his girlfriend was doing tonight? He knows me and Trilce are friends."

"He is such a dickhead," my boyfriend concluded. "You know once I punched him in the face until his nose bled?"

No!

"We were kids. But that was the first and only time Jacob was ever proud of me. He even broke his piggie bank to bribe Mason so he wouldn't tell on me."

"Malefic, as always."

He sipped and clicked and ate and clicked. "Let's do this: We'll play good cop, bad cop. You apologize for throwing your drink at him. And I'll tell him to knock it off."

Mason had to apologize to me for making me look like a racist ass. But if I wanted Cliff's intervention, I had to do what he said.

"You humiliated him in the club," he went on. "If you had apologized when I told you the first time, this wouldn't have happened."

I nodded. "OK."

"Good."

"Is he gonna take off the picture?"

"Better. I'll ask him to acknowledge the picture wasn't real. Maybe we can blame it on a prank or something."

"Are you serious?" I exclaimed in disbelief. "I wanna kiss you so bad right now."

"No one is stopping you, stupid."

I hugged him from the side and kissed him repeatedly. "You're the best."

"I know! I wouldn't let you go down like that." His smile wiped away the feelings of doubt I had earlier.

From now on, I was going to stay faithful. I wouldn't give in to temptation if Varun Dhawan himself hit on me.

"And I'm not gonna let a petty spat between you two threaten *my* job." Cliff had too much pride to confess he did this only for me. He was going to confront his best friend from childhood for my sake.

"You're a superhero," I hugged him as tight as I could.

Contraction

/kənˈtrækʃn/ *noun*

As I tended the fitting room, I put sensors on new Logg men's shirts that I unpacked from the tote and put them on hangers to run to the floor. Was I mistaken or were my colleagues just too quiet today? No one came by to chat or to run the new merchandise that I was putting on the rack. Wondering if anyone had seen that picture from the other day, I decided to be quiet and let this pass by. I pricked my finger with the sensor when I saw Mason was coming to me.

He came in, carrying so many items he could hardly walk. "So you got a job. Good for you. Heard you got fired from the last one."

If I did anything he didn't like, he would complain to my manager. He might do so anyway, regardless of how much I tried to appease him. I should have apologized earlier.

He walked to the wheelchair access room.

I had to swallow my pride and do it. "Mason?"

He opened the door. "It's Mr. Lombardo to you."

Ignoring the remark, I continued, "I'm sorry for the way I behaved…"

He put his hand on his waist and paused for a second. "Talk is cheap. I need proof that you're truly sorry."

I stared at him. "How?"

"You get an employee discount, don't you?"

He was going to make me pay for his purchase. And I had to make him happy, for him to take down that awful fake picture of me.

He left a number of items on the fitting room counter for me to buy for him. On his way out of the store, I saw him talking to Phillip, my manager.

I went back to the fitting room. He had thrashed the place. All items were off their hangers and thrown around the room, on the bench, on the floor, and hanging from various hooks.

"Abdul," Phillip showed up. "What happened? It's such a mess here." He pointed to the totes that I hadn't yet unpacked.

"I'll take care of it."

"You know, what you should really feel sorry about? The blackface picture."

He might have seen it on his own, but I suspected Mason had shown it to him. "That was just a prank. It wasn't even real," I explained.

"I can't be the judge of that. But I know this." He paused for a second. "I will have a store-wide staff huddle at the end of the day. And if one of them, just one of them, objects to your continued employment here, I'll have to let you go."

Most of my colleagues were African American and I was probably going to lose my job today.

"And what are these?" He had noticed the pile of clothes on the counter.

I wasn't going to buy Mason's clothes if I was going to be fired anyway. "A customer wanted to put these on-hold until tomorrow."

He shook his head and walked away.

At the huddle, I just shrank into myself, contracting my existence. Phillip was speaking but I couldn't hear anything he said. I just made out the word "objection," but I didn't dare look up at my colleagues to see who would respond.

"You all have another day to think about this. Abdul, your shift tomorrow is canceled," Phillip announced.

A few minutes later, my phone vibrated in my back pocket: a message from Ty.

"I have no future" — Surviving child sexual exploitation

By Rakesh Luthra

Lashkargah, Afghanistan (Compass News) — The sadness in the eyes of fourteen-year-old Mojtaba (not his real name) is overwhelming. He lacks the playfulness of a teenager. He says he dances at parties for men. "They do bad things," he whispers, his voice devoid of youthful confidence. "They force me." We don't ask pointed questions, mindful of not subjecting him to re-traumatization.

"What am I going to do now? I have no future," he lowers his head. "The best-case scenario is for me to age out. If I'm lucky, I get to leave this town and work as a day laborer or something in another city."

If a teenager succeeds in escaping, the options remain few. It's taboo to discuss this specific form of child abuse. Families are under tremendous pressure to keep the entire thing secret. The men who exploit these children are warlords and police officers. They can easily intimidate families into silence and submission.

"These children cannot go to the police for protection," says Kabir Sadat, the executive director of NGO Jawana. "It's likely that the police officers would also sexually assault the youth. They may even bring charges against him for being a so-called child prostitute." The latter is a misguided notion of holding children accountable for illegal acts they committed while under the control of someone else. "The concept of a child prostitute is invalid because children do not have the capability to understand sex work and how it impacts their mental and physical health and growth. The idea of children wanting to do such a thing is irrelevant because the question is self-contradictory. Children cannot consent to sex work," Mr. Sadat elaborates.

An official of the Ministry of Interior has told Compass News that these boys should be prosecuted. But Mr. Sadat disagrees. "There's no legal basis for that," he explains.

Unfortunately, escaping from situations of forced sexual exploitation can be life-threatening. Nazif, whom we met in an earlier installment of this series, was killed during his attempt to escape. Another civil society activist, who spoke on the condition of anonymity, knew of a case where the child who had escaped was later found dead. "Sometimes family members cannot tolerate the shame, and they resort to extreme measures," Mr. Sadat confirms. "Other times, they try to keep their sons safe but they don't always succeed."

Another way out of this type of situation is simply to age out. "I hope my beard grows soon and they won't want my company anymore," Mojtaba says. However, if a boy brings in a lot of money, he may not be able to leave his situation into his early twenties.

Some teenagers end up in a vicious cycle of abuse, becoming traffickers themselves after aging out of dancing or serving as a chai boy. "I want to have boys of my own," says another teenager, who asked to remain anonymous. "This can be a lucrative business. People are making a lot of money off of dancing." The last option is to engage in sex work as an adult.

The spokesperson of the Afghanistan Independent Human Rights Commission, Gulbahar Mirdadzai, tells Compass News there are no shelters for male survivors of human trafficking, including boys. She did not know of any medical or psychological support for these children.

The Commission is not a service delivery institution. UNICEF supports several educational programs but no services for children who have been trafficked or sexually abused. The head of UNICEF in Kabul, Karla Ziegler, reiterates that this is a complex issue but does not explain why her organization is unable or unwilling to provide any support.

"These kids are not disposable," Mr. Sadat adds passionately. "They've endured some of the worst of what humanity has to offer and they deserve a chance at rehabilitation. But if we can't talk about their pain, how are we supposed to create a path forward? How can we expect them to reintegrate into society and, God willing, prosper in it?"

Unfurl

/ ˌʌnˈfɜːrl / verb

Ty's words kept echoing in my head: "I can't stop thinking about you. Perhaps we could just maintain a platonic friendship?" I wished I could tell him that I also couldn't stop thinking about him. But if I overreacted, he would slip away. For good, this time. Playing it cool, I told him that we could hang out a bit the next time he was in town. I hoped he hadn't seen the blackface picture.

I slowed my pace as the Knoll Lighthouse became visible down the street. Reaching too early only meant more anxious waiting. After months of looking forward to a simple message from him, even the promise of a simple friendly encounter lifted me into a state of elation. And now I was here early, letting anticipation build up even more. Ty didn't know but I considered this encounter an early birthday gift. My white sneakers gently kissed the brown brick pavement. The blue sky gave the red and black structure a particular prominence, as if a spaceship was about to take off.

I hope the two of us are inside as it propels into the air. No, I shouldn't wish that. I'd decided to commit to my relationship with Cliff, so this must be free of sensuality. The lighthouse stood, like a tack that pinned down life onto the earth, into reality.

The knot in my stomach tightened. Maybe I shouldn't have suggested going to the aquarium. The TV ad portrayed a date. I could switch my desire for a more acceptable wish. A little secret that, if shared, would scare him off. Like a scarecrow had to be still if he wanted to make friends with sparrows.

A breeze caressed my face. As I approached, a flock of birds flew away, creating little accents in this picture. Baltimore was so beautiful over here.

I turned around to look for Ty. A white woman was pushing a stroller toward the water. I looked away. And then I saw him. He had a nice fade. Even from afar, his eyes reflected the entire sky. A low-cut V-neck tan sweater showed off a hint of his pecs, his skin glowing. Several bead necklaces dropped over his chest. He was wearing a white blazer, with sleeves pulled up, displaying numerous bracelets. His jeans matched the color of the brick pavement. His smile radiant.

My heart rate increased.

"Greetings, Mr. Abdul."

"Hi." I couldn't help smiling like a chipmunk.

"It's so good to see you." He wrapped his arms around me.

He smelled like a thousand roses had rained over him. Not the usual common rose. *Gol-e Mohammadi*, with a more penetrating perfume. I took a deep breath to take in as much of him as I could. Wishing this hug could last a few hours, and fearing that I may seem too intrusive, I embraced him loosely, allowing enough space in between so he could pull away with ease at his discretion.

He squeezed before letting go. "You look good." He lightly grabbed my chin, his finger emanating a magnetic pull.

I looked down, shy. His dress shoes looked so gracious that my white sneakers appeared clunky and rude.

"Shall we?"

"I hope I didn't totally mess up your schedule."

"Nah, I wanted to see you."

He wanted to see me.

"How have you been?"

Was he going to ask if I ever called the number he left me? "Like usual. Nothing has changed much." *Such a boring answer.* "I'm still studying for the SAT."

"That's great."

I grinned, imagining he would have liked it, if he'd known I used his writings as a study guide. As we approached the ticket window, I offered to pay for the tickets.

"What, you won the lottery or something?"

"No, but I'm the host."

"Nah. You're too kind. But if you win the lottery, don't forget yours sincerely."

"Please. It's nothing."

"I appreciate the gesture," he reached for his wallet, "but allow me to pay for myself."

A crowd of four women and some thirty to forty children spilled into the aquarium.

"I'm not sure about your take on this, but I think we probably should get a head start," Ty proposed.

Fish always mesmerized me. Calm and tranquil. They literally lived in a different world, unperturbed by the tribulations of ours. The first fish I noticed was as long as my forearm, had grey fins and something like hair under its jaw. Its eyes passed over me as if I didn't exist. The next one hardly looked like a fish, and more like a yellow triangle: longhorn cowfish, according to the sign. "That one looks so weird," I announced, lacking eloquence.

I looked around. Just a few kids behind me. "Ty?" I walked toward the end of the walkway. Was I allowed to call him by the shortened version?

He was already ahead of me. "Here," he waved at me. "I thought you were next to me."

"Sorry, I didn't realize you moved on."

"I used to have angelfish as a child," he said.

Some of them had a zebra pattern. A red fish like the one in the movie swam by.

"Look, Nemo." I felt Ty's two fingers gently hook onto mine. I rubbed my fingers against his.

"Better hold on to my host before he ditches me for some fish," he justified.

Am I imagining it, or does he want an excuse to hold my hand?

"I love clownfish."

"Which one is that?"

"Hey," a young girl exclaimed as she ran towards us. "Nemo," she touched the glass.

"Nemo," a group of children yelled in unison and ran toward us.

Ty chuckled, half-covering his mouth as if the world wasn't pure enough to witness his gorgeous laughter. "I think it's safe to say your name stuck." He pulled away his hand, even as more children congregated around us.

I didn't get the joke, but I smiled.

"I'd forgotten all about those dimples."

We stepped away to let the kids enjoy the sight. A boy around the age of ten followed us and stared for a moment.

"Hey man," Ty noticed him too. "You enjoying your field trip?"

"When I grow up," the boy paused, "I wanna be gay like you."

"Yeah?" Not even Ty, the pensive poet knew how to reply to that.

"And I want a friend like him," the boy pointed at me.

Ty fist bumped him, "That's a plan, my man."

"Marvin," an older teacher called out. "We don't point at people, remember?" She walked closer. "And you should stay with the group." She put her hand on his shoulder. "But you guys do look really cute together," she muttered as she guided Marvin back.

I waited until they were far enough then asked, "Do you think he's safe speaking like that?"

"I trust God is watching him."

Why hadn't God looked after me when I was a kid? This child lived in America. Maybe God cared more here. "These kids are so full of life. So exuberant."

He frowned. "Didn't you say you're studying for the SAT?"

"Yeah?" I didn't know where this was going.

"You sound too advanced for that. 'Jolly' would be an SAT word. 'Exuberant'... That sounds like GRE."

"You only say that because you're my friend," I dismissed the compliment, while soliciting a commitment to our fledgling friendship at the same time. It didn't come.

In silence, we proceeded to the seahorses. I read the sign next to the display. "It's the male seahorse that gets pregnant," I summarized the writing. "What if we were seahorses? I would *not* be looking forward to pregnancy at all."

"Our kids would be gorgeous though. With your genes and mine," he smiled at his own joke but quickly caught himself. "It's hard to be your friend," he scratched his head. "You make me betray my values," Ty whispered the knockout punch. "You make me want to act on my primal instincts." He kept hitting me with his words.

"I..." I wanted to turn around and face him.

He put both hands on my shoulders to keep me in position, a foot apart. "Did you ever call the number I gave you?" He succeeded in finding the least sexy subject of conversation.

We were standing close, yet miles away. Even his body seemed to get smaller in the distance. It felt like hours passed. He should have guessed the answer by now.

Next was the jellyfish display. Long strands of luminosity, dragging behind a radiant soft umbrella that opened and closed on a loop, pushing forward. Beautiful but fatal. Cliff was my jellyfish. Was I Tyrique's?

"You don't have to confide in me," Tyrique finally said. "You and I are…"

If Tyrique with his boundless eloquence couldn't define what we were, I couldn't put a label on us either.

"Just find someone you trust. You need a support system."

"He has been really good recently." I hovered on my fingertip by the glass, wishing the jellyfish would sting me, just so I wouldn't have to have this conversation.

The day continued to get worse. I thought Tyrique didn't want to cut it short just to prove to himself that he could resist the urge to touch me, flirt with me, like me.

We ended up in Maharaja, a small Indian restaurant on South Gay Street, the street name being the main reason we walked that way in the first place. "Abdul, I wanna ask you something. I don't want to appear insensitive, but you said you Googled me so I feel like it's not inappropriate."

"OK," I granted the permission to be asked an insensitive question.

"I wanted to find out more… and I saw this article about dancing boys in Afghanistan."

"You made that disclaimer for this?" Of course, he needed to ease into this topic, but I wanted him to feel comfortable with me. I was going to allow any tactless question, as long as *he* was the one posing it. "It's on the cover of American newspapers often enough."

"Is it something common?"

"It's called bacha bazi. It's when men of power keep boys to dance for them in women's clothing, generally in parties. They can be warlords, police chiefs, commanders, or what have you." I said as a matter of fact, with academic detachment.

"In girls' clothing."

"And the powerful man gets to sleep with the boy after the party. Or someone else who's willing to pay the right price."

"That's absolutely horrifying."

Neither of us had any interest in the tikka masala chicken anymore.

"They say women are for children, boys are for pleasure." For an unknown reason, I confessed a deeply shameful thing I had never told anyone else. Not even Rakesh. Even though he probably heard it elsewhere.

"What happens to the boys?"

I felt thankful that he didn't say, "I can't even imagine." What was the point of stating you were unwilling to empathize with survivors while trying to express sympathy? "They eventually age out, I guess." I replied, sanitizing what I wanted to say: That they got thrown out. They might become beggars, addicts, prostitutes. But some survived. They'd have to move to another city where no one knew their story. Families generally weren't accepting of such shame. Although some families would move to another city with their sons. Ty didn't need to know all this. Too much detail would hurt him and would depress the mood even further.

He sighed. "Tell me about you," he gave up on the topic. "I don't really know much at all."

"What do you wanna know?"

"The regular stuff. Like where were you born? Where did you grow up?"

"I was actually born in Mashad in Iran. My older brother was born in Bamiyan but then my family fled. That was right before the end of Soviet occupation."

"When was the first time you visited Afghanistan?"

"In 2003. After we thought the US war was over. My grandparents were getting too old to take care of themselves, and my father, the oldest son, wanted to go back to Bamiyan and look after them."

"So you all left?"

"In Mashhad, we were constantly being harassed everywhere we went. Once I was in line at a bakery, and a woman jumped the line in front of me and started yelling that no one wanted refugees from Afghanistan. My father was paid less than his Iranian colleagues. Going to school was an ordeal because we didn't have *amayesh* cards. At the beginning of every academic year, our school registration would be on-hold until the Ministry of Education issued a *bakhshnameh*, deciding whether refugee children could attend school or not."

Things had gotten much worse since then. During the Syrian civil war, some Hazaras joined *Sepah-e Fatemiyoun* either because they wanted to protect Shi'a holy sites from *Da'esh* or because they were tempted by the bonuses that the Iranians promised. But I'd also read that in addition to encouragement through mass media, Iranian authorities sometimes arrested undocumented refugees from Afghanistan, and threatened to deport them and their families, unless they joined the war. After fighting in Syria, when they returned, they and their families would get a residence permit.

I didn't want to say all of that to Tyrique either. No one wanted to find out too much about Afghanistan, Iran, or Syria. The problems were too egregious for American audiences.

I decided against delving into any of this. Why would I? He was just a friend. A distant one at that. I wrapped up the story. "They said after the US invasion, Afghanistan was a safe country and that refugees had to go back. No one likes refugees."

Tyrique seemed content with the abridged version. "Where are your parents?"

"My father's dead. The rest..."

Tyrique's hand froze, holding a piece of paratha roti. A blob of gravy dropped from his mouth on the table. "I'm sorry." He wiped his mouth. "I'm afraid of asking what happened. Tell me only if you're OK with sharing that." He slightly pushed his plate away.

I told him what happened with as little detail as possible. He didn't have to know more. Only Rakesh knew the full story. He never asked if he could print it in his reports. My story remained entirely mine. A lump started to take form in my throat.

"That is devastating. I'm so sorry."

We sat in heavy silence. Or was it the burden of the story, truncated as it was.

"How's your family now?" He dared to ask when I thought I'd pushed him to the limit.

"I never saw them again. My brother threw me out. Not that I blame him."

Tyrique cleared his throat and put his fist in front of his mouth. He made a noise, his voice cracking under the pressure of fighting tears. Ty inhaled but his chest tremored, breaking his breath into small staccato fragments. A layer of haze covered his face.

I upset him. When I looked back at him, Ty was crying. Not streams of tears, more like balls of water, hailing down on his face. I wished I could kiss his eyes, right then, in front of everybody. Taste the saltiness of his tears and console him.

I wished I could hug him and make him feel better. "Don't be sad. It's OK."

"No, no, no. You lived through all that and now you're trying to console me? I should be consoling you."

"I'm fine." My voice came out robotic, devoid of the dregs of pain that was settling on me.

He stared at me in silence.

"You don't need to cry. I'm still here. Even if I don't deserve it. I'm still..." I couldn't console him more than that. Not without breaking down.

Ty took a sip of water and took his time to think of something to say. "These are your tears that are trickling out of my eyes. I feel like I have to take on your pain and just let it unfurl in me."

He thought if he took this on, I'd have a bit more breathing space. That didn't make sense to me, but a beautiful sentiment, nevertheless. "I shouldn't have told you. I'm sorry."

Tyrique shook his head slightly. His eyes still locked on mine. Shining more than usual behind a curtain of sparkling tears, I felt guilty for smearing his beauty. I had been looking forward to spending time with him for months. And now that he was here, my despair had infected him. I wanted to rise to his heavens of bliss. Like the first time we met, hoping I could savor another stolen moment of joy. But instead, I had depressed him too.

Stolen joy.

That was why I couldn't hold on to it. Our time together was never mine to start with. This precious, adorable, considerate man was not mine. And he shouldn't be, because I upset him. Because I made him weep.

He reached out and took my hand. "If you were my boyfriend, I..." He stopped himself.

We stood on a cliff. At the slightest trace of an invitation, I would jump with him. But he didn't want to. He just left me with my Cliff.

Tyrique wiped his eyes. "Abdul, I'm sorry but I can't do this."

"What?"

The wordsmith was helpless.

"I only answered a few questions that *you* asked me." *And even then, I didn't tell you the half of it.*

"I know. You're so precious to me. I want to hold you and support you and listen to your darkest memories and carry you through the pain but..." He sighed. "I can't do all of that without crossing the line. We agreed to be just friends."

If I wanted to save this strange friendship, I had to pull him out of this lagoon. "I overshared. That was my fault. I'm sorry."

He smiled, his eyes wet and red. "Don't take this the wrong way. But I think you could benefit from a good therapist. You've gone through a lot." My expression turned cold because he added, "I don't say it to be hurtful. I'm on your side, remember? I've gone to therapy too."

I steered the conversation to Trilce. Talked about her dates with Ben. Her convincing him to bring cats to his yoga class. Him agreeing to do it despite his allergies. About Cliff doing well at work, hoping that we could move to New York City. About the fire in the bathroom.

Talking about superficial matters helped ease the unease between us. People *thought* they wanted to know the truth. But they didn't. They wanted everyone to be covered behind the cheap yellow smiling emoji. They asked questions just to hear that everything was fine. This way, they wouldn't have to invest any time or energy.

But avoiding the topic reinforced the distance between us. He was sitting across the table, soon eating again. But he wasn't fully there. He hadn't made his heart available. As soon as the emotions got intense, we both retreated.

Despite his physical presence, he had already left me there. All by myself. Cold.

Frozen.

Dalliance

/ˈdælɪəns/ *noun*

Despite his tears, the non-date with Tyrique gave me a strange sense of hope. I had the power to deal with all that life had thrown at me. He pulled back after hearing a watered-down version of my past. But I had the capacity to have managed the whole situation. And he stayed despite his urge to flee. We both had trimmed our wishes into a shape that was acceptable to both of us. I mattered enough for him to do that. If we could continue to have a normal friendship, maybe we wouldn't even have to hide. Maybe our stolen moments of joy wouldn't have to be diverted.

In the food court, the parmesan cheese and oregano on my pizza smelled appetizing. Between bites, I checked Ty's Instagram. Half an hour ago, he'd posted a photo of a tiny plant growing between the bricks of a wall. The caption said, "Happy Birthday, Abdul." I grinned.

"Excuse me," a male voice interrupted. "Could I ask you for a big favor?" He was wearing a black baseball cap with a picture of a marijuana leaf. "I need to use the restroom but I don't wanna take this in there. Could you keep an eye on it? I'll be right back." He showed me a large H&M shopping bag.

I agreed.

"Thanks so much." He put the bag on the chair next to me and walked away.

Why me? I could have easily taken his brand-new clothes and disappeared. I took another slice of the pizza.

"Thank you so much," he showed up after a few minutes. "I definitely didn't wanna take... I'm Esteban." He extended his hand, still partially wet.

"Abdul."

"I know. Nice to meet you."

I probably had a puzzled look on my face because he explained, "You have your nametag still on." He sat in front of me. His dark brown eyes reflected the light from the windows. His hair was just messy enough to appear as if he hadn't spent a considerable amount of time styling it this way.

This was my birthday. And I wanted him to be my gift.

"You have a bunch of nice stuff at the store right now."

"Yeah, we've been lucky these past few weeks," I replied.

"Today, even luckier to get such a lovely customer."

His eyes twinkled. "I'm so sorry to interrupt your lunch."

"No problem. I need something sweet for dessert." I winked.

He chuckled. "You have a good sense of fashion."

I had to think to remember what I was wearing: a floral-patterned long sleeve button-down with a bowtie.

He leaned over the table and reached into the H&M bag on the chair next to me. "Tell me what I can match this with." As he got closer, I could smell his cologne: an aroma of jasmine? No, roses. I had learned that these were called Damask Roses. The same scent that Ty had been wearing a couple of days ago.

Esteban pulled out a dark blue shirt with gold patterns of galaxies and constellations.

"You look like Nicholas Gonzalez."

He was taken aback by my declaration. "You think so?" He adjusted his cap.

"But younger and hotter."

He gave me a shy smile.

"Let me think what you can wear with that shirt." I tapped on my chin. "I mean the safe choice is a pair of simple dark-colored slacks, or even jeans. Come sit next to me. Let's see what we can find."

He did. Our knees were now touching.

"You could pick pants that clash with it."

"Like something red?" He opened his browser app and started typing.

"Or maybe a dark maroon, with subtle black patterns. Maybe something to resemble rocks or mountains. So that your top can hint at the sky, and your bottom can remind of the earth."

He snapped his fingers and pointed at me. "That's exactly the type of fashion guru I was looking for."

I put my hand on his thigh. "You're welcome."

"You know what? My phone is out of data but I have Wi-Fi upstairs."

"Let's do it." I took out my phone and texted Philip. "Can I please take a longer lunch break? I have to tend to a personal thing. But I'll be back as soon as the new shipment arrives."

We went upstairs to an office. There was a stack of newspapers by the front door. The headline read, "Police officer charged with second degree murder in Mosher shooting case." Esteban picked up the newspapers and dropped them in a basket inside and complained, "No end to this madness."

I nodded and entered the office. The furniture reminded me of a psychologist's bureau.

"You work here?"

"My sister-in-law does." He stood behind an armchair.

"What cologne are you wearing?"

He opened a desk drawer and took out a pink bottle the shape of a heart.

I read the name: Seduce Him. "It's a women's perfume."

"The men's version is blue. It's called Seduce Her. And it smells like feet." He pinched his nose. "Do you want a... puff?" He was ready to spray it on me.

"I'd rather smell it on you." I pulled his collar and took a deep sniff. "And it works... to *seduce him*." I kissed him on the lips, my finger hooked in his belt loop. The flap of his cap was in my way. I reached to remove it.

"Nobody's allowed to touch my hat."

"I'm sorry." I took off his hat and let it drop on the floor. "What are you gonna do about it?" I kissed him before he had a chance to reply. "Your hair looks great. Don't withhold the world of that beauty."

He undid my belt and slipped a condom in my hand.

Corrode

/kəˈroʊd/ verb

The dessert we made for Nowruz needed *senjed*. But the symbol of love was missing in my life, as was Ty. Or perhaps it was a sign from the universe: Cliff was all the love I needed. Without *senjed*, it wasn't *haft mewah*, rather *shesh mewah*. But when you didn't have all the ingredients, you had to improvise. I used several types of raisins to compensate.

"Did you always know how to make it?" Cliff asked.

"I remember how my mom used to make it." Maybe my mom thought of me today as she prepared the same food. Karim must have a few kids by now. She might be too busy with them to reminisce about me. Did she blame me? Like Karim did? I felt tender in my nose. Thinking about family never cheered me up.

The clock on the stove read 7:32.

"It's gonna be the new year in thirteen minutes," I announced, happy that I had avoided Cliff's questions about Nowruz and why the new year started at an unusual time. I didn't know all the details about the moment of *sal tahvil*. I wasn't an astronomer.

How was Ty doing? I had a couple of minutes to spare. I visited TyriqueWilliams.com. The entire page was gone and replaced with a black background with grey writing: "On a digital sabbatical. You too should try it."

I looked at my phone contacts, pausing over "Terrence H&M," my code name for Ty, just in case Cliff showed a sudden interest in my phone again. If I could only bask in his rose cologne.

"Hey Abdul?" Cliff was looking at something on his phone.

My favorite burgundy velvet jacket that he had given me was hanging on the back of the chair. I'd wear it in about eight minutes when my body cooled down from the cooking. We used to buy new *yakhan qaq* for Nowruz when I was a kid. I enjoyed showing it off when we went *eid-didani*. Karim thought mine was too girly, having noticed I was different from most boys. Perhaps, that was why the more I grew up, the more he disliked me. He didn't like what he saw in me. He knew I was gay before I did.

"Yo? I called you," Cliff sounded aggravated.

What now? I walked into the living room.

"Where were you on Monday?"

With Ty.

"Are you deaf?" his voice got louder. "Where were you on Monday?"

"I…"

"Are you cheating on me?"

"What? No," I denied.

"Tell me the truth. Something is up with you. I can feel it."

"Nothing's up," I tried to sound normal.

"Mason warned me that you are flirting with every man in sight."

"What does he know? He changes boyfriends more often than socks. He hates me. He'll make up anything to attack me. Can't wait to go to New York so I don't have to hear about that piece of garbage anymore."

"You say a lot, but I haven't heard an answer yet. Who were you with on Monday?"

"Trilce."

"You were with Trilce on Monday? In the aquarium?"

How did he know I was in the aquarium? Was Mason following me? "Yes."

He got up and paced in the room. "Prove it. Show me pictures."

"My phone was dead. I don't have pictures."

"You're lying." With one sweep of his arm, he hit the vinegar cup on the table. It fell on the floor and spilled, smelling rotten. "If your phone had died, the tracker app wouldn't have worked."

"You're tracking my phone?"

"Damn right I am. I wanted to prove Mason was wrong, but it turns out you *have been* hoeing around like a little bitch." He yelled so loud that particles of spit flew in my direction. His face red.

If he finds out I cheated on him, he will lose it. Is this the moment he kills me? Finish off the job that my brother attempted?

"I was with Trilce. You can call her and—"

He slapped me in the face. "You think you can find someone better than me? Someone whose muscles are more ripped? Whose apartment is more stylish? Who pays more for your living expenses? Who entertains your stupid dream of college education?" With another slap of his hand, my chair was toppled and with it, my velvet jacket.

I tried to get away from him. But I was too close to the wall.

"You have anything to say?"

He lifted his arm. I jolted. I stared at him, petrified and almost pinned to the wall as he stepped closer.

"What are you looking at?"

I felt his hot breath on my cheeks.

He had me up against the wall. "Do you have anything to say for yourself?" His forearm hit against my Adam's apple. The Scorpio tattoo about to sting my neck.

If I said anything, he'd get angrier. *Come on, Cliff. If you wanna kill me, do it already. I'm tired. Get this over with.*

"Say something," he yelled as he lifted his arm, my whole body brushed against the wall. His arms dug deeper into my neck.

I did cheat on you. I am as worthless as you think. I couldn't keep my man, nor the man I had a crush on. Nor any of the random ones. I'm so tired of all of this.

"Fight me. Tell me I'm wrong."

I couldn't breathe. My body was struggling to get in some air, my limbs moving in all directions, like a marionette under the hands of a demented puppeteer. My mind was determined to stay still. I defied the animal instinct to fight back. How long would it take for my lungs to give in? One minute? Two?

That is what Commander Aseel had seen in me. That is why he picked me. I was always a disgrace. Too willing to surrender to any man who wanted me. It's time to pay the price.

Cliff lifted his arm a bit higher. My feet no longer touched the floor. I was attached to the wall by the neck where his forearm applied more pressure than I thought my windpipe could take.

"What is wrong with you? Why don't you defend yourself? Kick me. Hit me. Say I'm wrong."

My face started to feel like a bowl of boiling water. I pressed my teeth together so that my mouth wouldn't open. I wanted to asphyxiate. Choke all the way until I couldn't breathe even if I wanted to.

Cliff, please. Don't back down now. Just a little bit more. See it through. Get rid of me once and for all. I don't wanna hurt any more.

"You're always pathetic like that. You can't even fight for your life. How would you fight for me?"

My jaw hurt from pressing my teeth together. They were about to crack. As much as I wanted to fight it, a gasp for air broke out of me with a heavy sound.

"Do something," Cliff shouted.

Don't give up, Cliff. It's gonna be over any moment now. How long does it take for the strangulation to freaking work?

I was losing control over my muscles. I pressed my feet against the wall so I wouldn't kick him. But I forgot to keep pressing my teeth together. My mouth opened, still desperate to breathe.

Just a little more. Let the Scorpio wrap its claws around my neck.

"You're not even worth it." He lifted his forearm.

My feet hit the floor. My body plummeted and folded in front of him. My hands involuntarily found their way around my throat as if to open up my windpipe.

"Little bitch." He picked up his keys and stormed out.

I drew in air like a drunk swimmer who had been pulled out of water. My face brushing against the carpet. I saw the velvet jacket on the floor a few feet away. If I had only landed on the soft velvet.

I didn't reach out for it. I wanted to feel the carpet coarseness into my skin. To feel the pain.

Vacillate

/ˈvæsəleɪt/ *verb*

The next morning, I found myself at Trilce's door. I had to delete Ty's number from my phone. Even though I'd saved it under a fake name. If Cliff had been monitoring my activity on the phone, this was the only way to escape his control. I knocked on the door and waited. Trilce opened the door, wearing a pair of slippers that had rabbit ears. "Abdul?" She stepped away so I could enter. "You look… Are you OK?" She was wearing a matching gray sweatshirt and pants.

I put my index finger on my nose, gesturing the "quiet" sign. I needed her to slow down with the questions. "Hope you haven't had breakfast yet. I brought bagels." I took off my jacket, my phone in its pocket. I rolled it up and asked her to put it in the bedroom, in case Cliff knew how to remotely activate the microphone.

"Cliff called me," she sat on the sofa. "He thanked me for keeping you company and being such a good friend."

"He's installed a tracking app on my phone. He might be listening or viewing my screen. He knows everything."

"Please tell me you were in the aquarium. You were meeting Tyrique there, right?"

"Shhh!" Even uttering his name could awaken the monster.

She reassured me. "Your jacket is in the closet in the bedroom. He can't hear us."

The bagels on the coffee table smelled good, but I had no appetite.

She continued, "I googled a picture of a turtle and sent it to him. And then I panicked that he might run a reverse image search and find the picture online. Does he know you're here?"

"Yeah. I said it's a Nawrouz tradition to visit friends. Which is true. Damn it, I should have said 'happy Nawrouz' when I came in. In case he's listening."

"What's Nawrouz? Never mind. Where did you guys go after the aquarium? If I were supposedly with you..."

"To an Indian restaurant. Maharaja."

"OK. Got it."

"It gets worse."

She raised an eyebrow and sat in silence.

"I was with somebody."

"What? Do you *want* Cliff to..." She exhaled noisily as if trying to calm down.

"He smelled like Ty. And he was... my birthday present."

"It was your birthday?" She raised her voice. "You're a crappy friend."

I looked at the bagels on the table. Too insignificant to point out. She was right. I'd had so much to tell her.

"Where was this? You know, if Cliff knows your GPS locations at all times."

"In a psychologist office above the food court."

"The one above H&M? Well, then on the tracker it would look like you were at H&M the whole time."

"What if he finds out what floor I was on?"

"I don't think trackers do that."

"But he knows how to do stuff. He could have hacked into the security cameras. He can…"

Trilce put her hand on mine. "Stop shaking," she pinned my hands to my lap.

I nodded, my foot now shaking.

"Is there something else you wanna tell me? Did something happen? Something more than a simple argument?"

I looked in her eyes. She knew. Ben had told her.

"He was gonna kill me last night. He choked me." My voice cracked. "I wish he had gone all the way."

"Damn it, Abdul," she slammed her hand on my knee. "This is so much worse than I thought."

"I'm so tired."

"You have options. You have friends. I'm…" She swallowed. "So sorry for not asking you earlier. Ben told me after the baking class. I was waiting to see you in person. I…" She gasped.

"I only cause pain for everybody around me," I whimpered.

"I'm here," she ignored me. "I have a big crazy Mexican family. We can hide you, protect you… do whatever it takes. I won't stand by and watch some asshole threaten your life." She paused. "Come. Let's make some coffee." She led me to the kitchen. The rabbit ears flapping up and down on her slippers. "Bring the bagels."

I followed her and sat at the table.

"You're already jittery. I'll make some green tea." She opened the faucet and filled the kettle. "You need to leave Cliff. He's bad news."

"He has a temper."

"Can you stop taking the enemy's side for a minute? Who's gonna take *your* side?"

After a period of silence, the kettle started to whistle. She got up and dropped a pinch of tea in the pot, then filled it with boiling water.

"When we're in public, I hold onto his arm or something to show him off."

"A pretty face isn't everything."

She poured two cups of tea. "You can leave him, Abdul. You can come and stay with me until you figure things out."

"Then he'll just show up here. He can get vindictive. He can have Ben fired."

"Ben's a big boy," he said as he entered the kitchen. "He can take care of himself." Ben was wearing only a pair of navy pajamas. He kissed Trilce on the cheek.

"I need my passport that he locked up in the safe," I continued. "And my SAT book and other stuff." He had confiscated my savings prior to H&M. As for the new balance in my account, his buddy used it up forcing me to pay for his shopping spree.

"Call the cops and say he took your stuff," she suggested.

"If I humiliate him like that, he'll have me killed. I'll have a car accident somewhere or a random guy will shank me on the street."

"He's not that gangster," Trilce countered. "Although, what do I know?"

Ben poured himself a cup of tea and stood by the table. He didn't object to not having coffee. Always going with the flow.

"You can't go on like this." Trilce concluded. "I don't wanna call the cops one day because you're hurt."

"Why are we calling the cops?" Ben asked.

"Cliff had yet another outburst last night," she explained.

Ben looked at me, as if checking for any wounds. "I'm sorry. You OK?"

I nodded. "We're not calling the cops."

"I know what you're saying," Ben replied.

"Here, come sit." Trilce offered him. "Abdul brought bagels and cream cheese. We're celebrating...?" She stared at me.

"New Year," I completed her sentence.

"Happy New Year, Abdul," Ben said. "We don't look too festive." He left the kitchen.

"I need time," I announced.

"If you're not leaving him soon, you need to change your behavior to stay safe," Trilce advised. "Don't reach out to Tyrique. Do you think you can stop… hanging out with other guys until you find a solution?"

"You think I'm a hoe?" I thought I'd break down at this question. But I had no more tears.

"I think you're unhappy. You can enjoy other men's company. I'm not a judgmental closed-minded lunatic. But…"

"I'm happy when I… explore."

"Maybe you need some time on your own. To detox."

"It's exciting when I can get someone to pay attention to me. To want me."

"And? After a few episodes? Do you realize you're desirable?"

"Maybe a little," I smiled. "It's so messed up. It's like my happiness triggers Cliff."

"It's not your behavior that triggers him. Abusers always want to project their rage onto others. As if it's you who's doing something wrong and not them."

"I *am* doing something wrong." I must have looked miserable, because she hugged me.

Ben returned, wearing a tan T-shirt and holding several Mardi Gras beads in his hand. "I thought we should look up to par to celebrate the new year." He put a few around her neck.

She adjusted her long hair.

"Thanks for celebrating your new year with us." Ben put a couple of beads around my neck.

"Who just had a birthday," Trilce chimed in.

"Oh wow. How old are you now?"

"Twenty-five."

Ben still had one necklace left.

"You have to put it on him," Trilce explained to me. "It shows that you think he's cute."

I did.

"Well, if a gay man approves, you got yourself a keeper, Ms. Salinas." Ben brought plates and opened the bag of bagels. "Not 'cute' though. I would say 'freaking hot.'"

"Always generous with compliments for himself," Trilce smiled and handed him a bagel. "And the birthday boy celebrated with a hot guy of his own, did he not?"

I felt embarrassed. Ben didn't know about my indiscretions.

"Who was he?"

"Just... some guy." I changed the topic, "I need to stick around and get my passport back. Cliff wants to move to New York. He will have to unlock the safe at some point," I reasoned.

"Do *you* wanna go to New York?" Ben wondered.

I didn't.

"Do you know when the company is gonna transfer him?" Trilce asked Ben.

"I'm not sure. In a couple of months, maybe?"

"That's too long," she concluded.

I looked down at my cup.

"Whatever you decide," Ben sat down, "you can count on us. We got you."

"He knows that," Trilce added softly. "You do, right?" She grabbed my hand to emphasize.

Redemption

/rɪˈdempʃn/ *noun*

The air in our apartment suffocated me. I had no one else to blame but myself. Giving in to infatuation, admiration, or lust, and cheating on Cliff. Worse still, I had betrayed who I used to be: a kind, loving, devoted boyfriend. A tiny attempt to atone for my sins as a child. A sign that I could be good. That on this corner of the world, living in a different culture, and forever cut off from my ancestral land and language, I could be worthy. That if I hadn't been fooled by Commander Aseel, I could still be a good son. Respectful of my father, loving toward my mother, and as always obedient to my older brother, whom I loved so much.

But he was right. Karim threw me out because he saw something in me that I hadn't yet realized. Even in that moment of rage and loss, he showed me mercy. He gave me a second chance. And I got everything I wanted. Yet, I failed to become worthy. I had evil in me. Why couldn't Cliff strangle me all the way, and get the job done once and for all? Pulling the last breath out of me.

My stomach wringed as if trying to free itself from its own acid that sizzled into my chest. I pushed a pillow into my belly.

A quick visit to Ty's website confirmed that he was still cleansing his soul from digital residues. The entire page gone now. All it said was: "Error 404, Page not found."

Perhaps I could try to write my own poem. I closed my eyes and sank into the pain that kept twisting. I went to the bedroom and took a pencil.

Once in a long while,
You discover a gem.
Do you not?
My nails are cracked
And fingertips colored by soil so
I can't see blood.
Searching, digging, despairing, and
Then digging more.
Should I admit defeat
Or make up excuses that
I'm covered in dirt?

My attempt at poetry seemed shallow and trite. It didn't have the complexity and beauty of Ty's writings. Nowhere close. It didn't truly express how I felt either. Despite the image, I didn't think that Ty, Alex, Derrick, and Esteban were somehow stained, tarnished. They treated me with respect and kindness. It wasn't their fault that I'd broken my commitment to my partner.

The poem was rubbish: in form and contents.

I tore off the page and crumpled it. The cracks in my soul were expanding into a full breakdown. I didn't know I could sob so woundedly.

I felt something on my shoulder. When I opened my eyes, Cliff was sitting on the bed next to me.

"Cliff," I hated how my voice sounded between the sobs.

He wiped the tears off my face. "Here," he gave me a glass of water.

I took a sip.

"Some more," he almost whispered.

The water diluted the evil in my belly. The pain abated.

He took the glass. "Come here, baby." He embraced me. My head on his shoulder. He was warm, strong, and protective. Why did I ever betray him? I bawled as he patted my hair. "It's OK," he said several times. Then he took my head in his hands and kissed my cheek, wiping the tears with his thumb.

"Cliff, I—"

"Shhh. Let me talk." He took a deep breath. "Abdul, I'm so sorry I lost it the other day. I shouldn't have acted like that."

A mixture of tears and mucus on my face. I wiped it with my sleeve.

"I totally lost it. I thought you were cheating on me. Mason said… I should've known better."

"I love you, Clifford." Saying his full name should show my sincerity. A hidden apology.

"You do?" He sounded so vulnerable.

There was still hope for us.

"Remember Mason's crazy joke? The picture of you in blackface? Well, it's gone. I made him take it down. He spent hours tracking it on other websites and asking them to take it down as well. I can't say it's one hundred percent deleted from the web, but most of them are. Maybe he accused you of… Maybe he was upset that I'd forced him to spend so much time on that. And he made up a lie to hurt you."

My tears subsided. "Thank you."

"I'm sorry. I will behave better from now on."

"Me too."

"I get so mad. I love you so much that I can't stand the thought of you even looking at another man. You're mine, Abdul."

"I don't want anybody else. All I need is you." I wasn't lying. I was ready to do anything to get him back. To prove I deserved the life we shared.

"I wouldn't get so jealous if I didn't love you."

"Yeah."

"Here, lay down." He moved the pillow and laid my head on it, cautious like I was the most precious thing he'd ever touched. "How was your day? Any crazy customers?"

"I don't deal with customers anymore. I'm in the stockroom."

"Really? They wanna hide this pretty face in the stockroom?"

"Customers act obnoxious sometimes." *Mason had.* "It's all good."

"You're right. If you're hidden away, there won't be a thousand guys hitting on my boyfriend every day."

"Nobody's hitting on me."

"They'd better not. Or I'll break their necks."

You almost broke mine. I had to change the subject before he heard the irony. "It's good to lay down. I'm so tired."

"Oh, little baby. Here. Take off your T-shirt. I'll give you a massage." He extended his hand and picked the essential oil from the nightstand, next to a large chain.

"What's that?"

"I brought in my bicycle from the storage room. That's the chain for the bike. We should ride some time."

"Isn't it cold?" I undressed.

Cliff gazed at me for a moment. "You're pretty."

I patted his thigh. "You're gorgeous."

"And always a flirt."

I lay down on my stomach. His hands felt warm and caring.

"That's why Mason hates you so much. You know that, right?"

"What?" I tried to get up, but Cliff pushed onto my back.

"You never flirted with him. The night we met. Mason saw you first. He wanted to ask you out."

"That's not true."

"Yes, it is. He came to me and showed you to me. We had a pact of not going after the same guy. Bros before hoes and all that. So we both came to you to see which one of us you liked."

"I don't remember him at all."

"Yeah. And that's the problem. You acted as if he didn't even exist. Like he was transparent." As he got more excited, he pushed harder onto my back. But it felt good. Like a professional massage. "You looked at *me*. You talked to *me*. You smiled at *me*. Mason tried hard to get your attention. But you did not even look at him. It was fun to watch."

"I only remember you. In that blue tank top, showing off a bit of chest hair. Your dog tag necklace. Your biceps that bulged as you gestured."

"That always works," he sounded triumphant.

"I couldn't believe that you showed any interest in me. No one had before."

"Their loss," he playfully spanked me. "And Mason's loss. I mean, he's not hot like *me*. But he's not bad-looking. He's short. But he couldn't even get a glance out of you. Obviously, he holds the grudge to this day."

I thought he hated me because I was with Cliff. Mason wanted to be with Cliff. "But didn't you say—"

"He'll have to let it go at some point," he interrupted. "It's not like he would've been your boyfriend. He sleeps around. Never had a serious relationship."

"He's a dick. No one wants to be with him."

"Damn, this whole story didn't make you feel any bit of compassion for the guy?"

"He calls me, 'Yo bitch.'"

"*I* call you that."

"You are my boyfriend. What you call me is between us. He's an outsider. He doesn't get to say the same things you do. Even you shouldn't call me that. What the hell?"

"I only say that when you act up."

"You just promised to do better."

"I know." He pressed both palms on my shoulders and lowered his body over mine. "I bet it sounds sexy if I say it right!" he whispered in my ear.

"Hmmm... Only when I'm in the mood," I corrected. "I can't wait to move to New York so we don't have to see the Malefic fellow." Although I would miss Trilce so much. And Ben. And Shane.

"He's still my best friend."

"I'll tolerate him for your sake... sometimes."

"You're so bossy tonight," he approved. "I like it. And see what you've done." He pressed his body onto me, his manhood fully awake. "I guess you're getting a massage with a happy ending."

I lifted my head. He gave me a deep kiss, his tongue warm and inviting.

"I always knew you never cheated on me," he said softly.

"Really?"

"You love me too much to do that. And," he put his mouth next to my ear. "You're still as tight as ever," he murmured.

My face got hot against the pillow. My anatomy concealed my transgressions. I hoped my mind would soon cover up the guilt I felt inside.

Volatile

/ˈvɑːlətaɪl/ *adj.*

The next idea Trilce came up with was a boxing class. She saw it on Groupon. Apparently, by mid-April, most people had forgotten about their New Year's resolutions to work out. So, gyms offered discounted classes to attract new members. She herself didn't have an interest, but Shane was willing to check out the scene. The two of us had workout clothes on, walking down the steps into a large basement with neon lights and hip-hop music.

"I hope our instructor is cute," Shane remarked.

"You're always on the lookout," I teased.

"I'd like to surround myself with beautiful things," he confessed.

Maybe I was one of them.

The space was cool and smelled like chemicals, possibly disinfectant combined with spray deodorants.

"Good morning, gents. My name is Roberto. You can call me Rob. And I'm gonna be your instructor today. We're going to go over how to wrap your hand and some basic safety instructions. Then we'll cover the stance, the jab, the one and the one-two, and the hook if we have time. It's gonna be around fifteen minutes of prep time and just about forty-five minutes of active workout. Any questions?"

With his soft baritone voice and attractive face, he wouldn't have any problems holding our attention. He explained that the wrap protected fragile wrist and metacarpal bones. This was necessary since the glove didn't have much to protect the hand, other than some foam cushioning.

Next came the stance. We were right-handed, so we stepped back with the right foot and placed it at an angle. Contrary to what I'd believed, he said the power came from the legs. We had to bend the knees slightly, stand at the right distance from the heavy bag, and punch with the left hand.

"In fighting, timing is everything. You need the element of surprise. With good timing, you can beat someone who's stronger than you and maybe has a better technique. Like you, my man." He went to Shane. "Are you punching with the beat? Your jab looks like it's synched with the music."

"Girl! I mean… sir, there's a whole ensemble of Meghan Trainer and Iggy Azalea in my head."

"There shouldn't be no real pause between your one and two. Your opponent shouldn't have the time to react. Let's see what your buddy is doing." He moved to me. "Good focus. If it helps, you can imagine hitting someone specific."

I jabbed the heavy bag.

"Who are you hitting?" Shane asked.

"I don't know," I replied. "A cop."

"That's a bit too on the nose," Roberto objected.

I lowered my elbows and punched again.

"Raise your hand. You had a good position."

I thought he told me not to hit it on the nose.

"You can picture you're fighting someone specific," he turned back to Shane. "Someone who did you wrong."

Maybe a policeman was too generic. It had to be more precise.

My foster family lived in Philadelphia. I was in high school for some time until the bullying became intolerable. After I dropped out, but before aging out of the awful fostering situation, I worked at a gas station. The bullies soon found me and started visiting.

One day Kara showed up. The gas station offered car washes that were entirely manual. She wanted a car wash. I cleaned her car and vacuumed it. She refused to pay, claiming she had cash on the dashboard that was now missing.

We started arguing. I only wanted her to pay for the service. She accused me of theft. An African American teenager who was passing by saw her yelling at me and asked if everything was all right. Kara went ballistic. "If you don't get the hell out of here, I will call the cops. We both know what can happen when the cops catch someone like you." The smirk on her face made her the ugliest sight I'd ever seen.

The guy left. She still called the cops: Officer Blue Eyes.

I hit the bag, thinking of him. Pow! His cap would fall on the ground.

He banged me against the wall, legs spread, hands over head.

Pow!

He searched me so roughly I thought he'd been trained as a torturer in one of those clandestine secret prisons. He pulled out a couple of singles out of my pocket.

Pow!

Kara said she found the money. I'd never forget her face as Officer Blue Eyes escorted her to the car and asked if she felt safe enough to drive alone.

Po-po-pow!

"Now *that's* the hook," Roberto announced enthusiastically, bringing me back to the gym.

"Jeez! Remind me to never get on your bad side!" Shane was also watching me. "You look like an assassin right now."

"Good job," the instructor approved. Then he turned to Shane, "See, you can also put more force into the jab. Your feet can propel your body forward, so all the kinetic energy ends up in your punch."

"I kinda feel bad for the heavy bag," Shane said, still looking at me.

"I'm punching a specific cop," I said, jabbing a one one two.

"Get out that anger, girl!" My friend egged me on.

The instructor covered his mouth to hide his laugh.

Shane laughed too. "Right?"

"You're doing good," he endorsed my technique.

Acrimonious

/ˌækrɪˈmoʊniəs/ *adj.*

Perhaps the SAT book was mocking me with the word "acrimonious." It was almost May, and I didn't feel any more prepared to take the test than I did last year. Maybe I should check my Facebook. I opened the app and saw the video of a cat trying to catch a cardinal behind a window. I clicked on the account and un-liked the page. *How many cat videos can I watch?* Ben had shared a story that the police officer implicated in the Mosher shooting case had his charges reduced to involuntary manslaughter.

I looked at the article. The autopsy showed traces of marijuana in the deceased teenager's body. The police officer's lawyers claimed it proved that he had reason to suspect the guy of drug trafficking. How can these people sleep at night? I'd be ashamed of ever showing my face in public again if I made ridiculous claims like that.

I checked Ty's webpage. More than a month later, it still had the same digital cleanse "Error 404" message. White letters on a black background, an unusual font, so you knew the error was intentional. A poetic nod. Even in his absence,

Ty was creative. It wasn't my fault that I was intrigued. Infatuated. Another word that mocked me.

"I'm making some decaf. You want some." Cliff treated me with so much care, ever since the choking episode.

"Yes, please. I'd love that."

"Your wish is my command, my lord." He touched the side of his imaginary top hat and bowed.

My phone lit up. It was Trilce. "You saw the news? They downgraded the charges."

"I know," I texted back. "It makes me so angry that I'm thinking of picking a fight with Cliff."

"Don't do that," she replied.

"Here you are, my lord." Cliff gave me a cup.

I couldn't move.

"What?"

"You saw they lowered the charges against the killer cop?"

"Oh that? Yeah. I thought something was wrong with you."

"I hate this."

He sat next to me. "Drink."

I did.

"Was he a drug dealer?"

Moments like these made me want to punch him with all my strength. In that sense, I wasn't any better than Cliff with his violent outbursts. If not for my promise to Ty, I would have. What could I say to that? That not every Black man was a drug dealer? He would reply he already knew that. Or if he thought, my statement somehow accused him of racism, he might treat me with a good slap of his own. *He* hadn't made a promise to be peaceful.

"Look. They're following the process," he pointed out.

Which law enforcement process has ever led to justice? I didn't voice my opinion. His hand on my shoulder expressed concern and kindness. I didn't want to change that. His hand could express other emotions too.

"You have a soft spot for drug dealers. I wonder if it's because you have this bad boy fantasy. You probably knew a lot of drug dealers in Afghanistan. Isn't like ninety percent of the world's opium coming from there?"

"I grew up in Iran." Most of what Cliff imagined about me was false. But I was the one who evaded most of his questions until he gave up asking. It wasn't his fault.

"Still. You lived in Afghanistan for a few years. My baby is so kind." He kissed me. "I can be your bad boy myself."

"You gonna be a drug dealer too?"

"If it makes you love me more," he winked.

I wanted to fend off any accusations that I didn't love him enough. "That's not possible." It sounded flirtatious. I didn't mean it to be.

"Come on. Cheer up. You look like your mother just died."

"I wouldn't know if anything did happen to her."

Sometimes things like that just came out of my mouth. Cliff was in a weird position because any hyperbolic disaster might have in fact happened to me at some point in my life. He probably thought he was constantly walking on eggshells with me.

"I love you." He put his hand on my lap. "Sometimes I wish I could take away all of your sorrow."

"It's OK to hurt sometimes."

"I know you hate Mason. But if you ever consider smoking, Mason can get you some top-notch weed. It'll relax you."

I didn't know how he couldn't see the irony of our dialogue just now. In addition to pot, Mason also took pills when we went out clubbing. I would not trust anything he gave me. "I don't need any substance to relax."

"Come on," he rubbed my thigh. "Smile for me. I know of a certain something that always cheers you up."

"I don't feel like it." I didn't know if he meant sex or a Bollywood movie. I wasn't in the mood for either.

"How can I make you feel better?"

"Just hold me."

"Come." He did as I told him. He put his arm around me, his hand softly roaming on my arm.

Like two doves cooing, I rested my head on his shoulder.

He kissed my hair. "You're so fragile. I'm here. You're safe." He wrapped his other hand around me, enveloping me in a blanket of safety.

I pressed my body onto his.

"We can watch something. Oh, I know. One of those dog movies where the dog dies in the end. Hell, I'll be crying even louder than you. Awo awo," he imitated a baby crying.

He made me laugh.

"That's what I'm talking about. Why would you wanna deprive me of that? Those dimples."

The idea of him needing my laughter made me chuckle even more.

My phone lit up. Probably Trilce saw another update on the case. I hugged Cliff and closed my eyes, waiting for him to find a movie. To take my mind off the news.

Forlorn

/fer'bːrn/ *adj.*

Trilce was filling out the J in her protest sign. Mine differed from hers and consisted of only two words that expressed all I wanted to say: "dignity, humanity."

"Thanks for getting the supplies," Trilce moved on to the U in "justice."

"Sure," I answered.

We'd planned to join the rally in opposition to reduce the charges against the policeman from second degree murder to involuntary manslaughter. His body camera had magically stopped functioning right before the fatal shooting, in what many locals believed was evidence tampering by the police. We suspected the police had destroyed their evidence of guilt. Then, the police claimed that the charges should be reduced because the evidence was widely believed to have been altered. Basically, they altered the evidence and then used that as an excuse to lower the charges. The trial would start on Monday.

"Pass me the red marker."

I did.

"I hate how they're trying to play both sides. If it could exonerate the cop, why did it go missing all of a sudden? The footage was in their custody."

"Initially they didn't want to release it at all. Protesters forced their hand," I objected, remembering Derrick going to a rally for this. Not that I expected any rhyme or reason. Breathing would be a crime if the cops decided so. "I hate cops," I reminded her as if she didn't already know. "They're always the worst. In all three countries I lived in."

She tucked her hair behind her ear and continued making the sign.

I needed to ask her something. She'd tell me the truth. That would also be a break from thinking of the latest police killing. "Trilce?"

"Tell me."

I inhaled, hesitated. "Do you think I should leave Cliff?"

"I thought that was already decided. Didn't you say you just wanted your passport? What's changed?" She had no patience for indecision.

"He can be so loving sometimes. He gave me a back rub the other day. Watched a movie with me. Unlike me, he's been loyal this whole time."

"And made you miss a wedding that really mattered to you. And let's not forget that he almost choked you to death. Don't you think you deserve better?"

My sign was finished. "I did cheat on him. Several times." I wondered if I could survive Cliff's anger if he ever found out.

"Because you're unhappy with him."

"I love him," I proclaimed. "Sometimes," I corrected myself.

She took a deep breath. "What's changed since your new year?"

I shook my head, "Not much."

"You're in constant fear."

Biting my lips, I started to fill in the letters of my sign a bit more. "I just want to know for sure that I have a chance with Ty."

"Does he have a gun?" She refused to let go.

I swallowed. "I'm not sure. I've never seen one."

"You need to get out. And you don't have to rush into another relationship. You can be single. Didn't you say you were happy to explore?"

"Yeah. But what if Ty is the one? I don't wanna lose him just because I wanna try other things. I had several other experiences, but I don't think about any of them the way I think about Ty. I think he feels the same. He reached out to me, saying he couldn't stop thinking about me."

"If he loves you so much, he will wait for you."

Maybe. "I had one-night stands. But… If I should lose Cliff, I want to be sure I won't be alone for the rest of my life."

"You want life to give you a guarantee?" She made it sound ridiculous. "I'm pretty sure I can convince Tyrique not to get serious with anyone for a year. Until you're ready."

I looked up at her. "I bet you can."

She chuckled. "If I can persuade two gay guys to take a boxing class, I can convince anyone of anything."

"That was actually fun."

"I'm telling you. Good things happen when you listen to me." After a short pause, she opened her mouth to say something, but I preempted her.

"Please don't push. I'm still processing."

"Fine," she gave in. "But take your passport out of his safe."

Ben opened the apartment door and came in. "Hey guys."

"Hi honey," Trilce got up.

He put the enlarged picture of the guy on the floor and went back outside. Probably he had more things to carry up the stairs.

"He was so young," I stared at the picture. "It could have been me." I thought of Officer Blue Eyes who roughed me up at the gas station.

"Yeah," she sounded doubtful.

We looked at each other, asserting silently that he looked most like Ben. It could have been Ben. The thought frightened me more. I could sense she was worried about it too. *He just left the apartment again. What if he doesn't come back?*

I imagined my mom would have been worried about me every time I left the house in Bamiyan. When Commander Aseel took me.

Ben entered with some long sticks in his hand. They looked like the ones from Home Depot you mix paint with. "You guys OK? I sense a weird energy."

"We're worried," she replied. "And sad."

"Yeah."

"I'll make some green tea." She got up.

"Thanks."

"You need any help?" I offered.

"I got it." She hugged her boyfriend on the way to the kitchen.

I didn't know what to say. That no one should be treated this way? This was so messed up. To be so easily detectable because of your skin color.

Gays can try hard and blend in. To pass. But you can't do that if anyone can just look at you and know. Hazaras also stand out because of the way we look. A similar phenomenon in a vastly different setting. Can't America do better than Afghanistan? A country torn apart by decades of war and never-ending foreign interventions? Is evil so intrinsic to human nature we can't restrain it?

"Abdul," Ben interrupted my thoughts.

I forced a smile.

"I need to talk to you."

"Of course," I motioned to get up.

"Sit, sit. Continue." He sat next to me on the couch. "Abdul, I need to apologize."

I didn't expect that. "For what?"

"The day we first met. I came to your apartment with Mason and Cliff."

I remembered every detail about that evening.

"I should have stood up for you."

Embarrassed, I covered my face with my hands.

"Please don't be ashamed. If anyone must be ashamed, it's me."

"No, no," I objected.

"Please. Let me finish."

I was happy that I didn't have to say anything.

"I should have stopped them. They were so rude to you. But… Honestly, I didn't know what to do. I'd never been in that type of situation before."

At least, he didn't use the dreaded phrase, "survivor of domestic violence." I'd had it with these labels.

"I didn't know if it was my place to get involved," Ben continued. "And I didn't want to agitate Cliff. I was afraid he could get me fired," he shook his head. "I'm not afraid anymore. I know these are lame excuses. And I'm sorry." He looked at my sign. "Abdul, you should also recognize your own dignity and humanity. You have to take control of the situation. And you *know* Trilce and I are with you no matter what. I'm sorry I didn't have the guts to intervene when I should have."

I paused for a moment. "Thanks, Ben. For saying this and for telling them to stop the day we met. You did interrupt the tension. I know Cliff. He demands that I treat him with upmost respect, particularly in front of other people. If you'd been any more forceful, he *would have* had you fired. And he would have gotten more violent with me for causing him to lose a colleague."

"I mean it, Abdul. Whatever you decide to do, we got your back."

Trilce was still busy with tea. I could hear the opening and closing of cabinets. Either, she had the best timing, or she meant to leave us alone to finish our conversation.

"Cliff can have outbursts," I admitted. "But if you'd confronted him, it would've gotten worse. Plus, Mason does drugs. Pot. Pills. I don't know what they are, but sometimes his hands shake. I wouldn't put it past them to plant it on you and then call the cops. And if *they* don't frame you, the police can."

"OK. Good to know. But I won't go down without a fight."

"As long as the police don't get involved." I nodded. "Thanks for having my back."

"You got it."

"Tea's brewing," Trilce deemed it appropriate to enter.

He stretched, laid his head on the backrest of the sofa, and closed his eyes.

Within the hour, we drank tea, taped the sticks to the back of our signs, and joined the protest in front of the Western District Police Station. Someone was talking over a microphone about police brutality and their disregard for human life. Trilce and Ben walked closer to the speaker, away from me.

As I looked at them, I noticed a pair of small feet. A boy, around the age of ten, was carrying a cardboard sign that said "Stop Killing Us." He smiled at me.

I felt my chest implode. A cloak of sadness descended on me. I shuddered.

Trilce grabbed my shoulder as she stood next to me. She whispered, "Do not lose it in front of the kid. Keep it together." She said loudly to the boy, "That's a good sign you got. It's terrible that it's necessary to say that."

"I know," the boy replied.

I waved at him. Trilce directed me to walk away before I broke down.

"I think it's time for us to go home," she announced.

Ben gave me a questioning look. I guess he could see it in my face.

"I'm sorry." Of all the protestors there, I was the least entitled to feel upset. Still, I couldn't pretend to be strong for much longer.

"Yeah," Ben replied. "Let's go home."

Ablaze

/əˈbleɪz/ adj.

Since the beginning of the trial, the city witnessed two weeks of tense protests. Last Friday, the jury started deliberating, and the protests intensified. Every day, more and more cops appeared on the streets. Some reporters speculated that the jury may continue to deliberate through the following week, delaying the verdict until after Memorial Day.

Over the weekend, someone broke a window of a GAP store, a block away from our H&M branch. My manager, Phillip, panicked and closed up early. The police could shoot and kill civilians with impunity, but God forbid a shop window got broken. At work, my colleagues didn't avoid me as much. They probably had seen the recanting of the blackface picture.

Cliff casually told me not to go to the protests anymore. I knew right away that I wouldn't submit to this command. On personal matters, I listened to him. He had the right to tell me how to behave to conform to the American way of life. Most of the time, I loved him and trusted he had my best interests in mind. He'd allowed me to move in with him and helped me find my first good job at the Patapsco Fleet Inn. When he told me not to do something, I'd follow his advice. I had to sometimes compromise. If he thought college was a waste of money, I had to contemplate whether he was right. I couldn't afford it on my own. He had the right to make these decisions.

But when it came to the social conditions that were inherently unjust, I wasn't ready to blindly comply with his directions. I had to stand up for something. It wasn't a crazy idea. So many people did the same. Trilce and Ben went to the protests. Why couldn't I? My boyfriend didn't understand how much I despised the police.

Monday, I was supposed to be off at eight. But the verdict came in the afternoon: the officer was acquitted of all charges. It took the jury only a few hours to make a decision. Fearing heavy protests, Phillip decided to close at six and let us go home without the usual cleanup. I left the store with my colleagues Whitney and Vaughn.

He asked, "Are you guys going to the protest?"

"I'm going home," Whitney replied. "I don't wanna get tear gassed tonight."

I chimed in and said, "If a terrorist is Muslim, the media goes to every Muslim in the country, asking them to condemn the violence. But since our terrorists are cops, everybody's off the hook."

They both stared at me, taken aback.

I had never talked about social issues at work. After the photo incident, nobody wanted to talk to me anyway. "Sorry. I was just ranting."

Vaughn wanted to join his friends at one of the protests. According to him, the police had been pepper spraying and tear gassing children near Union Square Park. They had organized a rally after school. Instead of covering instances of police attacks on high school kids, all major media outlets zeroed in on a 7-Eleven that was burning. As expected, they started talking about "riots" and "looting." *Surprise, surprise. American media doesn't only suck at covering the war in my home country. They suck at reporting on events here too.*

I accompanied Vaughn for a little bit. But before long, we separated to go our own way. I texted Trilce. She said there had been clashes between the police and the protestors. She and Ben had decided to stay home this evening. Then, I texted Cliff, saying that on my way home, I got stuck in the crowd. He didn't offer to give me a ride. He was working on a presentation for an important meeting tomorrow. I passed police officers at every intersection. Where had they all come from? Did Baltimore always have this many cops? Some were in riot gear as if we were armed criminals.

Unsure of how to find a protest that the police weren't teargassing at the moment, I started checking Facebook and Twitter to look for ideas. I checked one of the hashtags and saw something that made my chest freeze: tweets from Tyrique's account. He was back online, and he was in Baltimore. He was witnessing and documenting the protests.

About an hour ago, he had tweeted, "Aside from fire in one 7-Eleven store, this is going on elsewhere. #Baltimore." The picture showed a group of protestors, walking down the street. Nothing unusual about it. I couldn't see a street sign or any other indicator to help me identify its location, where I could find Ty.

I read his next tweet. "Our media and politicians are quick to condemn the unlawful conduct of a few protestors this afternoon. Yet they choose to be silent about the unlawful behavior of BPD for decades."

I looked up from my phone, ensuring I didn't accidentally J-walk to give the riot police an excuse for pinning me to the ground.

How could I find Tyrique? Most protests were taking place in West Baltimore. It took me a long time to locate the all-important 7-Eleven. It was right on Penn North, where chaos reigned. Ty was in a calm area. Would that be near the Western District Police Station? I decided to walk against the traffic on Pratt until Mount Street and then turn right. This way, I could put my phone aside and walk mostly in a straight line. It would take me at least an hour to get to the police station. I passed by luxury apartment buildings and rows of beautiful townhouses. The Railroad Museum looked enticing. But as I walked on, slowly the houses looked smaller and less well-kept. The police presence got heavier. Once I crossed Calhoun, more and more windows were boarded up.

I checked my phone again to see how much longer I had before reaching Mount. I didn't see a new tweet from Ty. But something he had tweeted earlier in the day attracted my attention. "A white congressman from #Baltimore just compared protestors to Al Qaeda. #Shame. Meanwhile, a teenager was beaten unconscious by police." The rich and powerful were already expanding their definition to fit in more and more people under the umbrella they called "terrorists." If I got arrested, a simple look at my place of birth would be sufficient to label me as such. But now, I guessed all protestors were terrorists, so it didn't really matter.

I saw a shiny Honda parked in front of a dilapidated building with a boarded-up door and windows. The next building was a well-decorated real estate office. What a strange neighborhood.

Finally, I reached Mount Street and started walking north. I passed a church.

"Go home," a middle-aged man told me.

"Yeah. I am."

He looked at me like he knew I was lying but didn't say anything else. I increased my pace. I saw a helicopter fly above me, eastbound. From the next block, I could see smoke coming from that direction. The street was empty. A couple of buildings on both sides were entirely boarded up. One had its windows and doors shut by cinder blocks that were painted blue. I felt slightly unsafe, and I hated myself for it. I saw a nice building: another church. Of course, I was safe. What could happen in front of a church?

I kept walking. I blinked my eyes to see if I was seeing right. A building was missing its roof. My eyes were dry and itchy due to the teargas that hung in the air here. I heard sirens in the distance. Was I pathetic for trying to find Tyrique in these conditions? I had tainted intentions: I wanted to participate in the protests, but I also wanted to see Ty. Yes, I was pathetic.

I passed two armored vehicles. They looked more like army than the police. It looked like an entire row of townhouses were abandoned and boarded up. A couple of teenagers were coming in my direction but acted as if I were invisible. Another chopper could be heard from afar. I saw a street sign that said, "W. Lafayette Ave." I recognized the name, so I had to be close to the police station. A convenience store on the side was already closed.

"You can't go this way," a police officer yelled at me.

"But I—"

"You can't go this way," he yelled so loudly that I trembled.

"I'm going this way," I pointed toward the police station.

"Do you wanna get tasered, boy?" He mocked me. He was younger than me. But he had a gun, so *I* was "the boy" in this encounter.

I turned back and checked my phone, now in low power mode. I saw another tweet from Ty: "Media complains that the events on the streets tonight distract from the real message. Yet, they focus solely on the distraction. #Gaslighting #Baltimore."

Come on, Ty. Where are you?

The sky was getting dark. My eyes were burning. I could only imagine how much they'd hurt if I got actually teargassed. Not something I wanted to experience.

Tyrique tweeted, "Community leaders are strategizing on how to safely get the kids home tonight." *Where,* I wanted to shout at my phone. I enlarged the picture and saw a white, brick building with arched windows. It seemed like a church. I began searching for churches in the vicinity. After a few minutes, I located the church in question: Saint James Episcopal. I walked east toward Fremont. The air smelled like gasoline fire and rubber smoke.

"There's a police car on fire," a guy was telling someone else. "Up the street."

That's exactly where Ty would not *be.* He just tweeted, "Talking heads say the police are watching criminal activity without interference. And they trumpet unqualified praise for the police. The issue of police brutality is not even talked about anymore."

It was getting darker. I had been walking for two hours. My throat burned and my eyes itched. Occasionally, I could hear things being thrown, perhaps rocks.

I refreshed the page. My phone battery was now at two percent. A new tweet simply said, "#Baltimore." Attached was a picture of a few men in suits walking on the street. In the background, I could see a red building, a yellow bin in front of it. I had just passed by the same building. The bin was a clothes donation box. I started running back in the same direction I had come from.

Perdition

/pɜːrˈdɪʃn/ noun

I saw a group of protesters down the street. As I approached, I could see some of them were wearing suits. Someone was taking pictures with his phone. I ran closer, my heart pumping as though trying to punch its way out of my ribcage. I moved to the sidewalk so I could see their faces easily. There he was.

"Ty?" I tried not to sound too excited.

He didn't hear me. I called out his name again.

He stared at me for a second. "Abdul Ali?"

Why did he use my full name? Were these guys from the Nation of Islam? Maybe Ty wanted to point out my background. Or was he subtly objecting that I called him by a shortened name?

"What are you doing here?"

My tongue felt like it was glued to my mouth. My whole body solidified like a pile of rubble. I had been so desperate to find him that I forgot to plan what I was going to say. He could see the desperation in my face. He looked annoyed. I had clearly bothered him, and he wanted me gone.

"I was in the protest," I managed to say.

"Go home, Abdul," he instructed.

I had interrupted his journalism, covering the protest. But after all this effort to find him, I wasn't ready to leave. "Tyrique?"

He looked even more impatient.

"I need to talk to you," I begged.

"Abdul," he shook his head. "Go home. Things are tense right now. This is not the time, OK? You can't be here."

I stared at him without any idea what to do next.

"Go home, Abdul." He turned around and walked away.

I was frozen and couldn't move, petrified out of pain. But I forced my feet to move, without looking back. The smell of burning rubber made it difficult to breathe. My eyes hurt. I blinked. The tears were so big that they felt like hail, hitting my face. The streetlights looked blurry as if I had taken off a pair of prescription glasses. The elongated shape of the lights would change as my tears flowed. I was in emotional pain, but the tears were chemically induced. The police used teargas to compel the crowds to disperse. I walked, no longer knowing where I was, and where I was going.

Tyrique wanted nothing to do with me. Like a pitiful loser, I had turned a protest about social justice into a deplorable attempt to find love. And a tragic attempt at that. I walked into a random street in the opposite direction of the protesters.

"Milk can help," someone told me.

I looked at her.

"You've been teargassed, right?" she continued. "Wash your eyes with milk. That'll help."

I shook my head and kept walking. Tyrique had no respect for me. No interest in me. No feeling. Nothing.

Nobody wanted me. I checked my phone to see how to get home. It was dead.

I should have known he wanted nothing to do with me. He was kind at our dinner together. I had to learn the difference between love and kindness. I'd thought Commander Aseel was kind. But he didn't want *me* either. He just wanted a... After all these years, I still didn't know if he'd picked me because he knew I was gay. Or if I *became* gay because he'd picked me. I wanted my heart to ache. I wanted to feel the pain, let it envelop me. I was no longer afraid of it. The worst had already happened.

All of a sudden, I was fourteen again. I'd had a hard life, but that particular day left the deepest cut in my soul. It had since gotten infected. And it reeked. I had to live with it, knowing it was my fault that my father died. And if we did have to pay for our mistakes, then I deserved the beatings and the humiliation I got from Cliff. I deserved much worse.

Sometimes I wished my father hadn't saved me. Did he regret it before he died? A death I'd caused. I wondered if his soul regretted it now, knowing my daily existence brought shame to his name. A name that I should be passing over to my son. To show to my descendants that my father's sacrifice had been worth it. Now, all hope of keeping our name alive rested on my brother. And he would never speak a word to me again. I understood. That day I took his father too. His protector too. I'd never found out how Karim lived, how he made a living to provide for my mom and sister. And his own wife and kids. He probably had a son by now, who would bear our name. The name I had dishonored.

I was only fourteen. We'd just returned from Iran. Despite what my parents had told me about Bamiyan, it still felt completely unfamiliar to me. My dad and brother worked in a *khochalo* farm. But my mom, always overprotective, thought the work was too hard for me. So, I sold random items on the street. That day, I was selling matchboxes, or at least trying to. I hated hawking at the intersection. The fume from the cars bothered me. As they drove on the unpaved road, they unsettled the dust on the ground. I wished I could go to the mountains and breathe the fresh air. By noon, I still hadn't made enough money to even get something to eat. I decided to take a break. I walked to an open area with a few half-dead trees. There, farmers parked their trucks, out of which they sold cantaloupes, watermelons, and vegetables. I sat on an upside-down bucket and looked down at my feet. My *kalawsh* were dirty from the dust. My *pero-tanbo* was probably just as dusty, though it wasn't visible on the gray material. I took out the matchbox with the nicest picture, my favorite. A quail on a red background. I would sell it last. Then I saw an ant on the ground. It changed directions several times. It would climb my foot a little and then headed back to the ground. I didn't notice two bigger boys showed up behind me. Threatening boys always showed up in pairs to easily overpower me.

"Why don't you just kill it?"

"Waiting for it to climb your leg and bite your ass before you do anything?"

If I ignored them long enough, they would go. I didn't want to get beaten up. So, I kept my head down and remained silent. Nothing I hadn't experienced before. But I put the matchbox back into the plastic bag before they noticed that I was looking at the colorful picture.

"He doesn't wanna be cruel!" The first boy mocked me. A few days ago, I'd made the mistake of asking him not to kill a sparrow. "Don't be cruel," I was stupid enough to say. Now they used that against me. "He has a tender heart, you see," he snickered.

"What a tender boy," the other said as he stepped on the ant. I saw from the corner of my eyes that someone was approaching. A man in uniform. Hopefully, he'd chase them away if they harassed me too much. Adults could scare off the bullies if they chose to. That was why I always tried to be in public.

"Look at me when I'm speaking to you." The second boy interrupted my hopeful thoughts. He put his foot on a rock next to me, on top of the extra fabric of my loose pants. "Didn't your father teach you any respect?" He grabbed my chin and lifted it, so I had to look him in the eyes.

"Be gentle. He's a shy boy, you see," the other one laughed.

"Shy and tender. Like a girl." The first one slapped me on the cheek.

"What's going on here?" The man approached us. He was wearing a dark green uniform and carried a Kalashnikov.

The second boy lifted his foot, leaving dust stains on my pants. "Commander, good afternoon. How are you doing?"

"Hello."

"Commander, buy some pastries. I have fresh pastries. Sweet and tasty."

"Commander, buy some gum," asked the first boy.

"What pastries you got?"

"Rice cookies, Commander. My mother baked it herself. It's as fresh as morning dew."

"How much?"

"For you, I'll make a good discount."

"Give me a few."

"Yes, Commander. I can give you all. They're very good. With pistachios."

"Boy, I don't need them all. Give me three."

"Yes, Commander. I'm at your service. Anything you want." He handed him three cookies.

The man pulled out a stack of money from his pocket and gave some to the guy.

"What do you sell?" He asked me.

"He sells nothing, Commander. But I have chewing gum. All flavors. Very tasty," said the first one.

"Be quiet. I don't need gum." He turned to me again. "What do you sell?"

I reached into my plastic bag and showed him a matchbox.

The man sat next to me. "Good. I'd just ran out of matches." Then he looked at the other boys and gestured with his hand. "You two, get outta here."

"If you want anything, just come to me," the second teenager said. "I can bring you anything. I sell at a good price." He pulled on the first guy's sleeve and they both walked away.

"Are you gonna give me a matchbox or what?"

I gave him the one in my hand. He pulled out a cigarette and lit it. "Are the cookies any good?"

I looked at him and shrugged.

"What, they're not your friends?"

I shook my head.

"Not much of a talker, are you?" He took a bite.

I noticed his white teeth.

He didn't look like some old, scary army commander. His mustache and beard were trimmed, and his hair had a buzz-cut. And he had dismissed my tormentors. He also looked younger than most commanders. I guessed he was probably in his late twenties.

"You stare, boy. Nobody taught you manners?"

I looked down. He was wearing black boots. Not sandals like some soldiers.

"You hungry?"

I didn't respond.

"Here." He gave me his half-eaten cookie. I hesitated and then grabbed it with such an urgency that embarrassed me. I took a bite, and then another. Before I knew it, the whole thing was gone.

"I saw the boys bothering you. I got rid of them for you… Still hungry?"

I nodded. He gave me another cookie. I wondered how I could thank him. I thought for a second and then I looked into my plastic bag and found the matchbox with the picture of the quail. I gave it to him. "Take this one, Commander. It's better."

He took it. "How is this better?"

"It has a colorful picture." I smiled and then looked down.

"You're a good boy. But if you get harassed a lot, you need someone to protect you."

I was too naïve to know what he meant.

"You have a weird accent. Where are you from?"

"My family just came from Mashhad. But we're from here."

"Ah, born in Iran?" he concluded. It made sense to him now. "I can tell you're different from the other boys." He puffed on his cigarette. "You're kind. That's good. But it also means you need a man to ensure other boys don't hurt you. There is a war going on and people think kindness is weakness. But I have fought enough battles to know kindness is good."

I nodded and smiled again. He saw the goodness in me.

"You kinda cute too," he rubbed his chin.

I bit my lower lip.

"What's your name?"

"Abdul Ali."

"Nice name too. I'm Aseel."

I bowed my head.

"Tell me Abdul, how much you make, selling matchboxes."

It took me a moment to calculate.

"Can't be much. You should get tired, walking on the streets the whole day."

"It's not that bad."

"And the boys beating you up for... having a tender heart."

He picked on the one thing I feared the most: being discovered. I liked other boys and they hated me for it. But even at that moment, I liked Commander Aseel.

"And beating is not even the worst thing they can do to boys like you."

How did he know this?

"I've been looking for an apprentice. Someone who can help out around the house. Make tea and stuff. Can you make tea?"

I nodded.

"And I'll make sure you don't go hungry. I have money. I can take care of you. Is your father alive?"

"Yes, sir."

"The money I give him will make a big difference. He wouldn't have to work so hard. You do want to help your family, don't you?"

Of course, I wanted to help my family. I had already let down my father by not working at the farm. I wanted to prove that I could be useful, like Karim.

"You'll make your father proud. I will pay him well. What do you say?"

I didn't know how to answer.

"Plus, work is not all we do. We also have fun. We have music, we dance. You like to dance, don't you?" He looked at the matchbox in his hand, with the picture of the quail on the red background. "I see you like red. I have a nice red shirt for you. It has gold trimmings. It would look great on you. You're kinda cute."

I loved how he was so nice to me.

"I have a boy, as beautiful as the moon. I've already had him for a year. If it was bad, he wouldn't stay so long, would he? I'll be around to make sure nobody bothers you. You want me to protect you, don't you?"

Commander Aseel put his hand on my lap. His grip was masculine yet kind. Then he threw his cigarette butt on the ground and stood up. He bit the last cookie he had.

"The cookie is good." He walked away towards his pick-up truck. He opened the door and looked back at me. "You coming?"

I followed him.

"Good boy," he smiled.

His boy was about the same age as me. He looked stunning. Light brown hair, green eyes, and full eyelashes. I found it strange that his foot was chained to the bed.

Aseel showed me a lot of affection. He put some kuhl on me and let me wear the red long shirt with gold trimmings. Better yet, he gave me gold pants that matched the long shirt. He put anklets on my feet. They had bells that jiggled when I walked. That would sound nice if I danced. He kissed my cheek and patted my hair. We had rice and meat for dinner that night. I hadn't had so much food in a long time. But I was worried about my mom. He said he had his men go to my house and give my father some money. I would see him on the weekend, he said.

Even now when I was walking on random streets of Baltimore, my stomach churned when I thought about that fateful night. Even Aseel didn't find me attractive enough to take me to his room. At fourteen, I had no idea what he wanted to do. I was curious and I liked him. But he already had a boy in his room. I was there to be the house servant. That was the lie he told me. As much as it made me sick now, I felt jealous that he didn't want me.

Later that same night, I took off the anklets, but left the gold pants on. I wore my regular clothes on top of it.

I woke up in the middle of the night with someone banging on the door. Aseel got really upset. My dad, uncle, and brother stood at the doorway.

My dad yelled, "What do you want with my son?"

Aseel repeated that he wanted me as an apprentice and had already paid him my wage. My dad kept yelling and he called him a bad name. I wanted to tell my dad that Aseel hadn't done anything. I'd only been there for a few hours. What could he do in such a short time? But no one could hear me in the middle of the commotion. My dad was very upset and told me to get into his car. I didn't know why he was so angry. I obeyed, flustered about the argument. But in my haste, I tripped and fell down. Karim saw me wearing the gold pants under my clothes. If he had any doubts that I was gay, he didn't anymore. I was afraid he'd tell on me when we got home.

My father pushed Aseel and called him bad names. Meanwhile, Karim grabbed my hand and dragged me to the front door and onto the back of the pickup truck. My uncle ran to the driver's seat.

The next thing I knew, Aseel shot my father in the chest. He fell on the ground. My uncle turned on the engine and drove so fast that my brother and I fell on the floor, in the back of the pickup truck.

"You killed our father, you little faggot," Karim yelled at me and then punched me in the head.

My uncle slowed down to make a turn when Karim yelled, "Get out." I was too scared to react. He got up to his feet, took me by the collar and spat on my face. "Nobody wants you. Get out."

He approached me and kicked me in the stomach. I fell out of the truck and landed on my back. I was in so much pain that I couldn't move. The truck didn't stop. I was lying on the ground, breathing the dust it raised.

I never saw my family again.

That was how I left Bamiyan.

And here I was in Baltimore, still lonely. Still unwanted.

I had ignored my boyfriend's warning against joining the protest tonight. What was he going to do to me when I got home? He might throw me out. Like everyone else did.

I bumped into a trash bin. The townhouses seemed clean, and their lawns were manicured. *Where the hell is this? How did I end up here?* I zipped up my jacket and noticed that my calves were hard. They felt like hundreds of needles were prickling them. Another trash bin was in front of the next house. Beside it, a blue recycle bin sat quietly. A beer bottle shone under the streetlight. It reminded me of how Cliff had taken out his anger by breaking the beer bottle when Rebecca fired me. In a desperate attempt to feel better, I picked up the empty beer bottle and smashed it onto the pavement. It didn't diminish my misery one bit.

I walked on. Recycle bins were lined up all over the street. Maybe I needed to break some more. I took a tomato paste jar from another one and threw it on the asphalt. The lid fell off and rolled on the street. I didn't have any skills even at easy things like breaking glass items. The next blue bin had a wine bottle. I crashed it. But it didn't make me feel any better. I yelled as loudly as I could. My voice sounded like an animal: not a wounded wolf, more like a sick cat. I hated my voice. Another glass container winked at me. I shattered it. Then I turned into a darker alley.

I screamed so heartily it scratched my throat. Two blue bins were overflowing with beer bottles. Someone must have had a party. I broke one, and then another. When I picked the third, floodlights startled me. When I turned around, I saw red and blue lights flashing.

"Baltimore PD," the cop yelled as he came out of the car. He was pointing his gun at me.

My hands went up in the air without any conscious effort on my part. I wanted to counteract this capitulation. "Go ahead," I yelled back. "Go ahead, shoot me. I broke a few bottles. I surely deserve to die."

The cop approached me. The edge of his gun was shining like a sword.

"Come on, shoot. I'm just no better than—"

A second man came out of the vehicle. "Abdul?"

I couldn't see him from behind the headlights. The voice sounded familiar.

"I know him. He's chill," he told the first cop, who was now close to me.

He was tall and determined. And African American. His gun still pointing at me. "Keep your hands up," he yelled.

"He's no danger," said the second man. His plain clothes became noticeable as he paced toward us.

The first cop shone his flashlight directly into my eyes.

I turned my head, but the rest of my body remained in place, like dried fish. My desire to live was stronger than I'd thought.

He slapped on my pants pockets and sides. My phone and wallet were the only things he touched.

The second guy was now visible. He had locs.

"Derrick?" What were the chances that *he* would find me? "Are you a cop?"

"Nah."

I knew that. He worked at the coffee shop.

"What were you doing here?" The cop yelled again, apparently feeling no sympathy.

"I don't know."

Derrick moved his hands in a circular way, motioning for me to keep talking.

"I was in the protest but got scared and left."

They expected more.

"And I got lost."

"And you started damaging property," the cop admonished me.

"Just a bottle from a recycle bin."

"Apparently several bottles," he noted. "Enough for neighbors to call us."

People were being teargassed and brutalized, but the cops found the time to respond to a call about broken bottles. My body remained rigid. The way it had been under Cliff's chokehold. I couldn't force myself to move. I was literally scared stiff.

"You wanna go to jail?"

I begged Derrick in my mind to protect me.

"You wanna see how people are treated on the inside?"

I could now see Derrick's face. *Please.*

"My buddy here knows you so… Make it the last time I see you."

"We'll drive you home," Derrick announced.

The cop shrugged.

We remained quiet on the ride home. I wondered if Derrick had seen the blackface picture. Or if he knew it was bogus. Or if he cared. He didn't say anything. I wanted to be unnoticed and sink back into my thoughts. Maybe I could figure out what I should do after I got home.

"Do you live alone?" the cop asked.

"No," I replied. "With a roommate." I didn't want Derrick to find out that I'd been cheating on my boyfriend.

"I'll take you to him."

"It's not necessary."

"We found you acting erratically and vandalizing property. Your roommate has the right to know. Hopefully, he can talk some sense into you."

I was hoping Derrick would vouch for me. But he remained quiet. Maybe he was still angry with me. I had ghosted him. Not that he reached out many times. Now it was too late.

How long had I been wandering on the streets? I checked my phone to see what time it was. The battery was dead. I looked at the dashboard for the car clock, but nothing looked normal in a police car. I wondered if Cliff had been tracking my location until the phone died.

In a few minutes, he probably was going to give me a good beating. I didn't even care anymore. I had a plan: to think of my dad, drown myself so deep in emotional pain that my body would become numb to physical hurt. I deserved it. Karim was right: nobody wanted me. I was something between a nuisance and a parasite. I just wanted to sleep and forget everything. Wake up in a whole new body, an entirely different life.

The cop double-parked in front of 101 Ellwood. Our apartment building. I looked at Derrick to say thank you. He just nodded and looked away.

"Get the door," the cop told me.

I obeyed. "You don't need to—"

"Shhh," he said as if talking to a toddler.

I felt justified in my hatred of the police. When we reached the apartment, he rang the bell three times. Within seconds he knocked on the door, as if he were going to save the world and couldn't spare a single moment.

We could hear Cliff's footsteps.

He appeared in his boxer shorts, eyes half open, hair disheveled. He put his hand on the doorframe. A deep frown showed how much he hated to be woken up in the middle of the night. "What's going on?"

"Does he live here? Abdul Ali something?"

Cliff looked at me. His face didn't change but I could feel he was getting more agitated by the second.

"Yeah."

"He was vandalizing private property. He should really be going to jail but… I brought him home as a gesture of good will."

My partner's face started to redden. "Thank you, officer. I had told him to stay home but…" He paused for a second to perhaps make up a story. "He's not a hundred percent alright in the head. I keep taking him to psychiatrists, but no final diagnosis yet."

He didn't know that I'd introduced him as just a roommate. But I doubted the cop was homophobic. Not with Derrick in the passenger seat.

"Make sure he doesn't join the riots again. I'm sure you know about the curfew that's been announced?" He pushed me inside.

"Of course. I'll keep an eye on him."

"If he commits another felony, it'll be on his permanent record."

I kicked off my shoes and stood behind Cliff. He was going to protect me for now. Although, in a minute, he was about to attack me himself.

"I understand, officer. Thank you."

"OK. Keep him off the streets."

Cliff closed the door behind him. An angry Cliff was normal to me. I was back in familiar territory.

"You've really outdone yourself," he paced toward me, hand balled into a fist.

Without thinking, I stepped backward. "I—"

"Do not say a word," he warned. "You…" he raised his hand. But then, he paused for a second and his expression changed. "You know what? You're not even worth it. I have an important meeting in a few hours. I'll deal with you after work." He walked to the bedroom. "Get me a drink."

After taking off my jacket, I poured some Jim Beam into a crystal glass and took it to the bedroom, with the lights off.

He took it, gulped the whole thing down in one breath, and banged the glass on the nightstand. "Get out."

Did he mean out of the bed, out of the room, or out of the apartment? I chose the middle option. I closed the bedroom door. I lay on the sofa and covered myself with the knitted blanket he called an "Afghan."

All the walking had drained my energy, and unlike what I expected, I fell asleep. When I opened my eyes again, it was already morning. I got up to take a shower. Cliff was already dressed and now blow drying his hair in the bathroom.

"I'm sorry, Cliff."

"Stupid," he roared. "I told you to come straight home."

"The streets were blocked. I—"

"Shut up," he mumbled. "I don't even wanna see your face right now."

I went back to the living room. A few minutes later, he showed up. I wished he would smile at me.

"I can make you breakfast," I said in the softest tone I could.

He ignored me and put on his shoes. He took the chain off of his bicycle and put it around his neck. It was too cold to ride a bike, but I didn't want to upset him further.

He walked back into the bedroom. He knew I hated it when he kept his shoes on inside the apartment. He wanted to show me that he didn't care.

"Come here."

I did.

He was standing by the closet, considering which suit jacket to pick. "Come here."

I stepped closer.

"Next time I tell you to stay away from the riots, you listen." He pushed me into the closet and shut its door. I heard the jiggling of the chain. He was locking me in.

"Let me out," I complained.

"You're lucky I have this meeting. Otherwise, I'd beat you until you faint."

"Let me out of here." I banged on the closet door. "You can't do this. Let me go."

"Shut up. Think about how you want me to beat you when I come back. Bang my skull into your nose? Kick you in the belly until you throw up blood? Or break your finger? Think about *that*."

"No," I screamed. "Let me out."

Abyss
/əˈbɪs/ *noun*

It was pitch dark. What could I possibly use as an axis to force the door open? There was no stick in the closet. To take the doors off of the brackets, I needed to tilt them while they're half open. We had no screw drivers in the closet to loosen the brackets. Not that I could see the screws in the dark anyway. The pole, under the clothes hangers, was glued to its own brackets, possibly also nailed to the wall. I punched on the door, hoping it would break. Things looked flimsy until you wanted to break them.

I tried to kick the door, but there wasn't enough space for me to fold my leg up high. I couldn't use the strength of my thigh. Kicking the door with my foot would only get me broken toenails. Or broken toes.

The only thing we kept in the closet was clothes. Nothing big or heavy that could break the door. I squinted in the dark. The only thing I could see was the light of the safe, blinking green. The safe was screwed into the wall so I couldn't bang it against the closet door. Most probably, it was too heavy for me to lift anyway.

I stomped my feet and punched on the door. I screamed as loudly as I could.

No one seemed to be bothered by the noise.

Vortex

/ˈvɔːrteks/ *noun*

I couldn't breathe. That confused me because nothing was blocking my breath. The clothes left enough room for oxygen. Light showed in a small gap at the bottom of the door. I wouldn't die of asphyxiation here. But I couldn't imagine being stuck in the dark closet until Cliff came back with a punishment that he had so much time to prepare. My nose, unclogged, refused to let air in. I took a shallow breath. Something frothed inside me, like a bottle of fizzing soda that had been shaken. What if the foam covered my nose?

I swallowed. I couldn't allow this monster to come out of me. If the world saw the grime inside me, no one would ever dare to come close again. I had already lost Ty. And Cliff was about to send me to a hospital, battered. No one needed to watch me bubble out of myself. I gasped for air. Nothing was coming in. I opened my mouth, but I still couldn't breathe. This was the moment I realized I was nothing. Not worth the air that gifted itself to all living things.

I was a fraud. I cheated myself out of so many impossible situations. Even if my mind allowed me to think I deserved to exist, my body was shutting it down. Maybe all I had to do was to let the darkness in, cover me, until I no longer was.

Of everyone I schemed, only Cliff got a chance to stand up to me. Beat me down for the disrespect I showed him. Ty never got a chance to object that I made him an accomplice in my indiscretion. Derrick never got a chance to question me. My father never got a chance to let me sink in the shame of having caused his death. What kind of a son would do such a thing? What kind of a human would act like such a monster? Even the worst among us are still unlikely to hurt their own families, their own parents.

I gasped for air. I couldn't stand it anymore. This closet was making me crazy. I had to get out. There had to be a way to get out. As much as my eyes got used to the darkness, I still couldn't see much. Other than the blinking green light of the safe.

What if I…?

The meeting in Cliff's office must have involved his transfer to New York. I couldn't imagine much else that preoccupied him to the degree that not even my arrest merited a reaction.

There was a chance Cliff would answer the phone. If I interrupted the meeting, he would come home fuming with rage. That was a worse option than just waiting until he returned at a time of his choosing. But there was a chance he wouldn't answer the phone at all. If the meeting mattered so much, he might turn off his phone. Or leave it outside.

I squatted by the safe and entered 0000 for the passcode. A message told me, "Wrong passcode." The green light continued to blink. I pressed 0001. Same result. Next number. I didn't even concentrate on the numbers. It didn't matter what passcode I entered. I didn't have time to try to guess it. Imagine what combinations would make sense to Cliff. But I was hoping for a specific result, other than opening the safe.

It didn't take too long. The technology was made to assess risk in this type of situation. The screen finally said, "Wrong passcode." But this time, the blinking light turned red. The home security company would be calling Cliff in a moment. If he got the message, he'd be back in a quarter of an hour. Or simply tell the company that everything was fine.

But if I were lucky and he did not get the message, the company would call me first. My phone was dead so they couldn't verify that things were all right. They would call the police.

Of course, I had no idea what was happening in the city. Would cops even respond to such a call? Or were all of them already in riot gear, ready to attack peaceful protesters? In a neighborhood like ours, the police were likely to do something about a reported theft.

It felt like decades passed before I heard the doorbell. I stomped my feet, banged on the closet door, and screamed. The bell rang again. Maybe I'd been wrong. Did I trust a random police officer? Most probably a white straight man. He would take Cliff's side, not mine.

"Police," said the cop at the door. It was a woman.

This might be my only chance. I yelled "help me" and banged on the door with all my strength. Then I heard something. I thought she'd heard me. But... something strange was happening. I heard people talking, and then the key unlocked the front door. Soon, the padlock on the closet door clicked. I heard the bike chain rattle. The door opened. And there he was. Cliff was looking at me.

"Babe, what are you doing?"

I jumped out of the closet. Then the African American policewoman showed up. The flap of her shirt pocket said "Evans." She saw me outside of the closet. The chain hung from the closet door, but that didn't prove anything.

"I'm sorry," Cliff told the cop. "He has a mental condition. We've been to several psychiatrists. The tentative diagnosis is," he looked at me with pity, "mild schizophrenia."

She looked at me, frowning.

"That's not true," I sounded agitated. I wanted to pounce on Cliff and punch him in the ear. But that would only prove I had a mental disorder.

"The police brought him home last night. They caught him vandalizing property. He even set fire to the bathroom sink a couple of months ago," Cliff added. "He should be on medication. But I wanted to make sure he gets the right treatment. Doctors are only too willing to put everyone on pills these days." He sounded like a concerned boyfriend.

Officer Evans nodded slightly.

"That's not true. The fire was an accident. The fire department wouldn't let me off the hook if it were arson."

"I'm worried," Cliff added. "He was already fired from his job." He pressed the bridge of his nose, "I'll contact the psychiatrist right away."

"That's not true. He had me locked in the closet since he left for work this morning."

"Honey, you're imagining things again." He put his hand on my shoulder.

"He beats me." I yelled out.

"Oh, come on baby." He hugged me. "Stop the nonsense."

"You can ask my friends."

He rubbed my hair. "I'm sorry, officer. I'll take it from here. He says things like that. It's quite embarrassing sometimes. He really *believes* what he says is true." He patted my cheek. "It's not his fault."

I slapped his hand away. "Please, please. You have to believe me. I only want my passport and Social Security card that he put in the safe."

"Honey, we talked about this. I'll keep them safe. You constantly lose things. These are too important."

"I need to prove my legal status so the police won't call ICE." I made up an excuse.

"We don't call Immigration," Officer Evans corrected.

Is that all she can do for me?

"Thank you, officer. I'm so sorry for the trouble. I'll take care of him."

"Please. Don't leave me with him," I begged. "He will kill me."

"Baby, calm down." Cliff rubbed my back. "It's OK."

His hand felt heavy and strong. He could snap my spine in half.

"OK, then. You guys be careful," Officer Evans was satisfied.

"Thanks again," Cliff said.

She walked away.

"Please. Please," I continued to plead with her. "Don't leave me here."

"Come baby, it's OK."

The front door closed.

Cliff looked at me. Then he slapped me so hard I almost fell.

Officer Evans showed up in the bedroom again. She'd tricked us into thinking she was gone.

Cliff hesitated for a second. Then put his hand on his cheek, like I'd just slapped him. "Honey, you can hit me as much as you want. But I'm not going anywhere. I love you."

"*He* hit *me*," I objected. "Please, you have to believe me."

"I don't have the time to judge a…" she started saying but noticed something on my face.

My cheek probably had turned red with a handprint.

"I only want my passport and Social Security card. That's all." I pleaded with her.

"Baby, your documents are safe. Please calm down. You're OK." He touched the corner of his mouth and then looked at his own hand, as if checking for blood. "I have legal guardianship because of…" he dropped his head.

"You should have been an actor," I shot back. Then I turned to Officer Evans. "Please, if he has legal guardianship, it looks like to me, the documents would be there in the safe. Just verify that. I beg you."

"Mr. Edwards, just to calm him down, let's see that guardianship document."

"Of course," he stepped toward the safe. "The thing is if we want to take him to the doctor as quickly as possible—"

"I'm sure one more minute wouldn't make that much of a difference," she counteroffered.

"Yeah. It's no problem for me. I'm just thinking of him," Cliff reassured.

"I only want my passport and Social Security card," I reminded her.

"Baby, you're spinning out of control again." Cliff wasn't about to drop the act. He started going through folders that he'd taken out of the safe. "Did you mess with these?"

I wanted some clothes and my phone charger. But I didn't have the time to pack them.

"What have you done to it?" Cliff feigned innocence.

"No luck?" Officer Evans intervened.

"I don't know what he's done to it," he replied. "Baby, when was the last time you were in here?"

"Please tell him to give me my passport and Social Security card."

"Mr. Edwards, unless you find the guardianship papers, I will have to ask you to return his passport and Social Security."

"Are you going to file a police report? I need some documentation to apply for replacements. He constantly loses things," my so-called partner objected.

She stared at him, letting the awkward silence linger.

"Fine. They're here. They wouldn't be safe in his hands. And then, who's gonna help him get new documents?" Cliff looked in the safe again and pulled out my passport. "Here," he gave it to the cop.

She opened it. My Social Security card was inside. She gave them to me.

I looked at Cliff. I couldn't read his expression. He was as beautiful as ever. How could such a beautiful face make up such a story about me?

Was this going to be how we broke up? Would our loving relationship just vanish in the presence of a police officer? No parting words? No apologies? No well wishes?

"You know I love you but," he hesitated, "if you leave again, you can't come back."

What do you mean "again"?

"I can't let my heart break again. Remember how I looked for you everywhere the last time you had an episode?"

I couldn't believe it. I remained unfazed.

"Fine. You and I are over, Abdul. I can't go on like this." Cliff's voice trembled.

For some reason, I told him, "I'm sorry."

"Officer, I need to report a looter. I saw him on TV last night, looting a store. I know his name. I thought I'd save you guys some time."

"I'm listening."

"Tyrique Williams. He's an agitator from out of town. He came to Baltimore to cook up trouble."

Officer Evans wrote down Ty's name in her little notepad.

"He's lying. He's being vindictive because I cheated on him with Ty."

"You see what I'm talking about?" He asked the cop. "If he'd been cheating, I would've dumped him a long time ago.

But that's him. Abdul imagines things. I should have got him on medication when I had a chance."

"Cliff, why are you lying? What do you get out of this? They could kill Tyrique for no reason. You know that. If you wanna punish someone, punish *me*. It's not his fault."

"Abdul," he answered calmly. "You need help. I did my best but I failed. Just make sure the next man who's generous enough to open his heart to you doesn't get crushed. The way I did."

I looked at the policewoman. Ty was in so much trouble.

Crucible

/ˈkruːsɪbl/ *noun*

Officer Evans climbed down the stairs with me. "It was a smart decision to let *him* break up with you. But your troubles aren't over yet."

"He has years of my savings in his bank account."

She ignored my statement. "In domestic violence cases, the survivors are in most danger immediately after leaving the abuser. Do you know where to go?"

"I have a friend."

"I don't know a shelter for male survivors. There's a homeless shelter but I can't guarantee they have space. Or if they welcome gays."

"I'm going to my friend's apartment."

"Does Mr. Edwards know this friend? He can come looking for you. Like I said, this is the most dangerous time. Even though it may not feel like that."

I didn't know what to do.

"Do you know where you're going?"

I shook my head.

"I suggest leaving town if possible. If he's very angry—"

"Angry and vindictive," I interrupted. "What he said about looting, it's a lie. He just wanted to cause trouble for Tyrique."

She walked to her vehicle. "If you know where to go, I can drop you on my way."

"Just drop me anywhere that's not here." I couldn't believe I volunteered to enter a police car. But I wanted to get away from Cliff as quickly as possible.

She signaled to me, and I got in the car. She said something on her wireless.

I was too distracted to pay attention. An armored vehicle passed us on the street, reminding me of a war zone. Were we at war now? I just wanted her attention so I could insist on the false report. "Tyrique Williams is a writer. A journalist. I had an…" I hated that word, "affair with him a while back."

Oh my God. I just confessed to Cliff that I had cheated on him with Tyrique. Was he gonna kill me? Or Ty?

"Where does he live? I take it he's not from here."

"Chicago."

"Well, it shouldn't be that difficult to verify he's been in Chicago the whole time."

"He's visiting," I had to admit. "To cover the events. He's a journalist."

"Were you with him last night?"

She was probably hinting that I should give her a certain response. "Yes," I lied. "The whole time. Other people were with us too. They can confirm he wasn't looting or anything like that."

"Was he with you when you were vandalizing?"

"Yes. He was trying to stop me. That's why when the police came, they only took me. They didn't arrest Tyrique. They left him alone."

She stopped at a red light.

"Please. I beg you. He can get shot based on a false claim."

She sighed. "I don't get it with people. After a whole night of looting and vandalizing and chanting 'fuck the police,' you still call the police at the first sight of a problem. And now you're accusing me of randomly shooting civilians. The nerve."

"None of this is Tyrique's fault. He just got caught in my mess."

She drove without saying anything. Military-style vehicles were moving about the streets.

I couldn't remain silent. I felt like my blood was getting hot. It was burning my flesh from the inside. "We constantly bury unarmed innocent people that your colleagues kill. You all take your time to compare notes and make up a narrative to make everyone else look like criminals. Your tactics and weapons are from war zones. You try your killing machines on my people in Afghanistan, and then come back here and use the same methods on Americans. If you don't like it, you only have yourself to blame." I couldn't believe what I was saying. But words came out without me having the power to stop them. I hadn't spent years under Cliff's violence to be subjected to more violence by the police. "The least you can do is to make sure Ty doesn't get punished for no reason."

"Didn't I just…? Boy, you got some nerve."

"Drop me off. I'm not charged with anything and you can't kidnap me without cause. Drop me off," I yelled.

She stopped the car and I jumped out. I wondered if my tirade was going to harm Ty. Maybe it would have been more prudent if I'd just shut up. "Ty is innocent," I said as I closed the door.

I had no idea where I was. Another police car passed me. People were sweeping the street and cleaning up broken glass in front of stores. I walked for a few blocks until I found an ATM. I withdrew the maximum daily limit of $250. That was a fraction of all the money I had saved in Cliff's bank account. That was gone now. But I was still alive and, according to Officer Evans, that was a success.

There was a Five Below store where I bought a phone charger. Soon, I ended up at the Greyhound bus station, still not knowing where to go. I plugged in my phone to an outlet.

A message from Ty lit up the screen. "I'm sorry. I didn't mean to be short with you. Just under a lot of stress."

Trilce had also texted me several times. They all had the time signature of a minute ago when I switched my phone back on.

I texted her: "Trilce, I left Cliff. A police officer escorted me out. She told me to leave town. I'm scared."

To Ty, I replied: "Ty, I left Cliff. He filed a false claim against you, saying you've been looting. I have to leave town."

Trilce replied.

And so did Ty. I looked at his message first. "It's fine. I've been surrounded by cameras and witnesses since yesterday. You OK?"

"I have to leave town," I texted back. I had already said that.

Trilce messaged, "Cliff asked Ben if he knows where you are. Ben told him he's sorry you've been unfaithful, and that he did the right thing to throw you out."

A way for Cliff to save face. Ben was so smart.

"Why don't you come over here?" Trilce asked.

"The cop told me that this is the most dangerous period. Told me to get out of town."

"Where are you going?" she inquired.

"Go to Chicago," Ty texted. "Sorry, can't talk now. But I'm going back soon. I will see you there."

I still have a chance with him.

Glimmer
/ˈɡlɪmər/ noun, verb

Trilce called me when I was on the bus. "I told Cliff I have a collection of recordings from your arguments. And pictures of bruises on your body. I threatened to report him to police if he tries to find you."

"What if he doesn't believe it?"

"He wants to go to New York. That's what he cares about most. He's not gonna jeopardize that. Make sure you disable your location tracker."

"Now that I'm leaving the city, I'm less scared."

"You got it. You managed to get out of the locked closet and still get your documents. He's not gonna bother you. He's probably already looking for the next victim."

"It won't take him long."

"And thank God for that. He doesn't have to obsess over you."

"Trilce, I'll miss you so much."

"I would miss me too," she joked. "I was the most fun person in your life."

I smiled. "You gonna come visit me?"

"A new excuse to visit one of the most beautiful cities? Nah! Baltimore has all the beauty I need," she laughed.

"You were my only real friend," I said in a low voice, not to bother the other passengers on the bus.

"I'm not dead yet."

I couldn't help but laugh.

"I guess this Tyrique of yours should be… a nice guy."

"In Persian, they say, 'grass should taste good to the goat.' I can't get Ty out of my head. I'm willing to risk it for a chance to be with him."

Tyrique had emphasized that I should seek therapy before he was going to consider dating me. "That's not negotiable," he texted.

I would do it.

Trilce replied, "I'm already planning our next adventure: horseback riding!"

"I'll ask him if he's interested."

"He'd better be nice to you. Otherwise, just leave his ass and come back here. By then Clifford will be gone to New York."

I didn't want to even consider that it might not work out with Ty. "Remember Phillip, my boss at H&M? He told me he doesn't guarantee a transfer. But he'll see what he can do."

"That's all you can expect from him at this point. I would have fired you on the spot for going AWOL," she teased.

"I told him a bit of what's been going on."

She was quiet for a moment.

"I think the other passengers are getting fed up with me on the phone. I'll call you tomorrow."

"OK, take care of yourself."

"Say hi to Ben."

I hung up and took a sip of my carbonated water. I enjoyed how the fizzy water felt in my mouth and throat. A bag of jalapeño potato chips sat on my lap. I had forgotten how much I loved chips. Leaning back on my seat, the tall back support felt good on my shoulder and neck. I sucked on my finger to taste every bit of salt and pepper.

In a few days, once he was back in Chicago, I was finally going to meet the man that I've been obsessing about, since the moment we met.

How crazy of me to think I was OK if Cliff choked me. That my life wasn't worth much. No wonder he called me "stupid."

Soon I may be dating Ty. Yes, I'd lost my savings and hadn't been admitted to a college yet, even in my mid-twenties. But I had plans. Hopes. And I was still here. Still alive.

The bus driver hopped on and announced, "We'll depart in about five minutes. If you wanna get any drinks or snacks, this is the time to do it."

"Are you going to Chicago?" A young Caucasian woman asked the driver. She had a backpack and a baseball cap that covered her brown hair. She turned around to the street and yelled out, "Ishaan! It's this one."

Her boyfriend approached her. His brown skin reminded me of Rakesh. They kissed and got on the bus. I wished Rakesh could see me. His efforts to bring me here had paid off. I just realized I wanted to go to Kolkata for their Indian wedding. That would be a dream come true. I would wear a burgundy sherwani. Ty could join me if he wanted. That would show Rakesh how much I appreciated all that he and Niloofar had done for me.

I thought of something. I jumped off the bus and ran back to the ticket counter. The woman wouldn't refund my ticket. But she said I could use the credit any time in the next year. She gave me the new ticket.

Darting to the new bus, I didn't have the time to rethink my decision. As soon as I sat, the bus moved. It soon exited one highway into another, going south. I saw one armored vehicle after another, going to Baltimore.

"Change in plans. I have to take some time and figure some stuff out," I texted Ty. "You will wait for me, right?"

I checked my contacts to make sure I had saved the address. When I saw it, I felt relieved. Thankful that Ty hadn't yet replied with many questions, I silenced my phone and put it in my pocket.

A green sherwani would look good on me. Or perhaps purple. With a burgundy turban.

I closed my eyes and took a deep breath, smelling the synthetic aroma of the air freshener.

How I was going to do it, I didn't have a clue. But I was going to find a way. I hoped Ty would join me. But I wouldn't miss Rakesh and Niloofar's Indian wedding for the world.

The bus passed by a green road sign. "Washington DC: 40 miles."

I smiled, eager to see Niloofar again. For no reason at all, or perhaps for all the reasons that could exist, I felt light. *I'm still alive.*

The phone vibrated in my pocket. That could wait. I wanted to stay in this state of delight. Weightless.

Still alive.

Author's note

Dear reader,
Thank you for picking this book and reading it to the end.
I wrote this story to imagine a path forward for a survivor of *bacha bazi* and how he can overcome barriers if he tries as hard as he can, and then a bit harder. Someone who has suffered through such an experience cannot always act in his own best interest. No one can. I tried to equip Abdul with the skills that can help him move forward.

Books on this topic are very few and mostly treat the survivor as a victim who needs to be rescued at the hands of others, mostly foreigners. It was important for me to make sure that Abdul has agency and that the most essential help came from Niloofar, an Afghan woman.

Domestic violence in a gay relationship is another rare theme in fiction.

Researching these topics took a toll on my emotional well-being. I cried several times as I read articles. Yet, I wanted to tell these stories that otherwise wouldn't be told. As an independent writer, I have the freedom to do so. But that comes with limited resources for promotional activities and publicity. I don't have the backing of a large publishing corporation to get the word out. Most media outlets openly declare that they would not review books by independent authors.

One of the most important ways in which you can help me continue writing these types of stories is by leaving an honest review on the platform on which you purchased this book. It doesn't have to be long. Just a few sentences would do. This can help me gain visibility, which is the most difficult asset to build for an independent author. Text me so I can thank you directly: 301 660 6165. You can also reach me at hamourbaika@gmail.com.

Many thanks,
Hamour

Discussion Questions

As an immigrant, Abdul doesn't take the race relations in the US for granted. How has he come to view them? Why is he so sensitive to them?

Abdul has lived through some very difficult situations and moved past them. Yet, he can't easily part with this abuser. What accounts for that?

Abdul is nice but distant. How is it that Trilce could break down the walls he's built around himself?

Tyrique has a profound influence on Abdul from the first glance. Why? How does he affect Abdul's view of himself?

Abdul is triggered by watching dancers and performers. What is the significance of him choosing to watch the go-go dancers at the DC night club, Secret?

Even though Niloofar and Rakesh played a significant role in safeguarding Abdul's life, he has his own agency and ambition. Does he always act in his best interest? Why?

Throughout the story, the story of an unjustified police shooting is unfolding and brewing in the background. In what ways does this affect the characters? Why is this event in the background?

The police shooting leads to protests in Abdul's adopted city. In what ways do these events align with Abdul's internal transformation?

How does Cliff's gaslighting and telling Abdul contradictory stories compare with the media coverage of race issues in the US?

Abdul is increasingly adamant about speaking against institutionalized racism. In what ways does his empathy for other minorities influence his empathy for himself and contribute to his bolstered self-confidence?

For more book club resources, please visit www.Hamour Baika.com.

If you'd like me to join your meeting virtually, please contact me at hamourbaika@gmail.com.

Acknowledgements

Andy, thanks so much for making space for me so I could write. Denne Michele Norris, you're amazing. I once heard that a good editor helps you write the book you thought you'd written the first time. That's how I feel about you. The incredible work you've done helped bring Abdul's story into light and life. Thank you.

Andrea Leeth, you were an amazing copyeditor. I truly appreciate your close attention to detail.

Calvary Diggs, your kind words brought tears to my eyes. Thank you for finding the final straggling typos and helping me make better stylistic choices. You're amazing.

MJ, Negina, and Khaliah Williams, I'm grateful for your insight and expertise to make sure that Abdul's story is authentic and that the themes are treated with dignity and care. You all went above and beyond and told me about other aspects of the story that should be strengthened. This book was improved because of your contribution.

Jessica Bell, as always, your design is beautiful. Thanks for wrapping the story in this amazing cover.

Finian Schwarz, the characters benefited from having borrowed your voice. Listeners to the audiobook and I appreciate it so much.

Anuj Chopra, thank you so much for reporting on *bacha bazi*. Your dedication to this topic reflects your compassion and kindness.

Justin Phillip Reed, I didn't know I love English poetry until I read yours. Thank you for blessing my world.

Mirajul Kayal, I appreciate your artistry in page design.

Abdul Ali, even in fiction I'm thankful to you. I learned vocabulary from you. In my most hopeful moments, I aspire to learn resilience from you. I gave you all I can. Now go into the world and have faith in yourself.

My amazing readers, it is for you that I write. Thank you from the bottom of my heart.

Also by Hamout Baika

On The Enemy's Side (novel, also available in Persian)

The Failure Plan (novella)

Unaddressed (short story)

Étant SFD (short story)

Lightning Source UK Ltd.
Milton Keynes UK
UKHW010722270223
417728UK00004B/467